Without you

WITHOUT YOU

MARLEY VALENTINE

Without you

Cover design by Emily Wittig Designs
Photographer: WANDER AGUIAR :: PHOTOGRAPHY
Models: Jacob Cooley & Luke Schaeffer
Edited by Shauna Stevenson at Ink Machine Editing
Edited by ellie McLove at My Brother's Editor
Proofreading by Jodi Prellwitz Duggan & Hawkeyes Proofing

This book contains mature content.

DEDICATION

To everybody who helped me get past the finish line.

We did it!

If someone makes you feel, let them.

— REYNA BIDDY

PROLOGUE

DEACON

ONE YEAR AGO

I hear my phone ring for the hundredth time and press the volume button on the side to silence it. Letting the call from my girlfriend go to voicemail, I wait for the notification telling me to listen to the message. I stand still in the doorway, anticipating Josie's usual string of texts, questioning why I'm avoiding her, halting any further movements.

Ping. Ping. Ping.

Like clockwork, my screen fills up with her inquisition.

Josie: I can't believe you're not answering.

Josie: I haven't spoken to you in two days.

Josie: You said you'd be back in two weeks, it's been four.

I bite my tongue in frustration, shocked and seething at her audacity. Is she for fucking real?

My fingers race over the screen in anger typing out my response.

Me: In case you forgot the reason I was here, Josie, let me remind you. Rhett is dead—my brother.

Jesus, my fucking brother, Josie.

Shaking my head, I power down the phone and shove it back into the pocket of my jeans. I don't have any energy to deal with the mess Josie and I are right now. We weren't always like this, at each other's throats, but the sicker my brother became, the harder I became to deal with. Now we're just a wreck. She wants more than I can give, and I, for once, just want what we have to be enough. Combine all that with grief, guilt and sadness, and it's inevitable that we're now struggling to make it work.

Leaving tonight and making the ten-hour drive back to Seattle, Washington is the last thing I want to do, but as much as I don't want to go back and face reality with Josie, I can't stay here any longer, either.

When it comes to hard truths, the mess of my life back in Seattle is a better option than what's left of it here. My family is now nothing but strangers walking around in a house that will never hold the same warmth and comfort it once did.

It's empty and cold—just like life without Rhett.

Knowing I need to keep moving, I continue shoving the last of my clothes and belongings into my duffel. I also manage to carefully slip in a letter my brother left me; one I don't think I'll open, but will take all the same.

I zip up the bag, wrap my fingers around the handles and throw it over my shoulder, before heading to my sister's room to say goodbye.

A quick unanswered knock isn't enough to deter me from walking in, knowing there's no way I can leave without saying goodbye. My eyes dart to the lump of limbs on the bed and I'm not surprised to see Victoria and my niece, Lia, curled into one another, sleeping soundly.

Kneeling beside them, I move Lia's golden-brown hair out of her face and kiss her forehead. The simple movement is enough to wake my sister, my eyes finding her open ones when I move back into view.

"You going?" she whispers.

Giving her a quick nod, I move forward and offer the same tender goodbye to my sister.

"Promise to text me when you get back to Seattle."

"I will. When are you going home?"

"Probably tomorrow. I'll see what Hayden wants to do when I speak to him."

Lia begins to move, and Victoria and I both stare, willing her to stay asleep. I lean over again and place my lips on the top of her small hand. "I'll call you. I love you."

"I love you, Deacon."

Kissing my niece one last time, I rise up to my feet, smile at my sister and quietly walk out.

Standing back in the hallway, my eyes lag on the only other closed off room and my body can't help but gravitate toward it. Inhaling, I place my hand on the cold, metal knob and turn it.

The hinges creak as I slowly push the door open, almost serving as a warning. Reminding me that it's been a few weeks since there was any life in this room.

The air is thick and musty, my mother's obsession with potpourri doing nothing to ward off the stale smell of sickness and death.

The sheer gray curtains are pulled closed, dimming the low glow of the sunset, but still providing just enough light to see all the untouched surfaces throughout the room. My eyes linger over my brother's childhood. Posters. Books. Drawings.

My chest aches at the bittersweet reminder of the teenager he was and the man that's not living. It's like being stuck in a time warp. Access to what his life was. What it could've been and what it will never be.

I walk around the room, skating my fingers through the thick layer of dust that coats everything. Nothing but a ghost remains in here, yet the unmade bed, with its rumpled sheets and slight body imprint has me wishing that was anything but the truth. It's almost a taunt, a false hope that life could be returning to the room at any moment.

My gaze lands on a wooden box sitting in the middle of his desk. It's shiny and polished, like a beacon of light; completely out of place in this room.

"Deacon." I turn to find my mother standing in the doorway. Her voice is dull as she stands there lifeless. She's nothing like the woman I grew up with, and I don't think she ever will be again.

Since coming back home, I don't know what's worse, that I had to watch Rhett die, or knowing that he took every-thing good with him. That he isn't the only thing in this house that's dead, that can never be the same.

"What's this?" I ask, walking toward it. My palm rests on the top, indecipherably drawn to it.

"It's for Julian."

My body recoils at the mention of my brother's boyfriend. I snatch my hand away in a hurry, not wanting anything to do with him or the box.

"Can you take it to him?" She leans on the doorjamb in exhaustion, like it's too hard for her to even hold herself up. "Rhett told me to give it to him after the funeral, but I just can't bring myself to do it."

A lump forms in my throat, a horrible feeling of jealousy begins to uncoil in my stomach, it's irrational, yet very familiar. It makes sense that Rhett would leave something behind for him as well. They've been inseparable since the day we moved here. Julian lived next door with his foster parents, and he and my brother hit it off straight away; their relationship growing and changing as the years passed.

Even though I was two years older than them, and had my own friends, and a close relationship with my older sister Victoria; I was always envious of what they had. The trust, the closeness, the complete confidence that this person understood you and would stand by you no matter what.

Even with my own family—I've never had that.

"Do you think you can drop it off at his place before you head back to Seattle?" she reiterates.

I want nothing more than to say no, but now isn't the time for arguments. Especially when there's no logical reason or plausible excuse as to why I can't. Instead, I give her a soft nod, pick the box up, and put it under my arm.

"You'll need this." She sticks her hand into the pocket of her cardigan and plucks out a single key.

"What's that?"

"He's probably not going to let you in."

"Mom." I shake my head and walk toward her, regret already washing over me. "I can't just let myself in there."

"Just check on him, okay?" She presses the key to my chest, not giving me any other choice but to take it. "For Rhett."

Knowing I can't say no to that, I tug the metal out of her grasp and slip it into my own pocket. "Do you know where Dad is? I want to say bye before I go."

"He's sitting out on the patio. You won't miss him."

"Meet me there?" I ask. "I'm just going to drop this stuff in the truck first."

She raises a hand to my face, looking at me wistfully. "Do you have something warmer to wear? It's freezing out there."

Leaning into her touch, I bask in her affection, wishing we could stay in this moment. Mother and son. A split second where the rest of the world doesn't exist and we're not a grieving family. "My coat is by the door," I respond. "And the heater in my truck works just fine."

Stepping out of her space, I jog down the stairs. With the box under my arm, I use my free hand to snatch my keys off the kitchen countertop and beeline for outside.

Once my bag, the box, and a week's worth of food my mother's trying to palm off on me, is safely stored in my back seat, I walk back up to where both Mom and Dad are standing.

My father looks like he's aged a million years. He's a hulk of a man, Rhett and I have always been miniature versions of him. But as big as his frame is, it still doesn't detract from the desolation and exhaustion on his face.

His ash brown hair is peppered with a new wave of grays that never existed before Rhett died. His cheeks hollow out as he takes a long, deep drag of his cigarette. With his reason for quitting no longer around, he's taken the habit back up with a vengeance. Almost like he's purposefully trying to kill himself.

Flicking the butt onto the sidewalk, he shoves his hands into his parka and blows out a large breath. Smoke mixed with the frigid air, surrounds him as he takes slow steps down the stairs. "You take care of yourself on the road, okay?"

A lump forms in my throat, and I swallow it down. I've

never felt more lost than I do in this moment. It's so obvious that Rhett was our talisman, the center of our family, the glue that held us together despite how different we all are.

When Dad's close enough he pulls me into his arms, hugging me with everything he has. Even then, there's little strength behind it, the hug a reflection of the weakness we're all left feeling. My eyes fill with tears, because it's one thing to know your parents love you, but it's another to know you're still never enough.

My mother joins in, her short arms stretching around us. Her touch is an added layer to the heartbreak. We're so broken, so lost. Unsure of the future, and unable to let go of the past.

I feel Mom's body tremble before the accompanying sob I've become accustomed to hearing follows.

"We love you, Deacon," Dad supplies, his voice hoarse and strangled. "We love you so much."

I wait for them to let me go, and rush to wipe my eyes, not wanting to break down in front of them, or at all. I'm not that type of guy, and when your parents are hanging on by a single thread, you don't want to be the reason it frays.

My grief has no priority here. I will myself to be the stone wall everybody expects me to be as we part awkwardly. I don't let myself dwell on the widening emotional gap between us, and I don't wait for the words of comfort that will never come.

This is what life will be like moving forward, and I may as well start to get used to it. I moved away to become my own man, and to be my own person. Selfishly, I wanted to stand out and get away from everything I grew up around and in the worst possible way, my wish came true.

With a soft, sad smile, I turn away from my parents and

walk back to my truck—head back to my life away from all
of this.

It's just me now. On my own. Alone.

~

THE HOUSE IS dark and cold, the last remnants of the sun
descending on the drive over. There's no heat on, no lights.
If I didn't know better, I would say nobody was home.

When my mother sent me over here with the spare key I
didn't anticipate that I would have to use it. But after the
fourth unanswered ring of the doorbell, I've succumbed to
the notion that Julian doesn't want anyone over.

Going against every single voice in my head telling me to
leave the box on the dining room table and the food in the
fridge and begin my drive home, I quietly make my way
through the moderately sized building, searching for him.

The further I walk into the empty house, the need to see
him and check on him, for Rhett, is overwhelming. Almost
like I'm indebted to my brother for all the ways I failed him
when he was alive, that maybe, just maybe, in death I can
make it up to him.

I find the main bedroom and contemplate whether to
knock or just walk in. Nerves wreak havoc on my body, as I
push past the need to turn back around and go home.

I rap my knuckles on the door to announce my presence
before making my way inside. I wasn't sure what I expected,
but a motionless Julian wasn't it.

A small bedside lamp casts just enough light for me to
get a good glimpse of the seemingly lifeless body in front of
me.

The ever-present cracks in my heart turn into fully-
fledged breaks as I take in what he's wearing. Laying on

what looks like Rhett's side of the bed, Julian is almost unrecognizable. Dressed in the suit he wore to the funeral, I realize he hasn't changed, and possibly not even moved for two days.

His arms are wrapped tightly around a pillow, and with his back to me, I can't tell if he's awake or asleep, but the urge to find out hits me harder than expected.

My feet move before my mind can tell them to stop, and I find myself walking around the bed, until I'm crouched down beside him.

His eyes are open, staring and still. Hollow and vacant, he looks almost catatonic.

"Hey," I whisper, hoping to break the silence. "I'm sorry for just coming by like this," I ramble. "My mom gave me the key. She sent me over with some food." Self-conscious, I scratch at my brow. "I brought over a box," I start. "It's from Rhett."

It takes no time for his name to register, and Julian's body and mind to react. If I wasn't sitting so close to him, I'd miss it. The way his eyes slowly shift around the room. The way the pillow compresses even further under his hold.

Finally, his gaze finds mine; desolation and hopelessness swirling around in his eyes. Desperate for a lifeline, he stares at me, as if he's waiting for what's next.

I itch to touch him, to comfort him, but I settle on placing my hand on his shoulder instead, offering help the only way I know how. "How about we get you out of these clothes, okay?"

I rise to my feet and begin searching for something more comfortable. "I'm going to look through the drawers for some clothes," I explain as I rummage through belongings that aren't mine. Eventually I find everything he needs and turn to hand it to him.

He hasn't moved, but the chill in the air seems to have blanketed itself over him. The numbness and stillness from moments ago is subsiding; his body now shivering relentlessly. His teeth chattering, loud and painful.

"Do you think you can get yourself in the shower?" I ask, wanting him to warm up. "I could turn the heat on for you while you're in there."

Without expecting a response, I exit the room to give him space and set off in search of the thermostat. Located near the kitchen, I turn it high enough to warm the house quickly.

Trying not to worry, I war with myself over whether or not to check on Julian. When I peek my head through the door and find him still lying down, I know there's no way he's going to get up and into the shower without assistance.

I'm doing this for Rhett.

"Hey." Using all my strength, I try to maneuver him into a seated position. Once he's up, I lower myself to the floor, kneeling in front of him.

I ignore my shallow breathing and the racing of my pulse as I slide the jacket off his shoulders. His head hangs between his shoulders, and I'm grateful he isn't staring at me. Our closeness is unnerving as I reach for the buttons on his shirt, trying not to overthink my actions.

Once they're all undone, I push the shirt off him. My fingertips hastily skate over his skin, and the way it pebbles underneath my touch doesn't go unnoticed.

He lifts his head, curious eyes boring into mine.

Why are you doing all of this?

Seeking some distance, I stand and take the pile of clean clothes I found for him and head to his ensuite bathroom.

I drop the clothes on the closed toilet seat and then turn

on the water. While I wait for it to heat up, I catch my reflection in the mirror.

For the first time in weeks, there's a flush of color to my skin. Beads of sweat pearl on my forehead, and I know they're not a result of the humid shower mist, or the strain of lifting another man. It's the product of an unknown heat. A slow burn unfurling at the idea of invading Julian's personal space and helping him. Taking care of him.

Shaking my head, I drag my eyes away from the man staring back at me.

This is for Rhett. Out of respect and love for your brother, you're taking care of Julian, because Rhett would want you to.

Not wanting to spend any more time poking holes in my logic, I step out to grab a still and half naked Julian. Stretching my hand out to him, I'm surprised when he takes it. I lift him up from the bed till we're standing toe to toe.

I clear my throat, trying to find the courage to talk. "I turned the shower on for you." I rub the back of my neck, feeling awkward. "I figured you could take the rest off on your own."

Without a second glance, he walks into the bathroom and shuts the door. The second I hear the lock click, my chest deflates, letting out all the trapped air from my lungs.

Pacing around the room, I don't know what to do next—wait that's a lie. I know I need to leave. He's fine. He's alive and safe, and I dropped off the box just like my mother asked. Considering we've never been in the same room together without Rhett, I've gone above and beyond what was expected.

I need to go, and we can go back to the Julian and Deacon who only ever tolerated one another for Rhett's sake.

As soon as the thought passes, the door swings open and a fresh looking Julian walks out. Brown eyes find mine, his face holding a bit more color, and his eyes alight with a little bit more life. He runs his hands through his thick, wet, brown hair, mussing it up every which way. It's then I notice the way his clothes are swimming on him.

Fuck.

"Shit. Julian," I say, the tone of my voice apologetic. "I didn't even notice."

He shakes his head at me. "It's fine."

We stare at each other, and I realize this is my cue to leave. I point my finger to the door. "I think I'm—"

"Thank you."

Two simple words settle in my chest and twist me up in a way I can't explain. There's something about being appreciated in this moment that makes my heart swell.

"Of course," I respond.

"Do you mind if I just jump back into bed? I'm not feeling too good on my feet."

"Fuck," I mutter under my breath. "Yeah. For sure. I'm going to get going soon anyway."

He walks aimlessly to the bed, unperturbed by the ogre of a man standing in the middle of his room. My gaze follows his every step, from the way he pulls the covers back, to the way he slides under them.

Determined to put this night behind me, I walk to the nightstand beside Julian and reach over to switch off the low lit lamp. As soon as the room darkens, the sound of ragged, pained breathing fills the air.

I try to ignore the way the sound buries itself inside my chest. The way his loss resonates with my own. With every step toward the door, I *want* to ignore *everything* about this moment.

But I can't.

I can't willingly walk away from him, not while his heart is breaking. Not while his world is crumbling. Not while the sadness that echoes throughout the room mirrors the sadness that surges inside of me.

Shucking off my shoes, I throw my coat to the floor and walk around to the opposite side of the bed. I can't explain the need, or what possesses me to comfort him this way, but that's what it is. A need. Not a choice. My parents have each other, Victoria has her family, and he has nobody—we both have nobody.

It's simple, but it's the truth.

I lay down beside him, on top of the blankets and wrap my arms around him. "Shhh," I say softly. "It's okay," I lie.

I pull him as close to me as possible until his back is curled nicely to my front. The second I apply pressure to his body, I feel him tremble and shake against me. The heaviness of Rhett's death blankets us as he begins to cry in my arms.

There's something about his vulnerability in this moment that triggers my own. The feelings I've been adamantly keeping at bay rising to the surface, threatening to spill over.

Through his cries, his arms manage to cover my own, holding me to him. It's unexpectedly soothing, knowing he needs this just as much as I do.

He's not pushing me away, and I'm not questioning why I don't want him to. Resting my forehead on his shoulders, I finally let go of the charade I've been holding on to so tightly and let my own tears fall.

Huddled together, I feel a strong bond forming between us. The understanding that we share a break that can never be fixed, a void that can never be filled; a life that is now irrevocably different.

With every salty drop of emotion, I feel understood.

With every salty drop of emotion, I feel a little less lost.

With every salty drop of emotion, I feel tethered to a man I've spent my whole life hating.

And with that last salty drop of emotion, I know I need to get the fuck out of here.

1

DEACON
PRESENT DAY

"Are you breaking up with me?"

With my head in my hands, I take a long, deep breath, trying to find some calm among the chaos. I have no desire to drag this out, or even fight for this pathetic excuse of a relationship. From the moment I got the news Rhett's cancer was back to the moment he died Josie and I have been on the downhill. Who am I kidding? There were red flags from the very beginning, and now I'm kicking myself for letting it get this far.

"Deacon, the least you can do is answer me," Josie whines. "I know I fucked up, but I just missed you."

I look up at her incredulously and wonder what the fuck we ever saw in one another. "You missed me, so you slept with someone else?" I narrow my brows at her in confusion. "Can you explain that one to me?"

"You're never here." She pouts, and my stomach rolls at the accusation.

"I'm here all the fucking time, and if I'm not, I'm at work."

She kneels between my legs and it takes all my strength

to not push her away. "You're here, but you're not *here*. I don't know where you are, but you're not here. Not with me." She takes hold of my wrists, dragging my hands away from my face. "Can you remember the last time you touched me? The last time you said I love you, and not because you *needed* to say it back."

Guilt trickles down my spine. "So, why are you fighting for this if all I've done is force you into another man's arms?"

"Once upon a time we were good together, I want to go back to that. You're it for me, Deacon."

Unceremoniously, I rise, needing some distance. Needing some fucking air. Josie's words are suffocating. Like swallowing a jagged little pill, I feel every serrated edge slice me open that little bit more.

I know I'm responsible for the majority of the issues in our relationship, but I can't forget the past or turn back time. I know the exact moment it all went to shit with us, and I know the exact reason why; I just don't want to continue to rehash it.

Right now, it's so much more than Josie cheating. We're not good for one another, and maybe if our circumstances were different, we could've had the life Josie thinks she sees for us. Instead, we ignored the signs and we both suffered in silence—and that is my biggest regret.

Josie is clearly hoping for a different reaction out of me. Wanting me to maybe hulk out and drag my woman back to my cave and claim her. To remind her of what we were and fuck her so she lives her whole life comparing every other man to me.

Maybe, a long time ago I would've done that. But not today. Not this Deacon.

"Look, Josie," I sigh in defeat. "I think we need to accept it's over."

"Deacon, please," she begs. She blocks my pacing, her water filled eyes locked on mine. "I'm so sorry. I never meant to hurt you."

I cradle her head in my hands, my thumbs wiping each falling tear. "That's the problem, babe. You didn't hurt me, I hurt you."

"Somewhere along the way we got lost, and I just don't think I can find my way back."

Her shoulders shake and every part of me wants to shut down and run away. The guilt of what we've done to one another, the relief that we're finally over; it's a war of feelings inside of me, and I don't know which of them I want to win.

This is more than I've let myself feel—because emotions are ugly and unforgiving—in such a long time, and it's a reminder of why I packed all the hard stuff into a box I never planned on opening.

"Why don't you let me get out of your hair for a couple of nights? You can have a bit of time to decide what you want to do next," I offer. "In fact, you can take all the time you need and I can stay at the shop."

Her hiccuped cries slow, her breaths becoming more stable. She wipes her eyes with the back of her hands and shakes her head at me. "I don't want to stay here alone, especially if we're not together. I think I'm just gonna go to my mom's."

I stop myself from asking if she needs any help, or telling her, again, how sorry I am, but they're not the words that will make this right. No words will. So, I sit back down on my couch, tense and still, letting the silence fester between us.

Josie places a small travel-sized suitcase in the middle of the dining table. My eyes follow every move she makes.

From room to room, and back to the suitcase, haphazardly throwing all that she might need in there.

She zips up the suitcase, and settles it on the floor, I start to rise, but she puts a hand up to stop me. "Don't."

Sitting back down, I lower my head and wait till I hear the lock on the front door click. The sound reverberates off the walls and the finality of it all hits me. There are many times in my life that I've felt alone. In my thoughts, in my experiences, in my feelings. But as another door closes, and another person leaves, I wonder, is this how it's always going to be?

My phone chooses this moment to vibrate across the coffee table, the word 'mom' large on the screen. I've spoken to her a grand total of five times in the last twelve months, and she's never been the one to reach out. That alone is enough for me to know I can't ignore this phone call.

It's the same battle I wage with myself every time there's contact between me and my parents. Be the dutiful son and clear all our consciences by checking in as if nothing's changed. To ignore the huge chasm in our family and add our strained relationship to the ever growing pile of fuck-ups I seem to be accumulating.

Left without a choice, I answer the phone but can't find the strength to even say hello.

"Deacon?" Silence. "Deacon, honey, are you there? I won't keep you long."

I clear my throat. "Hey. Yeah, sorry. It's a bad line," I lie.

"I'm just calling to make sure you're coming home next month."

Shocked, my words come out as a garbled mess. "What. Why?"

"Are you really asking me why, Deacon? Have you forgotten what time of the year it is?"

I laugh humorlessly. "That's why you called me yourself?"

"Of course it is. It would be disrespectful if you didn't come back home to visit him and spend time remembering with us."

I don't know why it bothers me that he's still on the forefront of their minds. He's their son, he should be. It's not like he's ever far from my mind, but every now and then I would love it if my mom remembered that I was still here. Still her son and still alive.

"Well," she probes. "It's the anniversary of his death, Deacon, can you make it or not?"

Focusing on my hand, I open and close my fist, tighter and tighter, holding on to the anger surging inside me. "I didn't know you guys were doing something. I'd have to check if I can get the time off work."

"Geez, Deacon," she spits out. "You practically own the damn garage. Of course you can get time off."

My teeth grind against one another. "I said I'll see what I can do."

"Well, if you can make time in your busy schedule, it will just be us, your sister, Lia and Hayden, and Julian. Maybe your grandparents. You could bring Josie."

Julian

His name shifts every part of me from irritated to curious. The mention of Josie and the fact that I'll have to tell them we broke up does absolutely nothing to sway where my thoughts are leading at just the mention of him.

I'd be lying if I said I haven't thought of him since the night I spontaneously held him in my arms, only to wordlessly rush out of there the moment he fell asleep.

Every now and then the image of him lying helplessly on the bed pops into my head, making my heart hurt for him, and my mind worry. The irrational feelings of contempt and jealousy I'd become accustomed to associating with him, in the years before Rhett's death, are nowhere in sight. They've been replaced with a baffling amount of concern, and a flurry of nameless emotions bubbling underneath my skin.

I've hung on to every morsel of information my family has let slip into conversation over the last eleven months. What he's doing, how he's coping, if they've seen him plenty or not enough.

"Deacon." My dad's voice comes through the phone, interrupting my wayward thoughts. "Sorry about your mother, she's just a bit stressed lately." *Well, that's the understatement of the year.* "How are you, son?"

Always the mediator, my father once again steps in and tries to salvage the conversation. "What your mom meant to say was that she would love to see you. We both would."

Growing up, my dad was my go-to parent. He was my hero—still is, but even for him, it's been too hard to pretend everything is okay between me and my mother. "Like I said to Mom, Dad, I'll try."

"Okay, well our door is always open for you." There's an odd pause before he speaks up again. "You know that right, Deac?"

"Yeah," I croak.

"Okay. Good. Love you, son."

"Love you too, Dad."

The call disconnects, and out of pure indignation, I launch the phone across the room hard enough to hear it thump against the wall and crash to the floor. Because all the words in the world will never explain how broken I feel in this very moment, I walk to the beat-up cell and throw it at the other side of the room for good measure.

Who the fuck needs to stay in contact with anyone anyway?

"Is that the last of it?" I ask Josie as I load another box into the back of her car. "I can do one more sweep."

"No. That's it."

It's been a month since Josie and I broke up, and every day since has been a whirlwind of emotions. From hurt, to anger, to some uncertain version of acceptance; Josie has taken this way harder than I expected. And I'm ashamed to admit I haven't felt nearly as upset by it all as I should be.

She had enough nerve to sleep with another man in a ploy to get my attention, yet she can't see the fact that I drove her to make such a consequential decision means we're not right for one another. We're no longer compatible, we're borderline toxic, and the most important piece of information is I don't love her as much as I should.

She deserves better. She deserves more. I just wish I could somehow get her to see that.

I slam down the door of her trunk.

"Will we keep in touch?" she queries. I must look at her confused, because she's quick to add. "As friends."

"Sure," I huff, not really seeing the point in arguing with her. "We can try being friends."

"When I get settled in my new place, I'll have everyone over for a small housewarming party. It will be great."

The lease on the apartment we shared together may be in my name, but I was willing to be the one to move out if Josie needed me to. But since she insisted she needed the fresh start, and wouldn't be able to do that with reminders of our relationship, we decided I would stay.

Truth of the matter is, I'm barely home, so I don't place too much importance on the four walls around me. I spend all my time at the garage, getting lost in all things cars. My love for anything on four wheels is the one thing that hasn't diminished over the years. In fact, the garage, around the guys I work with, the smell of oil, metal, and grease, is the only place that feels like home. The confidence I have under the hood of a car morphs me into a man not even I could recognize. Centered. Grounded. Whole.

Surrounded by metal and machinery, I'm content. I'm at peace. If I could bottle up that zen and use it for all the other times my life has turned to shit, I sure as fuck wouldn't be standing outside my apartment saying goodbye to quite possibly the only woman who will ever love me and all my fucked up flaws.

"Be good to yourself, Deacon." Placing her hands on my shoulders, she uses me for leverage and rises to her tiptoes, giving me a kiss on the cheek. "I know things have been hard since Rhett died."

I hang my head low, avoiding her gaze. "We don't need to talk about it, Jos."

"You're right. *We* don't need to talk about it, but *you* do."

Her hands rest on my cheeks. "I'm sorry we didn't work out."

"Me too," I offer gruffly.

"Be happy, Deac."

~

I'M STANDING in front of the coffeemaker in the breakroom when my best friend and business partner, Wade, asks me, "So how long are you going to be gone for?"

Removing the drip tray, I place my travel mug in the

machine alcove and press the power button. "I don't know," I respond. "Just the weekend?"

"Is that a question?" Wade frowns at me. "Are you asking my permission?"

"I just don't want to leave you here alone."

He sits down on the two-seater couch in the corner of the room. "You are so bad at lying. If you don't want to go, don't go."

I scrub a hand over my face. "You know it's not that easy."

Being my best friend, Wade is probably the only person who can see through my anxiety, and call me out on my bullshit. "Just stay for the weekend. Tell them that's all you can get and if it's going well, take the week. Hell, stay the whole two weeks until Thanksgiving even."

"I can't imagine it going well," I say despondently. I clap him on the back, his calm logic exactly what I need right now. "But thanks, that seems like a good idea, as long as you promise to let me know if things get a little too hectic around here."

"You do know we have five other full-time mechanics here, right?" He stands up and makes his way to the door. "You're good at what you do, but not that good."

"Get the fuck out of here," I call out to him as he slips out of the room.

Adding sugar to my coffee, I stir the hot liquid and then screw on the lid. When I've got a big day scheduled, I fill up the large insulated travel mug and keep it with me for most of the day. It stays warm enough that I don't need to stop and start what I'm doing in order to get my coffee fix.

Following Wade, I head to the main garage where he's bent down tinkering with the engine of a steel-colored '68 Charger.

Wade and I met when I first moved to Seattle after finishing high school. I never had plans to attend college, intending to study automotive mechanics at a technical school instead. But when I mentioned moving to Seattle, my parents insisted I go to college.

Seeing as I needed money from them to get me started, I agreed and finished a degree in Automotive Engineering. Part of me wanted to prove to them how well I could do on my own, and the other part of me wanted to experience what it would be like to be alone, independent, and not feeling overshadowed by everyone else's expectations of me.

It would be a lie if I said I didn't know when it started or how it happened, but the older I got and the sicker Rhett got, I just wanted to get away.

He'd been diagnosed with Acute Myeloid Leukemia. I remember it like it was yesterday. He had the flu for what seemed like forever, and when he finally went to the doctor to find out why he couldn't shake it, they discovered the leukemia.

Your body naturally produces white blood cells to fight infection and sickness, but for Rhett, the cancer meant his own white blood cells couldn't do that. Instead of protecting him, his own body was destroying him from the inside out.

Doctors told us it had been detected early enough to be treated and with many early cases, remission was highly likely if he remained cancer free for five years after the fact. We were all so optimistic, until we weren't.

He was seventeen when he received the initial diagnosis. Twenty-one when doctors discovered it had come back, and twenty-four when they told him it had spread everywhere.

I'd grown up feeling like the wrong puzzle piece, not really fitting in anywhere, not really doing anything exceptional. I was always on the outskirts, more out of choice than a dramatic familial exile. I plodded along, trying to find my feet within my own family, but it never felt like it was enough.

My mother wanted the best for me, I was her first-born son, and like any parent, she had hopes and dreams and expectations, and like any parent, she was disappointed. I didn't like the things she wanted me to like, and I didn't do the things she wanted me to do.

When Rhett came along, he eventually took the pressure off. I became closer to my dad, and my mother burst with pride over him, while my dad let me be me.

Until cancer came along and somehow both pushed me out of the way and brought it all back with a vengeance. My mother's comparison, her disappointment, her constant reminders that my brother could die and it was on me to live for him. This time I was older and my father couldn't mask it up with gifts, games, and distractions. So, I chose to leave, or run away as my mother so eloquently put it.

Seattle was supposed to be my fresh start. Wade and I studied, we partied, we got laid, we got jobs we loved, and I lived this life where I could forget that my parents were occupied and my brother was now never too far away from death's door.

Our friendship flourished as we bonded over a love of vintage cars and spent endless hours of our free time rebuilding, refurbishing, and fixing them for our boss. We started apprenticing for Mr. Duquette as part of our degree, and even though he wasn't required to, the relationship we'd formed while working had him offering us full-time jobs once we graduated.

He was old in age, but young and vivacious at heart.

Dedicating his life to his business, he used to say his love for cars was something no woman could rival.

A year after we started full-time work, Mr. Duquette dropped dead right in the middle of the garage from a major heart attack. Wade and I were shocked and devastated at the loss. He'd not only been our boss but our mentor and a friend.

Since he had no family, Wade and I were amazed to find out he left Duquette's Drives to us. His whole business. It was a surprise, but one we both welcomed.

Over the years we've put all our spare money, and all our spare energy, into making sure Mr. Duquette's legacy remains intact, while ensuring that our dreams and plans for the future were able to be carried out as well.

Now, we're known as one of the most revered automotive houses in the state. We specialize in repairs, services, exteriors, and interiors. We can handle vintage cars, new cars, wiring and electronics. The list is endless, and with a team of some of the best mechanics I know, this place is home. This place is my life. This place is everything I've worked for and everything I'll forever be proud of.

"Are you going to stand there staring at my ass or are you going to look over the schedule and decide what you want to pass off to everyone else while you're away?"

"Do you ever shut the fuck up?" I say in jest. The haze of anger from the anticipation of my trip to Montana is finally starting to dissipate.

"It's too much fun riling you up."

I grab the clipboard off the workbench and walk over to him. "If we closed on the weekends, this wouldn't really be a problem."

Straightening his body, he puts the wrench on the engine and stares at me. I prepare myself for the well-deserved abuse coming my way. "You're the one that wanted to stay open on Saturdays. I found the love of my life, and she wanted to spend every Saturday going to the markets and all I wanted was to hold her hand and hear her complain about the fish smell. I had to let go of that dream and now *you're* saying we should be closing on Saturdays?"

"You get every second Saturday off," I supply, trying to justify my selfish need to keep busy.

"Give me the schedule." He holds his hand out and I give it to him. He trails his fingers down the page and then raises his head up. "We'll rotate late nights on Thursdays and Fridays until we clear our Saturdays. And the weekend you leave will be the first weekend where the garage doesn't open on Saturdays."

I gesture for him to hand me back the clipboard. This is how it's always been. Wade is nothing but positive and practical; always there to remind me, if there's a will, there's a way. The advice helps a lot when you're the emotionally stunted one in the friendship. "I'm sorry."

He runs a hand through his hair. "What are you sorry for?"

"I didn't know how pussy whipped you were."

A bark of laughter leaves his mouth, and he turns to get back to work on the car. "I'm going to tell the other guys the new hours," I tell him. "I'll be back in a bit to take over."

He raises his hand to say bye, and just like that the tension between us is broken.

2

JULIAN

"What can I get you?"

A humorless laugh wafts across the bar. "I've been coming here every Wednesday night for the last year. Why do you insist on asking?"

I wipe the already clean bar top, giving my hands and body something to focus on, instead of the weary looking man in front of me.

Growing up, he was my best friend's father—the only father figure I've ever remembered. But now he's just a man in a bar that drinks to hide his pain, and I'm the guy that feeds his addiction.

Trying to ignore that he's looking worse than usual, I turn to the wall behind me and grab the bottle of whiskey. I slide the shot glass in front of him and pour till it's spilling over the rim. It's not his usual, but as I watch him shoot it, and push the empty glass to me for another; I know he needs it.

I generally try to steer away from heavy chit chat, because he's seeking as much distance from the past as I am, but tonight the words stumble out quicker than I can stop them.

"Are you okay?"

I know he isn't. Rhett, his son—who was also my boyfriend—has been gone for almost twelve months, and with the holidays fast approaching, emphasis on our heartache and loss, feels inevitable.

"You don't want to hear my shit, son. That's not what I come here for."

"Mr. Sutton."

"It's Bill, Julian. Nothing has changed in that way, just as I've been to you for years, you can still call me Bill."

My eyes quickly scan the bar, making sure there isn't anyone I need to attend. I walk around the countertop, and sit right beside Bill. "Is it Elaine?"

"She brought up Deacon coming out again tonight. Wanted me to call

him and harass him about coming even though she just did it last month." He squeezes his eyes closed and shakes his head. "She never calls him. That poor boy is doing his best to check in on her whenever he can and the only time she makes the effort to call him is to bully him into coming down for Rhett's memorial."

I also got the call from Elaine to attend, but unlike whatever is going on with her and Deacon, I haven't witnessed anything but compassion and warmth whenever she speaks to me. I try not to speak to her a lot. In fact, I've tried to distance myself from the only family I have, because it's just too hard to be faced with the life Rhett and I never got.

"You're going to come over, aren't you?" His tired eyes implore mine. "Elaine really—"

I put my hand up to stop him. "I know, but it's hard," I admit. "And from the sound of it, you guys might need to spend some quality time as a family. Victoria will be there too, won't she?"

"Wouldn't you rather spend time with people that loved him too?"

Noticing another patron walking toward the bar, I jump at the excuse and rise from beside Bill, leaving the question unanswered.

Logically, I would love to reminisce about the good times, but I really can't remember when they were. Rhett's sickness plagued so many of the years we spent together.

Cancer.

Remission.

Cancer.

Remission.

An endless rotation of hope and hurt that has scarred me so deep, I don't see myself ever climbing out of this hole. That constant up and down was my life for so long, and now I'm enjoying living it at a plateaued level of perfected monotony.

I work the same shifts, have the same conversations, and have no drama. It's not ideal. It's certainly not exciting, or probably even healthy. But it's safe and I've become accustomed to living this way. I like it this way.

No expectations. No disappointments.

"What can I get you?" I ask the older woman, who just slipped onto an empty bar stool. I hand her a small laminated sheet of cocktails. "We have some happy hour specials."

Without a second glance at the list, she points to the fridges behind me. "Can I get a bottle of Chardonnay? I'm waiting for a friend," she adds defensively.

"You can drink the whole thing on your own, honey. It's not my job to judge you." She smiles in gratitude, as I place the ice bucket and two glasses in front of her. "Have a great night."

Alone again, I shift my attention back to Rhett's father. "You need a beer or are you going home early?"

"One more," he replies on a sigh. "And then I'll get out of your way."

"I'm sorry, Bill," I offer, because I genuinely mean it. Week after week, month after month, nothing I say or do can fix his pain or mine. "I'll do my best to come to the church, and lunch, okay?"

His nod is appreciative, and with nothing left to say, and everything left to feel, we both sit in silence till he's done.

The next few hours drag, with only a handful of customers trailing in. I keep myself busy reading a bunch of book samples I downloaded on to my Kindle, hoping one story will suck me in enough to keep me occupied and make the time pass quicker. But it never works.

By the time I'm sticking my keys into my front door my body is exhausted, but I know my mind is ready to keep me up all night. I drop my belongings on the couch and kick off my shoes.

I stop at the kitchen and grab a bottle of water from the fridge before heading straight for my room. My eyes gravitate to the shiny wood box that sits on Rhett's nightstand. It's been there ever since I found it in my living room, screaming at me to pay it any attention.

I didn't find it till after the night Deacon dropped it off. To be honest, most of the days after Rhett's funeral are a blur, but the fact that he came over that night, and *he* kept me company till I fell asleep is something that didn't go unnoticed. Okay, that's an understatement.

If there was ever going to be another Sutton family member jumping in my bed, I expected it to be Vic. She's always been like my older sister. In fact, I have no problem calling her just that.

But surprisingly, it wasn't her, and I often lay awake at night thinking about the hows and whys of how it all panned out.

Did he draw the short straw?

My fridge was full and the mysterious box sat on my dining table so I knew what his motivation was for coming over, but one of life's biggest mysteries, is why he *stayed.*

Growing up it was like he barely tolerated his family, and as an extension of them, it seemed he didn't like me very much either. He moved to Seattle as soon as he could, and for the longest time he only came back out of necessity.

It's not a surprise his relationship with his parents, more so his mother, is strained. I've never seen it be anything else. The only person who has had a front row seat to his life, unconditionally, has been Victoria. And from the way Bill is describing Deacon and Elaine's relationship, I can't imagine Rhett's death doing anything to make the tension better.

Beginning my nightly routine, I take my clothes off and chuck them into the laundry hamper. Cross-legged, I sit in the middle of the bed. I reach for the box and just stare at it; like I do every day.

I run my fingers over all the grooves and begin what's become my daily ritual. The only time I let my heart bleed and feel all the things I've lost.

Lifting the lid, I stare at the six perfectly placed envelopes. I pick up the first one and trace every curve of my name on the thick pearlescent paper. Bold and black, Rhett's writing was perfect. He mastered the art of calligraphy, insisting that a person's handwriting revealed how they were feeling when they wrote the message. It was one of the many low endurance hobbies he picked up, insisting that dying didn't mean that a person couldn't still find ways to try and live.

Were they in a hurry? Were they careless? Was it important? Was the message life changing?

All those emotions are in every swirl of the dark ink. It's the reason I can't bring myself to open them. To see his feelings sprawled on the page, the words written with care and precision. To hear the sentences in his voice, and to breathe life into the future he expects me to have without him.

I put it back and then do the exact same thing another five times. I don't touch anything else he's meticulously placed in there. It's not just by choice, it's by necessity. I know the level of pain I can and cannot withstand. Every feeling has its day to be felt, and those days are far and away for me. In order for me to survive, I try not to feel anything at all.

Closing the lid, I shift the box back to Rhett's side of the room and swing my legs over the edge of the bed. I open the drawer on my own nightstand and pull out the cylinder of sleeping pills.

Popping the cap open, I pluck out a tablet, stick it to the back of my throat and chase it down with a whole bottle of water. It usually takes about half an hour for the drowsiness to settle in, so I choose to pass the time with a steaming hot shower.

Letting the water loosen my muscles, I stay under the spray, stretching and rolling out my neck. I wait till the heat fills up every inch of the bathroom. I wait till the air is thick and my breathing becomes labored.

Turning the water off, I tug at the towel and wrap it around my waist. I stumble out of the shower and back into the bedroom. Light-headed and lethargic, I fall onto the bed, welcoming the numbness. I let myself enjoy the nothingness and yield to my favorite part of the day.

A few hours a night where there's no Julian, no Rhett, no life and no death. There's no loss, no pain, and no grief. It's a blank space, a clean slate, a moment in time that just is.

Dark.

Quiet.

Peaceful.

A falsified moment of the only things I want, and the only thing I'll never get.

"THAT WILL BE one hundred and four dollars, thank you." The cashier gives me a strained smile. The one that they plaster on because they'll get fired if they're not friendly, but it doesn't quite reach their eyes, because their disdain for their job is too hard to hide.

I drag my wallet out of my back pocket and slide out my debit card. She holds up the credit card machine and I slip my card in the chip reader and punch in my pin.

"Do you want your receipt?" she asks.

"A reminder of the money I don't have but keep spending?" I say sarcastically. I give her a reassuring wink. "I'm good, sweetheart. Have a good day."

Pushing the cart out of the store, I stop beside my parked car and fumble around in my pocket for my keys. I unlock the trunk and then unload the bags inside. I don't know why I still bother shopping for groceries. I end up chucking the stuff every other week, because they're all the things Rhett used to love. The things he wanted to eat so bad but eventually the chemo and the medicine made it impossible.

It's more than I need to be spending on my week-by-week paycheck, but I do it anyway. I don't have any other needs besides my rent, so I splurge on food.

Climbing into the car, I turn the ignition, waiting for the rumble, but it never comes. I would like to say I'm surprised but this isn't the first time this car has refused to start. It's a black beat-up Toyota Rav 4 that Rhett's parents gifted him when we finished school. It's been nine years since then and this is just another thing of Rhett's I can't seem to let go of.

Some days I wake up and I want to eradicate every single thing of his from my life. I want to erase every single memory and all our history. And then every other day I pray that I'll never ever forget him.

Grabbing my cell off the passenger seat, I scroll through to find the one number I hate calling.

Closing my eyes, I rest my head on the steering wheel and wait for an answer.

"Julian."

"Mr.... I mean, Bill. I know you're probably really busy, but um..."

"What is it son, what's the matter?"

"I was wondering if you could meet me at Whole Foods? My car, I mean, Rhett's car won't start."

"Is it feasible for you to wait? Is the car blocking anything? I just have to tie up a few loose ends here and then I'll take my lunch break."

"Yeah," I say in relief. "Take your time, I'm not in a rush."

"Okay, I'll see you soon."

We both hang up, and I patiently wait, grateful that it's cold outside and my frozen food won't defrost in the trunk.

I know how lucky I am that I can depend on Rhett's family, but I hate it all the same. It's moments like these where I begrudge the man I've become. I'm twenty-seven years old, and most days I feel like a fumbling eighteen-year-old. I had plans and dreams. Wants and needs. And now I have nothing; not even a flutter of excitement for things to come and things that could be.

Rhett dying wasn't unexpected, yet that didn't make it any less tragic. And every time the cancer came back, it poisoned me right along with him.

It blackened my insides, darkened my soul, and killed every single living feeling inside me. Slowly, painfully, I didn't just lose Rhett. I lost me.

Sometimes I wonder if death really is the worst thing, because being alive and feeling so empty and hollow seems to be much worse.

It wasn't just that I lost my boyfriend, but I lost my best friend, and the future we planned for together. That's what hurts the most.

When I was four years old, my parents died in a car accident. It was a lot to process at that age. One day they were here and the next they weren't.

I remember them being good, I remember being loved, but the memory is never enough to combat the loss of belonging that followed.

My only living relative was my grandmother, and she took me in with open arms and brightened my world with her beautiful heart. When she died, I felt the loss more, I was four years older and our bond was stronger. She was my last living relative, and she was my last safe place, until I met Rhett.

I got shuffled around to a few different foster homes at first. And then eighteen months after my grandmother died, Mr. and Mrs. Anderson agreed to keep me on a permanent basis. There's no sob story that comes with it; they were nice people, but they were just doing a job; ticking all the boxes and collecting their checks. I don't begrudge them, I had a roof over my head and food in my stomach.

But there was no heart, no warmth, no love. I didn't have anyone in my corner, I didn't have a family, until Rhett and his family moved into the house next door.

We became fast friends, his parents and his home feeling more like mine than the four walls next door ever would. They never asked questions, and they never treated me differently.

When I turned eighteen, I was given access to some money that had been left to me by both my parents and grandmother. Not wanting to be anybody else's burden, I moved out of the Anderson's house as soon as I could. After a lot of convincing and what we hoped would be the beginning of forever for Rhett, he was twenty and in remission, he moved in with me.

Elaine couldn't part with him when he was sick, and he never had the heart to argue with her. Eventually, the idea he was finally healthy wore her down. It was his first step into independence, and the first step into the new phase of our relationship. And like the good parents Bill and Elaine were, they were behind Rhett and me every step of the way.

They were the kind of people that let you spread your wings just enough to make you feel free and hovered enough to make sure you didn't fall.

No matter how old I was, I was their kid just as much as Rhett was, and it was never a problem. Until now. I spent all my time with Rhett when he was healthy. And then when he got sick again? Well, cancer doesn't give you time to make friends, or keep friends. My world was always small, and now it's minute.

Now, I feel like a charity case. I'm the guy they check in on, because they feel obligated to their dead son. In fact, it's probably part of why Bill comes by the bar so often. He could just as easily drink at home. But I think he feels like he needs to see for himself that I'm functioning. I've tried to put some distance between us, but there's always a moment where I falter and I need them. And the truth is, they're the only people I can count on.

A loud knock on my window disrupts my thoughts and I turn to see Mr. Sutton, with jumper cables in hand, waiting for me on the other side. I lean forward, reaching for the lever underneath the steering wheel, and wait to hear the hood pop.

Once it does, Bill takes it as his cue to walk to the front of my car. He raises the heavy metal and attaches the cables to my dead battery.

He straightens them out till they reach his already prepped vehicle. I open my door and stick half my body out.

"Tell me when you need me to start my car," I call out.

He raises his fingers, counting out one, two, three. On three, I turn the ignition, praying for a miracle. The engine churns repetitively before cutting out.

I look up to meet his gaze. He gives me a nod and I try again. Thankfully after a few forceful pushes with my foot on the accelerator, and four more turns of my key, the car comes to life.

My body sags into the seat in relief, as Mr. Sutton slams down the hood. His face beams at me in success.

I smile back at him and step out of the car to thank him. Before I have a chance, he shakes his head at me. "Julian, it's time. You *need* to get rid of this car."

"What? And miss out on you rescuing me once a month?" I joke, trying to lighten the mood.

"It's okay to replace it, you know?"

I shove my hands in my pockets and blow out a loud breath. "I know all those things Bill, it still doesn't make it any easier to do." My eyes flick from the nothingness behind him and back to meet his eyes. "Thank you for helping me out."

"One day you'll stop thanking me," he states.

"And one day you'll stop helping me out."

"I owed you one, anyway."

I look at him quizzically.

"Every time I come into the bar, you just let me be. No questions. No judgments. No rushing."

"Guess we're even."

Bill looks down at his watch and then back up at me. "I'm sorry, I've got to run."

"Of course."

He pulls me in for an unexpected hug, and a ball of emotion gets lodged in my throat. "I know it's hard, but don't be a stranger, son."

3

DEACON

L eaving Seattle in the dead of the night, I arrive back in Billings, Montana by midday. Wade's always on me about being too stingy to buy a plane ticket when I visit, but I like the drive. I like the long open roads, the peace and quiet, and the feeling that you're constantly moving. It's the only time I don't mind being left alone with my own thoughts.

I also like to be in control of where I'm going and when I'm going. And on the off chance I need to get away, which happens a lot when I'm around my mother, I don't want to have to depend on someone else or awkwardly deal with public transportation. I want to be able to walk away, take a moment for myself, and just breathe whenever I want to.

I pull up at the cemetery and park in the row of spots opposite of Rhett's plot. Braving the winter, I drag my thickly padded coat and beanie off the passenger seat, before climbing out of the car.

Shrugging into the sleeves, and covering my cold head, I open the back door and grab the small bag of candy.

Dragging my feet, I wonder to myself why this never gets

easier. Isn't time supposed to heal all wounds? Yet, every time is like the first time, the reminder I'm living in a world without my brother crushing me all over again.

When I reach the gray-colored marble headstone, I place the bite-sized bag of candy corn on the top and hold my hand on the cold surface, feeling strangely close to Rhett.

"So you're the guy that leaves these here," a voice calls out behind me.

I startle at the interruption, but am quickly consumed by a prickle of annoyance and a heavy dose of recognition.

Julian

Wanting the ground to swallow me whole, I don't turn around or acknowledge his presence.

Fallen leaves crunch underneath his feet, every step warning me of his impending closeness.

"I wondered who it was that knew Rhett well enough to leave that god awful candy here every other week." Not sure what to say, I stay silent. "To be honest," he continues. "I thought it was your mom or your sister."

I don't know why the idea of my mom leaving little gifts for Rhett makes me laugh, but it does. It's not a loud bellow, but a low rumble in my chest that surprises me.

"She hated that he loved them," I supply, acknowledging his presence.

"That she did. Like his preferences personally offended her," he says with humor. Unexpectedly, his shoulder brushes against mine, as he steps up beside me. Caught off guard, I move a fraction so we're no longer touching. His tightly pressed lips tell me he noticed; but instead of calling me out on it he just continues rambling on about the candy.

"Actually, looking back, I don't know how I didn't know it was you. You had a never-ending stash when we were younger. You collected them and would sneak them into his room."

I turn my head to face him, and my thoughts stumble at the man looking back at me. Julian's cheeks are flushed from the cool, brisk air; his chocolate-colored eyes no longer the same lifeless orbs I encountered a year ago. Instead there's a low light that flickers, like he's stuck; unsure whether to burn bright or let the remaining sliver of life be doused out of him. It's a good look on him.

Taken aback by my own observations, I reluctantly pull my gaze away from his, and clear my throat. Swallowing, I lick my lips, ridding myself of the dryness in my throat before asking, "You remember that?"

"Yeah," he says softly. "There's not a lot I forget."

I lower my head, staring at my boots, and shove my freezing hands into my jacket. My gut and the ensuing pause in the conversation tells me he's referencing the last time we saw one another. The night I held him in his bed.

Getting lost in our own thoughts, we briefly give that single moment in our life the acknowledgment and reverence it deserves.

It's crazy to think I was party to such an intimate moment, and even crazier to contemplate the fact that he wanted me there... that I wanted to be there.

"So," Julian says, disrupting the quiet. "You visit a lot."

Perturbed, I snap, "Is that a question or a statement?"

"More like an observation," he answers, unruffled by my mood change. "I see that packet of candy corn here on his headstone every two weeks."

"Can I not visit my brother?" I bark out defensively.

He turns and looks at me exasperated. "I didn't say any such thing."

"Whatever," I mutter. "I should just go."

"Deacon." He places his hand on my forearm, stopping me. "You don't have to do that."

I pull my arm away from him, and he apologetically slips his hands into the pockets of his jeans. "What I was trying to say was, Seattle isn't really that close."

"I'm familiar with the distance," I say dryly.

I hear him sigh heavily. "I'm sorry. It's none of my business."

The apology sends a boulder of guilt to the pit of my stomach. Anybody would question why I would drive ten or more hours every other week just to drop off a 'gift'. It probably gets eaten by birds or squirrels, but once the idea came to me, I couldn't stop. I wanted to revisit those good times between my brother and I, and enabling his sugar addiction was one of them.

"You don't need to apologize. I'm just being a dick as usual," I say with much more self-deprecation than needed. "I really do have to go though."

He nods at me but keeps his eyes trained on the ground. Without another word, I leave him to his visit. My time with Rhett is exactly that; *my* time. No matter what happened between us that one day, or how surprisingly comfortable it was to stand beside Julian, that isn't something we do. We're not friends, we're not two people trying to fill that gaping hole in our lives by leaning on each other.

I won't let it happen. I'm not his new best friend and there's no way he'll be a replacement for my brother.

Climbing back into my truck, I slip the key into the ignition with the intention of starting it, but when I catch Julian crouching down in front of Rhett's headstone in my peripheral, I can't help but stare at him.

Why the fuck can't I stop staring at him?

Rising off the ground, he reaches for the clear packet of

candy and shoves it into his pocket. Every part of me wants to rush out of the car and call him out on it. Ask him what he's doing and why he's taking something that doesn't belong to him.

Has he taken all of them?

Twisting his body, he notices my car and stares directly at me. I don't know what expression I expect to see on his face, but I at least anticipate apprehension or even remorse for his petty theft, but neither appear.

His face is blank, and his eyes are indifferent, and it shocks me. He walks to his shit box of a car with long, purposeful strides, completely ignoring me, and it takes me a moment to recognize my own reaction to his dismissal.

I'm angry.

How dare he steal from me and then act like I don't exist? Aggravation courses through me, and before I can retreat or convince myself to simmer down, I'm opening the car door and stalking toward him.

"What are you doing?" I spit out, coming up behind him. He stills. With his back to me, he keeps his hold on the door handle, refusing to answer my question. "I asked you a question."

Turning, I expect a man ready to fight and argue with me. I expect him to tell me to mind my own fucking business, but all I get are eyes full of empathy and a smile so sad it hurts.

"Can you come to my place?" he asks.

"What?" I stare at him, confused. "Why?"

"You asked me a question and I want to answer it."

"About the candy?" I shake my head. "I just want to know why you took it."

"I know what you want Deacon, so can you please just meet me there?"

Do I want the answer that bad?

Without a word, I turn and head to my truck. I jump in and forcefully slam my door shut. *I guess I do.* Even though I know the way, I find myself waiting for Julian to take the lead.

I follow him, my palms beginning to sweat, and my mind racing with a million reasons why I should let this go.

I dislike the guy. I always have, and Rhett being dead shouldn't change that.

Julian and Rhett's place is only fifteen minutes from the cemetery. He swings his car into his driveway, and I haphazardly park behind him.

We both step out, the adrenaline that fueled my insistence to follow him slowly wearing off.

What am I doing here? Again.

I stand at the bottom of the stairs as he opens his front door. He cranes his neck, his gaze finding mine. "Are you coming in?"

Nervous, I scratch at my brow. There's no point backing out now.

Their place looks different in the light of day, the windows opening up the space and showing off all the ways they made it their own.

Accentuating their youth, and all the different stages of their life together, the apartment is decorated with mismatched furniture. Things they picked up from the thrift store and things they would've saved up to buy.

I remember how persistent Rhett was that he and Julian did everything on their own. Unless it was a hand-me-down, they didn't want anything they didn't earn.

It's weird, but I respect them for it.

Standing in the middle of the living room, I watch him

walk away and into his bedroom. He reappears with a box in hand, one very similar to the one I left here that night.

Placing it on his dining room table, he gestures to the seats surrounding it. "Please, sit down."

With no reason not to, I anxiously oblige. When we're both seated, facing one another, our expressions on display, he pushes the wooden box in my direction. "Open it."

I rub my hands up and down my thighs nervously, before placing them both on the table. "Look, Julian. I was angry, I didn't mean to intrude."

Impatient, he flicks the lock on the box open. When he removes the lid, my chest tightens in both confusion and appreciation.

There, in front of me, is what is obviously twenty-six bite-sized packets of candy corn. That familiar tongue twisted feeling that seems to happen around him returns.

"You kept them," I state in disbelief, the observation almost rendering me speechless.

"I didn't like the idea of a stranger finding them," he supplies, matter of fact. "Keeping them. Eating them. Throwing them out."

"They're just candy," I pacify.

He gives me a knowing look. One that says, we both know it isn't just about the candy. One that says, if it was as simple as candy, you wouldn't be so angry about me 'stealing' it. "It's a gift. From you to him, and I wanted to keep that sacred."

"Sacred?"

"I didn't know you were the one bringing them—not that the revelation changes anything—but I loved that someone else was trying to keep his memory alive," he explains, his eyes imploring me to listen. "Like someone, besides me, was still trying to keep him close beyond the grave." His body shifts forward and he places a warm, comforting hand on top of mine. "Driving ten hours every second weekend to see your brother. There's no way that should go unnoticed."

I lower my head, hiding the embarrassed flush that I can feel spreading across my face, and reluctantly drag my hands away from his, the intimacy making me feel uncomfortable. "It's not a big deal."

Appearing unaffected by my withdrawal, he continues, "It is. Do you care that I took them?"

Shaking my head, I reach for the small packets. "I may have been his big brother, but you were always his right hand." Even though there's nothing but truth in my words, the admission still hurts. "It's only right that you keep these for him."

Closing the box, I slide it closer to Julian and rise from the chair. "I should go."

Brown eyes watch me with interest. "Why do you drive all this way to bring them?"

"We don't have to do this, Julian," I say a little too aggressively.

He looks at me with confusion. "Do what?"

"Pretend we have things to talk about. You explained the candy corn thing and now I can leave."

Crossing his arms over his chest, he settles back into the chair and looks at me with disdain. "You always do this," he says.

My whole body stiffens at his accuracy. Disbelief and resentment at his observation coursing through me. He glares at me, his chocolate eyes challenging me.

I'm torn between wanting to reach over the table to grab him, shake him and ask what the fuck he means, or tell him to shove his opinion of me up his ass, because he's the last person on earth I'm going to try and make nice with.

Instead, I school my features and talk myself off the ledge. "Thanks for the chat, Julian."

Without waiting for a response, I turn and head to the front door.

"Deacon," he calls out. I don't look back at him, but the fact I've stopped moving acknowledges my interest in whatever he has to say. "I'll see you at your parents' house."

The reminder of why I'm here in Montana, and that this isn't the last time we'll be crossing paths, has me walking out without a second glance. It's bad enough that I'm going to have to sit through hours of watching my mother ineffectively deal with her grief, doing it in front of an audience isn't something I'm looking forward to.

Driving away, I contemplate going back to the cemetery for a few hours and delaying the inevitable with my parents, but the rain pelting down on my windshield makes the decision for me.

The weather doesn't slow down traffic as much as I want it to, and it takes less than half an hour to pull up in front of their place. Aware that my sister and her family aren't showing face till tomorrow, I keep my duffel bag in the back seat, still unsure if I'm going to stay.

Playing with Lia is the only upside to this whole visit. My niece is the light of our lives, the only real, and true thing holding us all together. And if she's not here to be the center of attention, I can't predict how long it will be before I feel like leaving.

Trying to take Wade's advice, I tell myself not to over-think the visit, and to not let the foul mood I'm in set the tone for the rest of the day. I'll take it all as it comes, and focus on the fact that I do miss my parents, and my sister and her family and hopefully that's enough for us all to tolerate one another for the next forty-eight hours.

Just as I'm about to climb out of the truck, I notice my father waiting at the front door. A mixture of nostalgia and anxiety washes over me as I take in his warm smile. He's the thread connecting me and my mother. The voice of reason, the one person I can depend on.

I don't even make it halfway up the steps before my dad is standing there with open arms, waiting for me.

"Deacon, it's so good to see you," he says. We hold on to each other, and I let myself enjoy the comfort and familiarity of being in my father's presence. "How are you?"

"I'm good," I answer honestly.

"And the drive?"

"Long. But you know how much I love the open road."

Together we make our way up the rest of the steps and through the front door. I'm immediately engulfed by the strong smell of my mother's homemade lasagna. Conjuring up memories of my childhood, and a reminder that irrespective of the loss and strain between us, not everything has been tainted.

"Your mom's in the kitchen," he informs me. It's a subtle request to go try and make nice, and I take the hint.

Heading to the kitchen, I stop and lean on the nearest wall and watch as she hurriedly cuts some vegetables. Wearing an apron Rhett, Vic and I made her when we were younger, covered in different colored handprints, she furrows her brows in concentration; her sole focus the task at hand. "Do you need any help with that?" I say as a way of announcing my arrival.

"Deacon," she gasps. "I didn't even hear you come in."

She gives me a quick once over and then frowns at me.

"Where's your bag? Did you bring a bag? Are you not staying for the weekend?"

"He just got in Elaine."

My father's stern voice has her lowering her eyes in a moment of shame. "I'm sorry, Deacon, it's just your sister said she couldn't make it tonight, and I was hoping we would get to spend some time as a family this weekend."

While the words attempt to be comforting and welcoming, the tone and her body language is anything but. She's stiff and awkward, enough so that I'm second guessing why she even wants any of us here.

The tension is short-lived when a voice I wish I didn't recognize reaches us in the kitchen. "Anyone home?" Julian calls out. "You left the front door open."

"We're in here," my mother shouts back. Dropping the knife and untying her apron, I watch the woman who, moments ago, seemed unenthused by my presence morph before me. Walking right between my father and I, she meets Julian in the foyer, her arms open to greet him. "It's so good to see you, Julian. I didn't think you were coming till tomorrow."

When he hugs her back, I feel like I've been kicked in the stomach. "Yeah, I got the night off work last minute," he supplies.

"Deacon," my mom coos. "Come say hello to Julian, it's been so long since you've seen him." Instinctively, I shift my gaze from the sight in front of me back to my dad. Like a kid who wants his parents to make it all better, I wait for him to say or give me more than the apology that's written all over his face.

It never comes.

My stare slides back to Julian, my attention fixed on him. Whatever expression is on my face causes him to step away from my mother and the pity in his eyes brings back the anger I felt at his place earlier today; the irritation that he's always managing to notice the things nobody ever has.

Every part of me wants to scream. Scream at him. Scream at them. Scream at nobody in particular. I just want to unload the hurt and disappointment that has followed me for longer than I can remember and stop feeling so inadequate every time I'm around my family.

But I don't do any of that. Instead I clear my throat and push myself off the wall, not giving my mother or Julian a second glance. "It's good to see you, Dad, I'm gonna grab my duffel, and then head upstairs."

4

JULIAN

My eyes follow Deacon as he rushes out the front door, and I have to fight the urge to follow him. Between the way he left my place, and whatever it is I walked in on, it's like he's teetering on the edge and ready to explode.

My intention wasn't to rile him up, I was just curious. I still am. So much so, I've shown up on their doorstep and invaded their family time, a day earlier than planned.

A part of me wanted Deacon to open up, to talk about the loss of his brother. I don't know if it's because hearing about someone else's grief might make me feel less alone, or in some weird way, it makes me feel closer to Rhett. But even if I was willing to talk and make nice, he made it clear that whatever hostility he's always harbored toward me is still very much alive and well.

Not sure how to proceed, I look at Mr. Sutton, and nod at him. "Hey, Bill."

Placing a hand on my shoulder, he gives it a tight squeeze. "Hey, son," he says with a resigned smile. "It's great to see you."

He heads in the opposite direction, and Elaine leaves me with no choice but to follow her into the kitchen.

"The lasagna is in the oven," she exclaims. "And I'm just cutting up the vegetables for a salad."

"Sorry, Elaine, I didn't even think. I won't stay for dinner."

"Don't be silly," she says, waving her hand at me. "I thought Victoria, Hayden, and Lia would be here tonight too, plus I still haven't figured out how to cook for only two people." She stops slicing through the lettuce and looks up at me. "Food or no food, you know this is still your home too."

Well aware she's referring to a time when Rhett was still alive, and I still lived next door; I choose to not focus on the melancholy statement and concentrate on the here and now.

"Do you need any help?" I ask.

Pulling out a bar stool, she pats the seat excitedly. "No. You just sit yourself down and tell me how you've been."

With my life pretty much on rinse and repeat, I don't have much going on since the last time she and I saw each other, but I rattle on about how working at the bar keeps me busy, and pays the bills. It's a simple life, but it works for me.

She hangs on to my every word, her eyes wide, asking questions whenever there's an opening. Filling every lull with an endless stream of words. If her need to escape her own thoughts and talk about her own life wasn't so obvious, her incessant rambling would be comical.

I've been so overwhelmed and drowning in my own grief, I realize this is the first time since Rhett's death I'm really seeing the woman who has always been like a second mom to me. The way she deflects everything on to everybody else and doesn't even allow herself a moment of reprieve. It's a mask she's so desperate to keep in place, but if she's not careful, the only option will be to break. The mask, and her.

Bill silently walks into the kitchen and grabs a beer from the fridge, and I don't miss the irritation that washes over his wife's face, while she watches him.

"Can I have one of those please, Bill?" I ask, hoping to steer Elaine's attention from her annoyance at her husband onto me. "You would think working in a bar would turn me off drinking."

The attempt at light humor falls flat as he wordlessly twists off the bottle cap and hands it to me.

"I'm going to watch the game on television," he announces to no one specifically. Not one for sports, I wouldn't know whether or not he's lying, but his hurry to be away from Elaine is an obvious motivating factor.

"How long till we eat?" I ask Elaine, trying to break the tension. "Maybe I could set the table."

"Deacon and his father will probably mope around and skip dinner, it might be easier if you and I just eat here at the breakfast bar." She stills and raises her guilty looking eyes to meet mine. "They're both just as stubborn as the other," she mumbles in justification.

"It's bound to be a tough time for everyone," I say, trying to acknowledge her feelings, while not really wanting to get involved in their family feud. "Emotions are high."

Thankfully she doesn't push the issue and instructs me to set the table however I like. Much to Elaine's dismay, the conversation is a little bit stilted from here on out, an unexplained irritation preventing me from wanting to exchange any more pleasantries.

Once I'm done, I excuse myself to check on Bill and find

myself sitting beside him in an odd but comfortable silence. We're both staring at the screen, not really watching when he says, "Why don't you go upstairs and tell Deacon that the food will be ready soon?"

Taken aback by the request, I turn and stare at him in confusion. "I don't think that's a really good idea. You should go up and do that."

He shakes his head and takes another sip of his beer. "He doesn't want to see me."

Wanting to argue, but knowing there isn't really a point, I leave the room, and trudge myself up the stairs. With heavy steps, I make it to the top and just stand there, staring at every closed door. I haven't been up here in so long, so close to Rhett's childhood bedroom. The place he took his last, labored breaths.

I fight the urge to step inside. The urge to reminisce, to unlock my feelings, and let myself miss him. Instead, I psych myself up to knock on Deacon's door.

I quickly rap my knuckles on the wood. When there's nothing but silence on the other side, I knock again; still nothing. I should be relieved, I should just walk back the way I came from and tell Bill that he should come and call Deacon down himself.

Before I can talk myself out of it, I take hold of the metal handle and push down. Expecting to come up against a struggle, I'm completely unprepared when it opens with no problem. I steel myself not to stumble inside and step in slowly.

With nothing but complete silence surrounding me, I stop and stare at the heap of muscle lying down on the bed in front of me. I stiffen, panicking that he's about to tell me off for entering uninvited, but when my eyes land on his face, I'm relieved to see he's asleep.

After the long drive, and the visit to the cemetery, I don't imagine it being that hard to have succumbed to slumber.

Feeling bold, I let my eyes linger over his body. Forced to fit in his childhood, twin size bed, he's splayed out on his back, looking even bigger than he actually is on the too small mattress. Still in jeans, his long legs are bent at the knees, stopping them from hanging over. My eyes shift higher and take in the expanse of exposed skin above his waistband. He's tucked his hand underneath the bottom of his shirt, causing the material to rise. His hand is resting on top of his taut, defined, stomach; covering a light smattering of hair that extends to a place I have to forcefully stop myself from looking at.

Surprised by my own train of thought, I drag my gaze up the rest of his body, and immediately regret my choice. No longer covered by the heavy layers of clothing from earlier, I take in his beautiful, sculpted form, and internally scold myself for even thinking that way about him.

When was the last time I thought that about anyone?

Even with his arm over his eyes and the peaceful rise and fall of his chest, it's impossible to miss the vitality and masculinity he exudes. I'm reminded of the night he wrapped those arms around me. Held me. Became the strength I needed to get through that very moment.

A small lump forms in my throat, and I turn away from him, not enjoying the trip down memory lane.

Focusing on anything other than Deacon, I check out the four walls around me instead.

I've been in this house no less than a million times and I've never stepped foot in this room.

Deacon's room.

I didn't have a reason to. It was off limits and we weren't friends; in reality, we hardly knew each other.

Cautiously, I walk to the side of the room, and inspect his large and full bookshelf, and realize we *still* don't know each other.

I let my fingers skate across the spines as I read the assortment of titles, trying to understand why there's this wall between us, who put it up, and why it's suddenly starting to bother me.

I look back at Deacon and drag one of the books out of its formation. It's obvious this room is his sanctuary, and safe place. I want to feel bad for invading it, but his annoyance is something I'm accustomed to dealing with, and it's not enough of a deterrent for me to walk out that door right now.

I'm curious.

Inexplicably so.

"What are you doing here?" With nothing but the sound of sleep in his question, I turn to find him sitting up, his elbows digging into his knees, his hands steepled together.

"Your dad wanted me to tell you the food is almost ready," I supply nonchalantly. A complete contradiction to the uncertain storm of emotions brewing inside of me.

I don't rush out the door and he doesn't seem eager to stand up, but he's staring at me and even though I can't read him, I refuse to look away.

"So, you like reading?"

Instead of answering, he rises off the bed and walks toward me. He grabs the book I forgot I was holding out of my hands and gives it a once over. He leans over me, and instinctively I inhale the smell of sandalwood. His chest unexpectedly brushes up against my shoulder as he slips the book back in its rightful place. The slight contact sends a shiver down my spine, and I don't miss his sharp intake of breath.

"I'm going to go," I say, needing, but not really wanting, the space. "I'll see you downstairs."

Stepping back, he gives me just enough room to walk away. And without a second glance, I do. I find both Bill and Elaine sitting on opposite sides of the table, waiting.

"Sorry," I say, trying to appear steady. "He said he won't be long."

"Not a worry, we can start without him," Elaine says.

"No," I retort, a little more forceful than I anticipated. "We should wait."

A look of gratitude washes over Mr. Sutton's face, and I give him a tight smile in response. I don't know what I was expecting when Elaine mentioned everybody getting together for the anniversary of Rhett's death, but this irrefutable chasm in his family wasn't it.

Deacon arrives in silence. Sitting beside his dad, he's got his head down, his eyes hiding, not looking at anyone or anywhere but the plate underneath his nose.

His mother talks like he's not there, while his father tries relentlessly to make the conversation about him.

"How come Josie didn't come with you?" Bill asks him.

I vaguely remember her from random occasions the last few years. She was uptight and unapproachable. She'd come with him for a few Christmases and birthdays over the years, and didn't seem the type of woman that suited Deacon at all.

Like you would know what suits him?

"We broke up," he says, continuing to eat and choosing not to elaborate.

"I'm sorry, son. I didn't know."

"She wasn't that great anyway," Elaine pipes in. "Couldn't even show up to your brother's funeral."

"Well, she cheated on me," he reveals. "So I guess it turns out I wasn't that great either."

His admission surprises me, and my chest tightens in sympathy for him. It appears everyone is stunned by the revelation, and another awkward round of conversation ensues.

It's really just a series of questions aimed Deacon's way and to which he only provides grunts and one word answers. Eventually it all becomes too much, and he pushes his plate toward the middle of the table, indicating that he's done, and with more than just the meal.

"May I be excused?" Deacon says, interrupting them. "I'm pretty beat from the drive."

"Well, don't forget we're going to the cemetery before the anniversary mass tomorrow. Be up and ready by nine," his mother orders dismissively.

"I'll just meet you at the church."

The sound of cutlery being dropped on the porcelain plate echoes throughout the room and the twisted look on Elaine's face is a good indication of the verbal vomit that's about to spew out of her mouth.

"Twelve months," she grits out. "Twelve months your brother has been in the ground, and even on his anniversary you can't make the time to visit him."

"Elaine," I interrupt.

His head snaps up, and his eyes bore into mine. It's a subtle shake of the head, but his message is clear. He continues to sit there while she berates him, laying into him about how being a good sibling doesn't just stop because your brother is dead.

I shift my gaze to Bill, whose head is in his hands, his body hunched in defeat. Uncharacteristically, I kick my leg out under the table, hoping it reaches the right person. When his head snaps up, I narrow my eyes at him in question. *Are you going to do something?*

He eventually straightens his back and calls out his wife's name. She doesn't hear it above her own voice, so he tries another time, with no luck. The whole process is too painful to watch, so I stand up in protest. My sudden movement has the desired effect, and everyone's eyes are on mine.

I watch the muscles in Deacon's jaw clench, and his eyes burn with fury. Contrary to what I know is going on in his mind, I'm not about to spill his secrets.

"I'm sorry, Mr. and Mrs. Sutton," I address to show off my annoyance. "I'm going to have to go. I'm not feeling too well," I lie. "I think it would be better if I went home."

"But you didn't finish your food," Elaine says, the only one oblivious to my ploy of distraction. "Let me put some in a takeaway container for you. You can reheat it later when you're feeling better."

"Of course." I nod, not wanting to argue with her. "I'd really appreciate that."

When she leaves, the tension level becomes stifling. Neither man can look at me, or look at one another. It's not my job to patch up the hole in this family that Rhett's death left, and the truth is, there's nothing I could do that would even work. But I can't, in good conscience, know what I know and watch her humiliate him. Our history is irrelevant; the fact he dislikes me even more so.

Elaine returns with a pyramid of containers. She points to the one at the top. "This one has dessert in it. It's apple pie, your favorite."

Great, something else Deacon can hate me for.

Stepping to the side, I tuck my chair in and reach for the

food. I give her a quick kiss on the cheek and direct a small smile at the Sutton men in front of me. "Thank you."

"I'm sorry you're not feeling well," Elaine adds casually. "Will we see you tomorrow?"

The answer comes out of my mouth before I even have a chance to second guess myself. "Of course, but I'll just meet you guys at the church."

Elaine's mouth presses into a tight line, but she doesn't say a word. I wait for a verbal lashing, I almost welcome it, and much to my disappointment it never comes. Apparently harsh words are reserved for Deacon, alone.

With nothing left to say, I walk myself to the front door and hop down the steps. Checking my watch, I mentally go through my work calendar and wonder if anyone would want to give me their shift.

Even though I don't usually work Friday nights, the thought of going home and stewing for hours on end about what happened inside makes me feel queasy.

Opening my car door, I stretch myself across the middle and place the food on the passenger seat. As I'm righting my body to climb in the car, I hear the screen door slam. Looking up at the house, I see an irritated Deacon racing down the few steps.

"What was that inside?" he grits out.

Playing dumb, I respond, "I don't know what you're talking about."

"Fuck, Julian, I don't need you to play nice for me."

I ignore the anger and the hostility in his voice, determined not to let it throw me off exactly what I want to know.

"Why didn't you just tell her?" I ask.

"It doesn't matter—"

"Yes," I shout, silencing him, and surprising us both. I

lower my voice, trying to regain some normalcy. "It matters. She was tearing into you, and you just let her."

He turns away from me, facing the house and running his hands through his short hair. Expecting him to walk away, I'm surprised when he says. "What am I supposed to do? She lost her son. She's allowed to be angry."

Coupled with his cracked voice, his words slice right through me. It wasn't what I expected. The honesty, or the pain. "We all lost someone," I remind him. "It doesn't mean it's fair. It's not your fault he's gone."

Looking back at me, he straightens his spine and slips his mask back into place. "I already told you to stop acting like we could be friends. I don't need you to fight my battles."

"Fuck," I breathe out. "What the hell is your problem with me?"

A sliver of shock graces his face before it turns into annoyance. "Nothing," he spits out.

"That's not how this works. If you've got such an issue with me, then fucking explain it. Tell me what it is, so I can make sure to live up to whatever fucking picture you have of me in that head of yours. Or better yet, so I can stay out of your fucking way."

"I'm just saying," he starts, his voice calmer than mine. "I'm not him. I can't be him. I can't be your fill-in friend."

A humorless laugh leaves my mouth. "Fuck, Deacon," I scoff. "Firstly, as I'm sure you already know, no matter what role he played in anyone's life; Rhett is irreplaceable. Secondly, whatever shit you've got going on up there," I point to my temple, "don't try and project it onto me. I was being nice, I was on your side in there, because it was the right thing to do. Nothing more. Nothing less. So, why don't you get over yourself, huh?"

I brace myself for a fight, but instead he reminds me of just how much he really doesn't want to be around me. Without a second glance, he walks away, and I watch him the whole time, hoping for something more. But it never comes. When he closes the front door, I accept the action for what it is.

Don't worry, Deacon Sutton, 'fuck you' too.

5

DEACON

As soon as I close the front door, I let my body sag against the sturdy wood. Exhausted, both mentally and physically, I close my eyes and let my head fall back.

What's wrong with me?

I don't know why I spewed all that bullshit to him, but having him witness my mother's outrage was just too much. It was humiliating. No matter how much leeway I give her and her grief, it doesn't mean it doesn't hurt.

I'm not actively trying to be a dickhead to him, but I'm not a people person on the best of days. I've never been *good* with the boy who got all my brother's attention growing up, and I'm not *good* with the man who has all my mother's focus now.

Footsteps have me opening my eyes, and I see my father standing next to the coat rack, grabbing his jacket. "Where are you going?" I ask him.

"Julian's car won't start," he informs me.

"What?" I turn to look through the window, and low and

behold he's still parked at the curb with his head on the steering wheel, exhaustion in his every feature.

Fuck.

He's hunched over and defeated, and the guilt that sits at the bottom of my gut blooms into a puzzling need to comfort him. I ignore it and tell myself my profession is the reason I should help him.

"Let me go take a look at it," I say.

"He needs a new battery," Dad says. "It's on its last legs and he just refuses to buy a new one."

I take hold of my father's coat and return it. "I said, I'll go."

"Did you thank him?" my father asks.

Confused, I shake my head. "Thank him for what?"

"You and I both know he's feeling fine."

It's not like I didn't know he was trying to save my ass, but the reminder coming from my father's mouth only confirms I am the self-centered asshole he made me out to be.

"I'll try and convince him to go and buy a new battery."

My father claps me on the shoulder. "You're a good man, Deacon."

Feeling anything but, I swallow my pride and head to Julian's car.

He doesn't notice me at first, so I tap on the window.

He winds it down. "Can you get your dad, please?"

"Open the hood," I demand.

"Fuck you, Deacon," he spits.

Unexpectedly impressed by his fire, I find myself smirking. "I deserve that, now can you please open it?"

I walk around the car and stand at the hood, waiting. He keeps me waiting, staring at me, and I raise an eyebrow expectantly. "Should I lean in and do it myself?"

Resigned, I see his body deflate with a sigh. I watch him reach down, and I hear the familiar pop.

Winning.

Pushing the heavy metal up, I find the rusted hood stick and hook it into the circular holder.

Looking at the car, there's no obvious corrosion or battery leak. Knowing how long he's had the car, and that I was the last person to replace the original battery for Rhett, there's no denying it's just losing its juice.

Detaching the stick, I drop the hood and move toward the passenger seat. Opening the door, I climb in and wait for Julian to turn to me.

Reluctantly, he does.

"Why do you still have this piece of shit car?" I ask him.

"For the same reason you drive all the way here and leave candy corn on his grave."

I don't let the wave of sadness at the mention of Rhett, or the revelation of how we're both clinging to the past, sit between us for too long. With my dad's words echoing inside my head, I try to compartmentalize and focus on helping Julian with his car and hope that it somewhat shows my appreciation for what happened at dinner.

"He would want you to drive around in something safe," I state. "This is way past its expiration date."

"Your dad said I just need a new battery."

"He's not as good as me when it comes to cars," I say smugly. "But he knows enough that you should listen."

"I'll look into it this week," he says.

Knowing he's already put it on the back burner, I surprise myself and push a little further. "I know a place we can go get a battery from. I can drive."

His eyes widen at my suggestion, but he quickly schools

his face before answering. "Can you just jump start my car, please?"

Unpretentiously, I hold out my hand for him to shake. "Truce?"

"You're kidding, right?" He rests his head back on the seat, closes his eyes and pinches the bridge of his nose. "Whatever you're playing at with your split personality bull-shit, I don't have time for it."

Pulling back my hand, I rest it on my knee and swallow my pride. "I'm sorry, okay?"

He stills, but doesn't look at me.

"Ninety-eight percent of the time, I'm an ass. And I'm not good company when I'm around my family," I admit. The words come out casually, but it's a painful confession that sums up my life perfectly. In and out, I breathe in my prox-imity to truth and try to blow out the ever present ache in my chest. "When I'm home, it ensures that the two percent that's decent is reduced to zero, and I become one hundred percent asshole. So, please, accept my apology and come with me to pick up a car battery."

He drops his hand and turns to face me. "I accept your apology, but can you get my car started? I will get a new battery this week."

I know he's lying, but I don't want to outwardly call him on it. We still have to see each other tomorrow, and while I can't predict my mother's mood, I don't need tension between me and one more person.

"What about if you leave it here tonight, and I'll just have a quick look at it and make sure everything is running smoothly?"

"Deacon," he protests.

"It's an old car, let me just check everything is in working order," I argue.

Huffing, he throws his body back on the seat in resignation and hands me the car key. "Fine."

"Thank you," I say while tilting my head toward my truck. "Come on. I'll take you home."

The drive is quiet, but the silence is comfortable. When we pull up to his house, he's quick to jump out, while balancing his food haul under his arm.

Leaning over the middle console I wind my window down not wanting to leave without saying goodbye.

"Thanks," he says as he plunges a hand into all his pockets, looking for his keys. "I'll see you tomorrow."

"I'll pick you up in the morning."

He shakes his head. "You don't have to do that. I can catch a Lyft."

"It's on the way," I retort. "And you know if I don't my dad will show up anyway."

A light chuckle leaves his mouth. "Okay."

"I can take you to the cemetery," I offer, even though it's the last place I want to be with my mother. My strong stubborn streak refuses to let her think I'm going because she bullied me into it. My grief is between me and my brother, and I don't need to prove anything to anyone.

"No," he says forcefully. "I meant what I said."

Moved by the idea that somebody--let alone Julian— would defend me, my throat tightens with emotion. "Thank you," I manage to croak out.

"I'll see you then."

Offering me a small smile, he extinguishes any lingering awkwardness by turning and heading straight to his front door.

There's no reason for me to watch him, but I can't take my eyes off him. I didn't expect him to be such an enigma, but the hard truth is I've always been jealous of a guy I clearly didn't know. When he showed up at the cemetery today, I never would've imagined the day would've ended up like this. He took every verbal punch I threw at him, holding his own and standing his ground.

He backed me up when I gave him every reason not to, and that sentiment alone leaves an odd sense of gratitude that I haven't felt toward anyone in a really long time.

Long after he's gone inside, I find myself still parked on the side of the curb. An idea forms in my head, and I'm hoping I've got enough time to put it into motion. I grab my cell out of the cup holder and send out a quick text.

Me: Do you have any new batteries on hand for a 2004 Rav 4?

$\approx$

"HE'S GOING to be so fucking mad," my dad says, with a chuckle.

I wipe my greasy hands on my jeans and then shut the hood. I take the cold beer on offer out of my father's hand. "If he's determined to keep the death trap, it's the least I can do." We both lean on the front of the car as I raise the bottle to my lips and use the cool liquid to celebrate a job well done.

"I've been worried about him," my dad starts. "I'm worried about both of you actually."

"What's up with Julian?" I ask, purposefully deflecting his last statement. I didn't come here to talk feelings with my dad, because even though I know his concern is real, there's nothing he can do to change any of our circumstances; no matter how badly he wants to.

"Nothing in particular," he says. "I think I'm just coming to terms that between you, your mother and Julian, there's no right way to grieve. You all handle everything so differently." He takes a sip of his beer, a contemplative look gracing his face. "I'm trying to work out if you're all okay, but it's not as easy as I want it to be."

My father has always been protective of his family. A man fueled by love, he has proudly owned his role as protector and provider. Even now, when I know his heart is just as shattered as everybody else's, he prioritizes everybody else first.

I see how split he is, especially as he plays peacemaker between my mother and me. He's not perfect, and every now and then I feel like he chooses the wrong side of the argument, but I'm not a complete idiot. While I've never experienced it, I can understand the torn loyalty, she's his wife, and I'm his son. Decisions like that should never have to be made.

"And what about you, Dad? When are you going to stop worrying about everyone else, and start taking care of yourself?"

"I'm fine, Deacon," he lies. We stand in silence, sipping on our drinks when he asks, "So, what really happened with Josie? You never mentioned that you'd broken up when we spoke."

I shrug. "I told you, she cheated on me."

"Well, how are you holding up?"

"My ego took a bit of a hit," I admit. "But I don't think I was as upset about it as I should've been."

"Dating is hard," he muses. "Why do you think I married my first serious girlfriend?"

"Honestly, the shop is getting so busy lately, I don't even have the time or energy to give anything else right now."

"That's such good news, son. You've put your heart and soul into that place." He pushes himself off the car and claps me on the back. "Now have you thought about how you're going to break the news to Julian about replacing the battery?"

"If I didn't know better, Dad, I would say you're scared of him."

A throaty laugh leaves his mouth. "You'll see what I mean."

Giving a once over to the car, I'm glad it's in working order for Julian. "I'm thinking I might go drive the car to him tonight," I tell my dad. "Just in case he needs it."

"Sure. Would you like me to drive behind you and bring you back home?" he asks.

"Nah, I'm okay. I'll work it out."

Raising the bottle to his lips, he drains the rest of his drink before speaking. "Well it'll be good for you two to catch up anyway."

"Dad." Whatever he can hear in my voice stops him. "You know Julian and I were never friends. We're not friends," I correct.

"I'm well aware of that Deacon, I was here while you were both growing up under this roof," he retorts. "But you've both been through a lot, and you can never have too many friends."

I'm stumped at what to say in return, the usual argumentative response nowhere to be found. I don't know why he's pushing it so hard, but seeing as I never in a million years would've expected to be holding a key to Julian's car, replacing his battery and driving it to his house, I don't really have any legs to stand on.

"Okay, well, I'm gonna get going," I tell him, heading for the door. "I'll see you later."

For what seems like the hundredth time today I drive to Rhett's place; well Julian's place now. And it isn't lost on me that I've made this drive more times now that my brother is dead than when he was alive.

Pushing that thought aside, I pull into his driveway and psych myself up for telling Julian his car is now fixed. Walking to the front door, I contemplate leaving the key in the mailbox. It's the easy way out, the option that makes the most sense, the expectation when two people are virtually strangers.

Before I chicken out, I ring the doorbell and wait for him to come to the door. The seconds feel like minutes, and instantly I'm taken back to the night I came in and found him helplessly laying on his bed.

Does he still get sad like that? Does he deal with that alone?

When the door swings open, an unexplainable sense of relief fills my lungs as I notice he doesn't look upset, or anything remotely close to that night. Out of his clothes from earlier, he's in sweatpants and a t-shirt, looking comfortable, and relaxed, and all kinds of confused.

His mouth opens and closes, his surprise rendering him speechless. I try to fill in the awkwardness by holding up the key.

"I brought your car over."

His eyes flick to the car and then back to me. "You got it to start?"

I lower my gaze and rub my hand over the back of my neck. I realize I'm not worried about his reaction, I'm more concerned with why I felt the need to overstep.

"I got you a new battery," I mutter.

"You what?"

I apprehensively look back up at him, and the anger and annoyance I expect is nowhere to be found. He's surprised, for sure, but it's the genuine gratitude in his expression that assures me, no matter how out of character this is for me, I made the right decision by him.

When he doesn't say anything else, I hold out the key to him again. "Take this. I still don't mind picking you up tomorrow morning, I just figured it was one less thing you'd have to worry about."

He holds the key, but doesn't pull it out of my grasp. "Do you want to come inside for a drink?"

Still connected by the object between us, we stare at one another in some kind of unexplainable standoff. We don't make an attempt to move and I can only give a feeble nod as my answer.

The air feels thick and charged as I follow him inside. Standing behind him, I see how rigid and stiff his back is, and I wonder if me being here is actually making him feel uncomfortable.

The invite was probably just him being polite.

"Is something wrong, Julian? My dad said you'd be pissed and the last thing I want is for you to feel obligated to be hospitable to me if you're mad. Especially after the way I treated you today."

He spins around, and I raise my hands on instinct to stop myself from walking into him. My palms brush against his chest, and a low, short gasp escapes Julian's mouth.

He takes a step back and shakes his head vehemently. "I'm sorry," he says, surprising me. "You just caught me off guard, that's all." He scratches his forehead. "I want to pay you for the battery."

"I didn't pay for it," I respond. Without any hesitation, the lie slips off the top of my tongue. I don't know his financial situation, and even though my dad may have thought that was the reason he wasn't quick to service the car, it wasn't the first thing to cross my mind when I decided to help him.

When I saw him sitting in the car outside my parents' place, the obvious fatigue and despondence on his face, I couldn't knowingly just do nothing. I still can't just do nothing.

Call it guilt, or call it paying a debt to my dead brother, but for whatever reason, leaving Julian to fend for himself doesn't sit right with me.

I have no doubt he's more than capable. I mean, hell, he's been fending for himself his whole life, but knowing I *could* help... that made me feel something else entirely. The solution was within my reach and there haven't been many instances in my life where I haven't been the disappointment in someone's story. Where I've had the chance to be helpful, if not a hero.

"I could afford a new battery, that wasn't why I wasn't getting it," he says defensively.

"Hey," I say firmly while putting my hands up in surrender. "That thought didn't even cross my mind. It was a simple fix. I'm a mechanic and you needed a battery."

There's a fair amount of logic to my argument, and while it seems to be enough to hold off his rebuttal, there's a long indecipherable lull hanging between us, as we both stare at one another.

His brown eyes bore into mine, and I stand there, waiting, wondering what it is he sees.

I could go, I could will my feet to move, but something in the way he looks at me makes me want to stay. It's not hostile or strained, but it's not comfortable or familiar either.

It's more of a pull. An inquisitiveness. A niggling feeling

that's wrapping itself around my body like a vine, keeping my feet planted on the ground.

Knowing I'm not going anywhere, I offer a shrug, because I really just don't know what the hell is happening or what the hell I'm feeling right now. But I'm here, and I may as well ride it out.

"So," I droll. "What do you say about that drink, huh?"

6

JULIAN

A drink? Shit. Yes. I asked him in for a drink. "Anything in particular?" I ask as I take hurried steps into the kitchen.

"Whatever you're having is fine with me," he calls out.

I open the fridge and stand in front of it, hoping the cool rush of air will extinguish the overwhelming tornado of heat swirling inside my body.

I try to process that Deacon—the very same man who has dismissed me more times than I can count in the last twenty-four hours—is at my house, swooping in with his grand gesture that brings up feelings I'm nowhere near emotionally equipped to deal with.

Curling my fingers around the two bottlenecks, I pull the beer out of the fridge and slam the door. Expecting to see him sitting on the couch, I'm surprised that he's still standing in the same spot I left him.

Nervously, I hand him the drink. "You don't have to stand up the whole time," I joke, hoping to break the tension.

"Yeah. Thanks." He shakes his head as if to rid himself of

something and then takes the beer out of my hand. He walks to the two-seater, and against my better judgment I follow. Sitting on either end, I maneuver myself into the furthest corner of the couch, bringing up my legs to cross and resting my back on the couch arm.

Deacon's posture is a little more stiff and I wait for the awkward and closed off version of him to return. When the silence lingers for a bit too long, I gear up the courage to break the ice, but once again he surprises me.

"Is it hard living here?" he asks. "Without him, I mean."

I want to say it's hard without him period, but I know that exact answer will shut down any further conversation, and I don't want that. This is the one thing we have in common, and as painful as it is to open those wounds, something in my gut tells me he doesn't speak about his brother or his death very often. That he needs this.

"Surprisingly, we didn't have as many memories here as I thought we would," I answer. "This place reminds me more of all the things that could've been, you know?"

He offers me a small nod before taking a sip of his beer.

"What about you?" I ask, cautiously. "Does living in Seattle help?"

Shifting his body, his position soon mirrors mine. He lowers his head, and absently begins picking at the label, clearly lost in thought.

"I make the trip down here more now that he's dead than when he was alive." There's a slight crack in his voice, a hint of vulnerability I wasn't anticipating. "I just wanted to be on my own when I got older. It wasn't personal, I just wanted to pave my own way."

"There's nothing wrong with that," I tell him. "You couldn't have known how it all was going to play out."

He rubs the heel of his palm across his chest. "Are you always so glass half full?"

I want to lie, because when it comes to me and my life, I live and breathe negativity. I wallow in nothingness and convince myself life is better on my own. With no feelings, no friends, no family.

But for whatever reason, I don't want that for Deacon. He needs to reprieve himself of the guilt and sense of blame that oozes out of his pores. Every word. Every look. Every move.

He's driven by the need to be better, because the right people didn't tell him he was enough.

"I just tell it how it is," I answer.

Sipping on more of his liquid courage, his eyes land on mine, holding my stare. "And how exactly is it?"

It's a subtle challenge, but I don't back down. Taking a large swig of my beer, I place the brown glass bottle on the coffee table and scoot closer to him.

I find myself wanting to be near him; not sure whether I want to comfort him or rattle him. "I don't know you," I answer, honestly. "I know *some* things, but for whatever reason, I never got the chance to know *you*. But I knew Rhett," my voice cracks on his name, and my tongue expands, feeling dry and thick. Like a lifeline, I reach for my beer and let the wheaty taste flood my mouth, and cool down my throat, as I will myself to say the rest. "He thought the world of you."

"I was never here," he argues.

"You were there when it mattered, and no more than a phone call away."

"God," he shouts, shooting up off the couch. "I don't understand why you're so nice to me."

He runs his hands through his hair and starts pacing around the living room, and I can't help but stand up too.

"It's infuriating," he adds. "I've never been nice to you. I don't visit my parents regularly, and I used my job to hide away when it was too hard to visit my dying brother."

Without realizing it, he's made his way to me, and we're once again standing face to face, but this time we're also toe to toe.

He's worked himself into a state, his breathing heavy and frantic.

"Deacon." His name is a strained whisper from my lips. I absently place my hand on his chest, my body trying to soothe him, before my brain can even say no. My palm connects with hard muscle and the contact reignites the heat I was only just desperately trying to douse.

I try to pull myself away, I tell myself to take my hand off of him, but I don't. I like the way he feels under my skin, and it takes everything in me not to let my fingers roam.

I watch him blink a few times, his eyes dragging themselves up and down my body, like he's just noticed how close we are. His gaze focuses on my hand, and I expect him to freak out.

Our proximity isn't logical. Not for us, and not for two men who are barely even friends. This borders on intimate, and I'm sure the role we play in the bigger picture makes this somewhat wrong.

Isn't it?

But when Deacon unexpectedly covers my hand with his, it doesn't feel wrong. It feels *anything* but wrong.

So, I let it happen.

I don't offer him words of comfort, because they're not what's going to make him feel better. Trust me, I know. It doesn't matter how many times someone tells you, if you don't believe it, it will never be true. Your own insecurities and your lack of self-assurance will win every time.

So, I let it happen. I let the touch happen, and I wait for the simplest and most overused form of physical contact to blow up in my face. Because that's the only way this can go, right?

Because I *can't* actually want to be touching him, can I?

"I think I should go," he announces. He lets his hand fall and takes an exaggerated step back. And I pretend his need for distance doesn't hurt.

"Yeah, I need an early night."

To try and take the sting out of this whole situation, I lower my head and walk to the front door. Swinging it open, I wait for him to take the hint.

Knowing he's only a handful of steps away, I look up to see what's taking him so long. The question must be written all over my face, because he draws in a long breath before speaking.

"I'm sorry," he says.

"You apologize a lot," I point out. "And you should really stop. Actually, what would be even better, is if we went back eight hours or so to when you and I never spoke."

He gives me a small nod, the look of shame on his face unmissable, and a guilt fueled sliver of victory runs through me at having the upper hand.

"Thank you for the battery," I say.

The second his two feet step over the threshold, I slam the door, not even caring how he's going to get home. Frustrated with myself for feeling anything else other than the numbness I've been so accustomed to.

Filled with anger, I do the only thing that will calm me down. Picking up the unfinished beer bottles, I throw them in the recycling bin and switch off all the lights in the living room.

I walk into my bedroom, strip off my clothes and take the spot in the middle of the bed. I reach over and pull the box to me. Holding it close to my chest, I hug the wood. As if it's Rhett, I hug it hard and hug it for dear life.

Tears stream down my face and my solitary living arrangement means I let them fall. I cry for the year that's passed, I cry for the man that's gone, and for the first time, I cry for me. I felt something tonight.

Something for Deacon?

Something with Deacon?

I felt *something* and I hate that for a split second *feeling* felt good at all.

When my emotions have mellowed themselves out, I place the box in front of me. Like a well-practiced ritual, I lift the lid and start picking out the letters. One by one, I give the unopened envelopes the reverence they deserve.

Thank you, Rhett, for thinking of me. I'm sorry you're not here.

My hold lingers on the one that says "One Year Anniversary" and I contemplate opening it. Curiosity has me wanting to, but self-preservation screams at me to keep it closed. The loss of Rhett is more than just a broken heart. It's more like the universe stole away and ripped every good thing in my life, tearing it into unrecognizable shreds.

It's an impossible heap of pain that can never be put back together, because there's too much missing, and what's left is too damaged. Too scarred. Too ruined. And opening those letters will only decimate that damaged fraction of what's left of me.

Finally ready for bed, I curl under the blankets and pray for a few hours of peace before tomorrow. I don't know what

I expected this weekend to be like. Actually that's a lie. With all the reminiscing and the sadness; I expected emotion, heavy hearts; I did *not* anticipate Deacon.

In any way, shape or form, I expected Deacon Sutton to be the very last thing I thought about before I finally fell asleep.

TAKING the last sip of my now ice cold coffee, I turn the tap on and run the mug under the spray, rinsing out the excess liquid. Sighing, I wipe my wet hand on my black jeans, wishing I didn't spend half the night tossing and turning, rendering me a complete mess this morning.

When I finally fell asleep, my thoughts of Deacon morphed into a constant reel of Rhett. Young Rhett, teenage Rhett, sick Rhett, healthy Rhett. Dead Rhett. Lots of dead Rhett.

My brain working overtime to dig up old memories and turn them into what felt like a live stream of dreams. The past meshing with the present, my subconscious playing tricks on me, messing with my reality.

Now, this morning, I'm just exhausted. Mentally, I can't sort through my thoughts fast enough, and my feelings are all centered around the debilitating ache in my chest.

I rest my hands on the bench and try to focus on my breathing.

In and out.

In and out.

My blood feels like lead, and it's making it hard to move. And I need to move if I'm going to make it anywhere on time. My eyes fall on the glowing numbers on the microwave, and I push myself into action.

When I make it to the front of the house, I pull my jacket off the hook that's nailed to the back of the door. Slipping into my thick coat, I grab my phone and wallet out of the bowl that's sitting on top of the buffet and tuck them into either of my pockets.

Just as I'm about to lock up, a knocking sound comes from the other side. Needing to leave, I pull it open, wanting to get rid of the unwanted guest, when I see Deacon staring back at me, looking equally fresh and weary.

I hold on to the solid wood for support, neither my body nor my mind prepared for his visit. "What are you doing here?" I ask.

Avoiding my eyes, he scrapes his hand through his hair. "I told you I'd pick you up."

I look away from him, and then over his shoulder at my car. "You replaced the battery in my car. It works now," I remind him. "And not to mention..."

The incomplete sentence is self-explanatory, as his gaze finally meets mine.

"Not to mention last night," he finishes.

I raise my shoulders and shake my head at him. "What do you want, Deacon? I thought I made my feelings very clear."

He shoves his hands in his pockets, and wraps the material around his broad body, and then brings his sea blue eyes to mine. His face is stoic, but his eyes tell another story. There's a storm brewing, a million emotions he's trying to contain. "I need you there."

His request winds me. My voice comes out a breath above a whisper. "What?"

He blows out a long breath, a plume of air mushrooming between us. "I need you to be my buffer."

My mouth falls open. "You're not kidding are you?"

"Look." A flush creeps across his cheeks, and he tucks his head into his chest to hide it. "This whole thing is embarrassing enough," he mutters. "But I can't deal with her today. I know how it sounds, and I know I need to man up about it, but she likes you." I don't miss the hurt in his voice, and I hate it for him. "She is less likely to bother with me today, now that she unleashed her fury yesterday. And you're..."

I raise an eyebrow in question.

"You're the perfect distraction."

As if he released a slingshot, his words land like heavy weights on my chest, and it's obvious we both feel the hit. The innocent words, strung together, and out of his mouth, feel anything but.

He doesn't shy away, like I expect him to, or even explain himself any further, for that matter. But the storm in his eyes is now a swirl of curiosity, with the slightest undercurrent of desire.

I may have only ever been with one man, but I'd know how to identify the kindling of attraction anywhere.

"I'm... um... I'm going to." I jerk my thumb behind me to stop my ridiculous stuttering, gesturing that I'm going inside. When he gives me a nod, I add, "We can go in your car when I come out."

I watch his shoulders relax and the intense look on his face fades when he realizes I'll do what he asks.

I head back inside for absolutely no reason at all, but to compose myself. I make my way to the kitchen and grab a bottle of water out of the fridge. Chugging it down, I wait for my heart to stop racing and my mind to stop spinning.

What the fuck was that?

Feeling stable enough to walk outside, I scan the house

one more time to make sure nothing is out of place before I lock up and leave.

Counting to five, I regulate my breathing and tell myself I can get through today. Today isn't about this awkward reconciliation between Deacon and I, today is about Rhett and *only* Rhett.

Stepping outside, I notice Deacon has already climbed back in and started his truck.

When I jump in, I'm greeted by warm air blowing from the heater. The change in temperature relaxes my muscles, but my mind is still on high alert, wondering how I managed to get myself into a confined space with Deacon, after I insisted we should stay out of one another's way.

Choosing to look out the window, instead of at him, I clear my throat, hoping it gets his attention. "I'm happy to help you out today, but I need you to promise me something."

It takes him a beat to respond. "Anything."

Turning to look at him, I hope he recognizes the serious-ness in my face. "If I say I want to go home, at any time, please take me home."

I watch his throat bob as he swallows before speaking. "I can do that."

Offering him a smile, I look back out the window, and choose to get lost in the blur of the buildings and greenery we pass on our way to the church.

"Will Victoria be at the church?" I ask, even though I know the answer, hoping to fill the silence.

"Yeah. I spoke to her this morning," he tells me. "They went to the cemetery with my parents and grandparents first."

The Suttons aren't extremely religious and aren't ones to push any beliefs on to other people, but when it comes to 'special' occasions, they expect their kids to be there. And because Rhett and I were joined at the hip, there wasn't an Easter or Christmas mass I didn't attend growing up. It's now become one more thing I want to hold on to.

When we arrive at the church, Elaine, Bill and Bill's parents are waiting for us at the bottom of the steps that lead to the entrance. If they're surprised to see us arrive together, they don't say anything.

Just as predicted Elaine's face lights up when she sees me, and her arms open in greeting. I almost want to rebel and move away, feeling resentment for how hurt Deacon is by her actions.

He may not be my favorite person in the world, but I'll never be able to unsee the vulnerability that consumed him this morning.

"It's so good to see you, Julian." She threads her arm with mine, and I feel Deacon's eyes on us. She should be doing this with him. "Let's head inside. Victoria, Hayden, and Lia are already seated."

"It's good to see you too, Elaine." I take hold of her hand and choose to pull myself away from her.

"Can you give me a second? I'll be inside soon."

Not wanting to adhere to my request, Bill places his hand on the small of her back when she doesn't move, and guides her inside, leaving me and Deacon alone.

"You don't have to stay here with me," Deacon states.

"I know." Wringing my fingers together, I look at his parents' retreating bodies to make sure they're out of earshot and then back at him. "I actually just want to apologize."

An obvious frown forms on his face. "For what?" But as the question slips out, he too looks at his mom and dad and then back at me. He places a hand up to stop me from talking. "You're apologizing for my mom?" He shakes his head at me. "No."

Dry as a bone, I lick my lips to try and find the right words I need to get my point across, but he beats me to it and steps in, closer.

A little too close.

With his mouth right by my ear, any fleeting thought I had is turned into dust as his low and firm voice coils itself around my spine. "I said, 'No'."

7

DEACON

I always end up here with him. Standing a little too close, the words out of my mouth a little too honest.

"Please don't," I say a little softer. "There's not one single thing you *ever* need to apologize for."

Our closeness means I'm privy to the hitch in his breath, to the slight tremble running through his body, to the beautiful blush of his skin.

Every single part of me is on edge, as I recognize the blurred lines between us for what they are. It's not a feeling I've experienced, it's not a feeling I'm familiar with, but the strength and intensity of it makes it very difficult to ignore.

Finally nodding at my request, he raises his head confidently. "I'm going to go inside now."

Just as I expect him to walk away, he surprises me. "Sit next to me, okay?"

Swallowing hard, I respond, "Okay."

It's not the answer I expected to give, but it isn't one I feel like changing either.

He doesn't wait for me, and I'm grateful for his sixth sense, because the moment of space is exactly what I need. I wait for him to extend the distance between us, before I let my ass land on the concrete steps, and bury my head in my hands.

Fuck.

My phone vibrates in my pocket, a message from Victoria on the screen.

Victoria: Where are you?

Instead of responding to the text, I give myself another sixty seconds and then I rise and haul my unsteady self, two steps at a time, into the church. I spot Vic first because her eyes are already darting around the place in search of me. When they land on me, and she smiles, I realize just how much I've missed her.

Standing up, she doesn't seem to care that she's seated in the middle of the pew, people on either side of her. She slides herself past each member of my family, not an ounce of concern for the disruption.

I reach her, just as she steps out, and catch her when she launches herself into my arms. We hold on to one another, squeezing away the sadness and the regret of not seeing each other in so long.

We're so busy, and Victoria is the only other person who's ever really understood me. She never balked at my moving or forging my own path, she never punished me for the physical distance between us; she let me be. She was and always will be the supportive and understanding older sister.

When we part, I don't miss the disgusted glare my mother aims my way at my tardiness. Choosing to ignore her, my gaze gravitates to Julian, who's at the other end of the long wooden bench, playing and whispering with Lia on his lap. They're in their own world and strangely, that's where I want to be.

With a perfect excuse, I kiss my sister on the cheek and whisper in her ear, "I'm going to sit with Lia and Julian, I want to see my niece. We'll talk after."

She gives me a small nod, and I watch her squeeze her way back past everyone's long legs. Thankfully the pew behind them is empty. I walk between the long planks of wood until I'm right behind Julian.

Sitting down, I lean forward, close enough he can hear me. "I'm just going to sit here, okay?"

Without looking back, or pausing his game with Lia, I hear him say, "There's plenty of room here."

My chest tightens at his insistence. *There's nothing wrong with doing what he asked, is there?*

I watch the priest walk to the lectern and realize if I'm going to move, it needs to be quick. Biting the bullet, I slide myself into the end of the pew, next to Julian, and repeat the half hearted lie I just told my sister to myself.

I want to see my niece.

It takes all of two seconds for Lia to climb into my lap, and that's all I need to relieve the tension.

"Hey Lia Lady," I coo, my voice just above a whisper. "I missed you."

"Missed you," she says back, her tongue getting caught between her small front teeth, her lisp hard to miss. "You play?"

"What are you playing?"

"Juledian," she says, the mispronunciation of his name making her even cuter. "You play."

"How about we practice being quiet?" He theatrically zips up his lips and throws away the key before pressing his index finger against his mouth.

"Shhh," I say into Lia's ear. "Let's be quiet."

"Shhh," she repeats. "Shhh. Shhh. Shhh."

"Lia," my sister hisses before we get too carried away. "That's enough."

While the priest starts his sermon, I give Lia my cell in the hope of keeping her occupied. When she tries to open the phone and the screen requests a passcode, she hands it to Julian. "Open."

"Open, what?" he says.

Her cute face scrunches in confusion.

"Open, please," Julian clarifies.

"Open, please, Juledian."

He's about to hand me the cell, when I lean closer to him and whisper. "Zero, six, two, seven."

Recognition of Rhett's birthday settles across his face as he punches in the digits, but it isn't till he hands the cell back to Lia, that he turns with a sad smile and looks at me. "I have the same code."

We stare at one another, and my skin tingles from the current of energy between us. We're similar in ways I don't understand and different in ways I do, and I can't get my head around any of it.

Lia's excited screech breaks the connection and echoes throughout the whole church.

It's so unexpected, I give her a little squeeze to quiet her down, but can't help chuckling at how adorable she is. I throw my hand over my mouth, as the sound comes out a little louder than I anticipated.

Quickly lowering my eyes in embarrassment, I try to stop my shoulders shaking, as I successfully stifle the laugh. It's useless and I can feel everyone's beady stares, disappointed at the disruption. But it's the feel of Julian's thigh pressing into mine that claims my full attention. It's both a distraction and a move of solidarity.

I tilt my head up at him, but he's working extra hard to keep his smirk in check and his focus on the front.

I can't even hide the smile that spreads across my face. Even if I tore myself open this morning and let my weakness fall at his feet, I can't deny I'm enjoying knowing there's someone wanting to watch out for me. Even if it comes attached to an onslaught of feelings I have no explanations for, right now, with Julian and Lia, I feel light.

Not better.

Not worse.

Just light.

Eventually, Lia settles, and Julian and I focus on the priest and his words. From what my father explained to me this morning, there will be a quick mention of Rhett and the fact it's been one year since he's passed, and if I blink for too long, we'll miss it.

When I asked why it was even necessary, he said, 'it's not. It's for your mother.' So, like everyone else, I try to focus on the sermon, so I don't miss hearing my brother's name. But I get lost in thought, staring at Lia and her sandy blonde hair. The way her layered curls fall across the span of her shoulders. How the only time I've seen her in the past year has been through a phone screen; missing every which way she's been growing.

I didn't know how much I would love being an uncle until Lia was born. It didn't matter what relationship we all had with one another, we always came together for Lia. Even with the distance between us Victoria never made me feel left out, sending me photos, using FaceTime once a week, making sure Lia knew who Uncle Deacon was.

But nothing, absolutely nothing, compares to holding her, watching her smile, hearing her laugh. As if she knows

I'm thinking about her, she squirms in my arms, working out her next move.

She crawls back into Julian's lap, and he glances up at me before smiling down on her. They're comfortable together, only solidifying that my sister has used her daughter to try and heal all of us. And for the most part, it works. Like a bandaid decorated in pink and purple flowers, Lia stops the wound from splitting any further. Like a bandaid, she stops us all from bleeding out.

Focused on the interaction between Julian and Lia, the only indication that I've missed something important is when I feel him shift, moving his leg away from mine. I immediately miss his touch, the hum in my body I was becoming accustomed to dissipates, and I search around us to understand what changed.

My ears perk up, my brother's name reaching the ears of the congregation. The weight on my chest increases as the priest 'remembers his short, but memorable life.' I watch my family tensing around me, and Julian shutting down as my brother is described in numerous, underwhelming adjectives.

I look back at Lia wistfully. She helps, but nothing will ever miraculously fix it.

As usual death and grief snuffs out any goodness in the air, souring the mood with promises of just another dark and painful day. The service is to honor his memory, but what it really is, is a day to acknowledge that time doesn't heal a single fucking thing.

It's a cruel promise. One the universe repeatedly doles out, only to repeatedly break.

It isn't long before everyone around me is rising from their seats, and we're all making our way outside. I'm on autopilot, the quick change in my mood annoying me.

For a moment there, I felt like I could breathe.

The air wasn't thick and stale. For a moment there I felt like there was more for me than always feeling like this.

We all congregate at the bottom of the steps, my mother and Victoria bickering about what to do next.

"Why can't we go out to eat?" Victoria suggests.

"It's cold and your grandparents don't need to be driving around in this weather," my mother responds harshly.

"Oh, Elaine," my grandfather interrupts. "We're just old, we're not incapable."

Victoria presses her lips together, hiding her smile. "If you want, Pop, I can drive your car for you and Hayden can drive our car with Lia." Victoria sneaks an apologetic glance at her husband but he just smiles and nods. The man would do anything for my sister.

Vic returns her focus to Mom. "Wouldn't it be nice to go to Rhett's favorite restaurant instead of being cooped up in the house?"

Cooped up with all the sad, sick memories is what she means. And she's right. Rhett died there. And no matter how many good memories we have in that house, none of them are strong enough to ward off the most painful one.

My dad's face softens in understanding. He plasters on a smile and grabs my mother by the elbow. "I think it's a great idea, Elaine. If my parents get tired or uncomfortable, I'll take them home myself."

Irrespective of the fact my grandfather stated he would be coming and driving his own car, my father's words leave her with no argument, no other reason to say no.

Her eyes scan all our hopeful faces, and she realizes she's been beat. "I had everything prepared to cook," she pouts.

I risk her wrath and wrap my arms around her shoulders. "You deserve a break, mom. You can take today off, and just cook it all tomorrow."

She tilts her head up at me. "Will you stay to eat the food tomorrow?"

Surprised that there's no sarcasm, and the request is filled with genuine hope, I nod. "Of course, mom. I'll stay as long as I can."

I feel everyone's eyes on me, but for some reason mine only search for Julian's. He's looking right back at me, his gaze knowing and perceptive. His mouth curves at the edges, a hint of a smile forming, one that I find myself wanting to reciprocate.

Feeling my face heat up, I school my expression, break our connection and look at my sister. "Are we ready to go?"

"Yesss," she cheers excitedly while clapping her hands together in victory. "Let's meet at El Sarapes."

All in agreement, we each split off to our respective cars, and I find myself once again alone with Julian.

"Is it okay if I ride with you?" he asks hesitantly. "I probably shouldn't have assumed. I can catch a ride with Victoria or your parents."

He's rattling on and it takes me a few seconds too long to catch on to his train of thought. "What?" I shake my head. "No. Yes. No."

We reach the car, and he stares at me in confusion. "What I meant," I say a little more coherently, "is of course it's okay if you ride with me." I unlock the car, pressing the key fob in my pocket and open his door. "I picked you up, I want you to ride with me."

Wordlessly, he steps up into the truck and I find myself watching the way his clothes stretch and pull against his body as he maneuvers himself into the seat.

"What?" he asks self consciously when he notices me

staring. "Did I scratch your truck or something?" He twists his neck to look behind him. "Did a bird shit on my clothes?"

What the actual fuck is going on with me right now? Was I just checking him out?

My pulse races. Frantic. Fraught. Overworked.

Unable to give him an answer, I push the door shut; knowing it's a dick move, but having nothing logical or relevant to replace it with.

It's my default.

When I don't know, or I can't get the words right, I shut down. He's witnessed it a million times over the years. A million more this weekend. What's one more time, right?

I walk myself to the driver's side but delay climbing in while I try to dissect the maelstrom of feelings and thoughts inundating my body and mind.

Shoving my hands through my hair in frustration, I acknowledge that if I stand out here any longer Julian will just ask more questions, or more likely, feel more self-conscious. I may not know much in this moment, or have answers to my own questions, let alone his, but I don't want him doubting himself, or worrying about upsetting me.

I've done enough of that to him, and I know wholeheartedly, I want to at least *try* to not do it anymore.

When I finally get into the car, Julian's eyes are glued to his phone, nonchalantly scrolling through whatever is on his screen.

My shoulders release the tension, internally grateful that it isn't awkward or strained. The restaurant is a good forty minutes away from where we are now, and while it's a comfortable silence, I find myself not wanting to miss the opportunity to talk to Julian. To hear him talk to me.

To try to work out when, why and how he's no longer the man I can't stand to be around.

Beating me to it, he says, "It's nice that we're all going to El Sarapes."

"It is, isn't it?" I agree.

"And your mom..."

I shift my gaze between the empty, long road in front of me and Julian. "It was unexpected," I admit.

"Did you mean what you said to her? About staying?"

We stop at a traffic light, and my fingers dance around the edge of the steering wheel, buying time. "I think the question we both should be asking is will she still feel warm and nostalgic once everybody else has gone and it's only me, my dad and her in the house?"

"But would you stay?" he presses.

"I love Seattle. I love living there," I explain. "I love living there more than I love living here. So... would I stay?" I shake my head. "Probably not." I let out a loud, vulnerable sigh, because there isn't a secret in the world I can seem to keep from Julian. "But, would I like to visit my mom and dad, and not go home feeling like shit?" I snicker. "Yeah. Every now and then I would."

"So," he stalls.

"So?"

"When are you going home?"

"Don't worry, I won't be around for much longer," I joke.

He shifts in his seat. "That's not what I meant."

"I know, I'm kidding," I assure him. "I'm just playing it by ear. I haven't seen my family in a year, and I made a promise to myself I wouldn't leave until we made some kind of amends."

"Do your parents know that?"

"Nah," I answer, shaking my head. "They can't be disappointed if I bail early if they don't know I had any plans to stay."

He nods in understanding, and I mull over my plan in my head. It's not a very good one, but I know all I can do is try. And I will.

"I haven't eaten Mexican food since Rhett died," Julian randomly offers.

"Yeah," I supply, appreciative of the segue into a new conversation. "Me either."

"I guess we have a lot more in common than we thought."

I laugh because it's a simple, but very accurate observation. In any other circumstances, we would and could easily be friends.

We fall back into the easy silence, this time I put some music on for an added layer of protection, and continue on the drive.

We're only five minutes out when a phone call comes through my Bluetooth system. Victoria's name pops up on the screen.

I press the answer button on the inside of my steering wheel. "Hello."

"Rhett must be looking down on us today, because we got a table straight away," she blurts out. "We're by the glass windows at the back. So, just bypass the front and walk right in."

"Got it. We're just pulling up in the parking lot. We'll be in soon."

"You and Julian are together?" she asks, the inflection in her voice makes it obvious this is news to her, and she is definitely surprised. "In the same car?" she adds.

"Yes, Victoria. And he can hear you," I snap. "What's the big deal? I picked him up this morning."

"Nothing," she sings. "I'll see you when I see you."

Annoyed, I turn into a parking space with a little more force than necessary and then turn the truck off. "You should go in without me. I won't be long."

"Don't do that," Julian scolds. My back stiffens, preparing myself for a fight. "That," he insists, his hand landing on my shoulder. "Don't go back into your shell because she asked a question. She's curious and just teasing you."

His fingers press into muscle, and my eyes follow the move. "Your mom is in a good mood, and you're with your family. Who cares if they're giving you a bit of shit. And for the record, you and I in a car together is a big deal," he says with a smile in his voice. "All of this doesn't happen very often. Enjoy the moment."

Looking back up at him, I huff. "You're making me sound like an ungrateful ass."

"Ungrateful, no, but an ass?" He tilts his head to the side. "If the shoe fits, maybe."

Turning to face him, I narrow my eyes.

"What?" he shrugs. "I can't help it if there's proof in the pudding. At least you've learned to tone it down a notch."

His confidence and the ease of our banter drags a slow smirk out of me. I don't know how we got here, but he's right, it doesn't happen very often; so I'm going to enjoy it.

"Get the hell out of my truck."

Luckily the walk from the truck to the restaurant is less than twenty steps, because the air is somehow colder, the wind much stronger than it was an hour or so ago.

We huddle close together, like we're trying to hide from the wind. When we reach the entrance, I pull at the glass door, opening it wide enough for us to both walk through.

My hand finds the small of Julian's back, guiding him in front of me.

The move is automatic.

Instinctual.

Muscle memory.

It feels natural, understated almost. Like something I've done my whole life.

Except there's the warmth that explodes inside my chest, as soon as my palm presses against him, and it... it definitely suggests otherwise.

8

JULIAN

We pass the threshold, and I wait for the sudden change. For the intimacy of his action to dawn on him, and for him to freak out and step away. But it doesn't come.

Not for either of us.

If I'm not mistaken, the pressure of his palm against my lower back increases, the further into the restaurant we walk. It takes every ounce of willpower not to turn around and look at him. Not because I want to alert him, or because I want to break our contact.

Because I don't.

I just want to see his face, read his expression; try to work out if the things going through his body and mind are as chaotic and confusing as my own.

When we reach the table, his hand slides off my back, almost like he was reluctant to let me go. My head swivels around, my torso twisting uncomfortably, desperate to get a glimpse of him at this moment.

He doesn't hide his eyes or turn away from me. He gifts

me a view of very visibly flushed cheeks that would be hard to explain to anyone that was looking at us too closely.

Every single part of me wants to drag him out of this place and insist he explain whatever this is to me.

Why is he touching me? Why do I want him to?

"Julian. Deacon," Victoria calls out, breaking the spell. "There's two seats here for you."

His eyes shift, no longer focused on me, his face now scrunching up in irritation at whoever it is behind me. Certain that it's Victoria, I turn to find her grinning in satisfaction.

I shake my head at her and smile. "Leave him alone."

She and everyone else around the table look at me quizzically, but I ignore them. I'm as clueless right now as the rest of them.

We take our seats, side by side; me next to Victoria and him on the edge. She nudges me, and I lean into her, avoiding eye contact. "My brother's being nice to you," she whispers.

"We're being nice to one another," I correct.

"Either way, it's really weird."

Her observation is harmless and completely natural for our relationship. Apart from Rhett, she's always been my closest friend. My closest family.

I haven't been very forthcoming over the last twelve months, but she never lets my mood deter her. She's always there. Offering an ear to listen, or a shoulder to lean on. It's not just her ability to share her loss with me, but it's her ability to understand the differences of what we lost.

Sometimes it's a smile, or just a playdate with Lia; a text or a phone call. She never gives up, even when I think I want her to.

She's the eyes and ears of the family, and that's why the

change between Deacon and I hasn't gone unnoticed. The only problem is, now that she's aware, she'll be watching and documenting our every move.

"Can we talk about it later?" I say, trying to end the conversation.

"Oh, we will be."

Picking up the menu, I distract myself and look through the list of dishes. When I notice Deacon's body turned to the side, his arm around the back of my chair, casually looking over my shoulder, I turn my head up to face him. "Get a good look?"

My voice is unrecognizably playful, and to my surprise Deacon smirks. "There's no point looking at the menu. Any time my parents are here, my dad suggests the set menu so we can have a taste of everything."

"Oh my god," I say, a smile stretching across my face. "You're so right. How did I never realize that?"

He looks up across the table at his dad and murmurs in my ear. "Three. Two. One."

Bill closes the menu and looks around the table. "Wouldn't it be easier if we just got the set menu? They have a bit of everything on offer."

Vic leans over, looking at Deacon laughing, she too obviously knew what her father was going to suggest.

When everyone agrees, a waiter returns and quickly writes down the easy order. Looking to Bill first, he asks, "Can I get you all any drinks?"

"Fellas," he calls across the table. "Beers?"

We all agree in unison, when he looks to Victoria for an answer.

"No beer," she informs him. She continues to muse over the drinks menu when Elaine pipes up. "What about if we share a bottle of Chardonnay?"

Bill's face lights up at Elaine's request, and I wonder if this is the first time in a long time she's truly allowed herself to enjoy the company around her.

I catch Victoria sneaking a look at Hayden before nodding at her father. "Chardonnay sounds great."

"Mom, Dad," Bill addresses his parents. "Same as us?"

"I'll have a beer," Mr. Sutton Senior says.

"He will have no such thing," his wife says. "His blood pressure has been high the last few days and the last thing we need is a trip to the emergency room."

"Can't a man grow old on his own terms?" he huffs. "It's just one damn drink."

Bill's parents continue to bicker, while Bill discreetly turns to the waiter, telling him to add a large pitcher of water for the table to the order.

While everyone waits for the food, we split up into our own conversations. Hayden and Deacon are lost in a conversation about work, and Victoria alternates trying to settle Lia down, and prying information out of me I'm not really willing to give.

"Why are you still working at that dive bar?" she asks.

"It's hardly a dive," I bite back. "And I like it there."

"You're wasting away there."

"I get out of the house. I talk to people," I state matter-of-factly. "That's more than what I actually *want* to do most days."

She rolls her eyes at me just as the waiter returns with everyone's drinks. He offers to pour the chardonnay, but Victoria stops him. "That's okay, I've got this."

"Can you hold Lia for a second?" she asks me.

Scooping the little girl off her lap, I place her on my own. As soon as the extra weight has been lifted, Victoria stands, immediately capturing everyone's attention.

She leans over the table, grabbing Elaine's wine glass. Pouring a generous amount of the yellow liquid, she hands it back to her mother and nestles the glass bottle into the ice bucket.

"So, I wasn't sure if I was going to do this today." Rubbing her hands together, she glances at Hayden. In sync with one another, he too stands and walks around the table to stand behind her. Giving her shoulders a squeeze, she nods in what I assume to be understanding.

"I figured it's very rare that we ever get together like this anymore," she starts. "Things change and time moves so fast."

"And while today will always be the hardest day of the year for us, it feels right to maybe try and change that by announcing Hayden and I are going to have another baby."

The table erupts in surprised gasps, chairs scraping against the tile floor, as each and every one rushes to hug and congratulate the expecting couple.

When Victoria announced she was pregnant with Lia, Rhett had just been told his cancer returned. It was bittersweet, being happy for his sister, and being sad because he wasn't really sure what the future would bring.

Lost in my memories, I bury my nose in Lia's hair, holding her tightly. I wish he was here for this. I wish, and not for the first time, that he was the one here instead of me.

I don't have anyone who would miss me the way his family misses him. My parents wouldn't mourn, I wouldn't miss out on being an uncle, and Rhett... well, Rhett would have all these people helping and supporting him to move on without me.

The bustle dies down, and I find myself staring at Deacon and Victoria's exchange. He's beaming at his sister, and I find myself wondering if I've ever seen him look so happy. His smile is wide, baring his straight, white teeth, his raised cheekbones giving way to the small lines around his eyes.

He looks so content. Relaxed and at ease, laughing with his sister. The sight is a rarity, and it's just so beautiful to see.

He's so fucking beautiful.

The errant thought bowls me over, unnameable emotions rushing through me. I can't go there. Not with anybody. And especially not with him.

As if he can feel me watching him, his gaze flickers to mine, his smile still intact.

I try to smile back, but it feels forced and fake. His face falters, and I hate myself for ruining this moment for him.

Lowering my head in shame, I busy myself with Lia, until Deacon returns to his seat.

When I feel Victoria sitting back down, I shift my body so Lia and I are giving Deacon our back. It's childish and unwarranted but I'm too unsettled and confused to act normal.

"Did you hear that, sweet girl?" I coo. "You're going to be a big sister."

Vic's face glows as she turns to me and Lia. Just like her brother, happiness radiates off her.

I smile at her. I smile the way I would've smiled at Deacon if my head wasn't in such a foreign place every time I look at him.

With nothing but the utmost happiness in my heart for her and her beautiful family, I smile. Because regardless of what I'm feeling and going through, she deserves this—they all do.

"Congratulations," I say, dragging her in for a one-armed hug. "When are you due?"

"In April. I only just passed the twelve week mark."

"Are you going to find out the sex?"

"Probably. I made Hayden wait with Lia, so it's only fair this time that we find out."

"Excellent answer," Hayden shouts across the table.

"Any preferences?" I ask them both.

"I know everyone says they don't care and they just want a healthy baby, but isn't that a given?"

"She wants a boy," Hayden interjects. "Said this is the last time she's going to let herself look like an elephant. No matter how much she loves me."

They're smitten with one another, Victoria giving her husband googly eyes, and Hayden completely enamored by the mother of his children.

"You guys are sickening," Deacon points out.

"I'm going to have to agree," I say. "It's not a surprise you're pregnant again. I bet you two just look at each other and poof it happens."

Victoria nudges me. "Come on, you know what it's like."

The words hit me, like a quick and fast jab to the face. I did know what it was like. I don't anymore, and fuck if I don't miss it.

Miss him. Miss his touch. Miss his voice. Miss someone knowing me. Someone loving me.

Her hands fly to her mouth, as if she's physically trying to push them back in. "I'm so sorry, Julian. I didn't even think."

"Hey." I rest a hand on her knee. "It's okay." Lifting Lia off my lap, I give her back to her mom. "I just need a minute, okay?"

I try to be as quick and discreet as possible. Needing fresh air, but not wanting to draw any more attention to myself.

When I finally make it out the door, relief hits me in the form of cool, brisk air. Realizing there's nothing but glass restaurant windows along the length of the building, I walk to Deacon's truck and lean on the passenger door.

"Julian." My head snaps up to see Deacon heading my way. My eyes drag themselves up his six foot three frame, and I inwardly curse myself at the newfound attraction I'm feeling toward him.

I'm not prepared for the avalanche of feelings. They're hitting me like a freight train, and suddenly I'm torn between wanting him to stay or wanting him to go.

"You shouldn't have come out," I reprimand. "I said I needed a minute."

"Hey." He puts his hands up in front of him. "I just wanted to check on you." Not waiting for an invitation, or caring if I mind, he stands beside me, against his truck. "You've saved my ass a lot this weekend. I wanted to do the same."

My heart softens at his words, but my mind rebels, pushing the harsh words from my mouth. "Can you leave me? I really don't want to be around you."

The lie burns my tongue, and I expect the usual, hot headed Deacon to strike back. I find myself itching for a fight, wanting an argument, but just like everything else this weekend, it doesn't go to plan.

He remains stoic and silent. Still and pensive.

"Did you hear what I said?" I say, harshly.

"Loud and clear," he retorts. "But I'm an expert at pushing people away, I know how this works. You're mad and hurt, and you think you want to be alone, but all you really want is for it to stop hurting."

Just like he said, he's an expert, and every single word and feeling rings true.

"She feels like shit for what she said."

"I'm not mad about it." I let out a long low sigh. "I just miss him."

Like our bodies have moved to this dance a million times before, he wraps an arm around my shoulders and my body turns into him. My arms find his waist and my head leans on his shoulder.

Tears slide down my face as I hold on for dear life, and he lets me.

Sometimes I feel like my grief will never measure up to the way his family must feel, but just like the night a few days after Rhett's funeral, Deacon is here for me. Taking care of me, validating my feelings; surprising me, and doing the absolute opposite of everything I've ever known about him, and I don't know what to do with all of it.

His empathy. His sincerity. His generosity. It's taking up space inside my chest. Space that isn't his, and space I shouldn't want to give.

There's no rush, or urgency, to get back to everyone inside. He waits. Quietly. Patiently.

Finding my emotional footing, I step back, separating us.

I wipe my eyes with the back of my hands, hang my head between my shoulders, and let my arms fall to the side. There is nowhere to go, nowhere to look, nowhere to hide when he's here, standing in front of me.

"I'm going to go back in," Deacon informs me, as if reading my mind. "Take as long as you need."

He neither expects or waits for anything further from me, walking away, giving me the space I needed all along.

Scrubbing my hands over my face, I give myself a much needed pep talk. I can do this. I can feel the way I'm feeling and enjoy the company of the only people who seem to understand me all at the same time.

Inhaling the fresh air, I exhale the tension and head back inside. I duck off to the bathroom first, washing my face, and buying time.

When I return to my seat, the crestfallen look on Victoria's face breaks my heart in two.

"Hey." I grab her hand in between mine, trying to soothe her. "Habits are hard to break. For all of us."

"I'm so sorry, Julian." She shakes her head. "I feel like absolute shit about it."

"Don't," I insist. "We're having a good day, and you have so much to be happy about." I pointedly look down at her stomach. "We all do, and that's what we should be focused on."

The traditional tortilla soup has come out and been served to everyone. Plastering a smile I don't one hundred percent feel, I raise her hands to my lips and kiss them. "Let's eat, okay?"

The mood is a bit more somber and my interest in conversation and food is a little more subdued, but I do my best to play the part.

The delicious, authentic dishes keep piling up in front of me, but the knots in my stomach are tied too tight for me to enjoy the taste. If the significance of all of us coming here, and eating together wasn't so important, I think I would've tried hightailing it out of here ages ago.

"Do you want me to take you home?" The hairs on the back of my neck stand at attention at the sound of Deacon's low voice near my ear. "It's okay if you're not feeling it."

"Don't be ridiculous," I say over my shoulder. "I'm fine."

He doesn't get the chance to argue with me because his

dad is tapping his knife against his beer bottle, calling for all of our attention.

"I'm not a man of many words," he starts. "But it wouldn't be right if I didn't thank you all for coming together today. I know it's not easy." Swallowing hard, his eyes well up with unshed tears, triggering the same blanket of heavy emotion around the table. "To have my family together, all under the same roof, is unheard of. It's not easy remembering and it's impossible to forget."

He doesn't stand as he talks or raise his voice. Somehow the noise around us fades into the background, the heartfelt message he's trying to get across taking precedence, reaching all of us in different ways.

"I wish it didn't take death, and anniversaries to unite us like this. We've all already lost so much, and we shouldn't let the business of life get in the way of sharing it with one another. Life is short. Life is precious. And we owe it to Rhett to remember that. Honor his memory by living."

Bill turns to Elaine, whose head is buried in her hands, her shoulders shaking in sadness. He wraps his arm around her, and we all individually fold into ourselves.

I mean, what do you say to the parents that lost their son? The grandparents that outlived their grandson? The brother and sister who are missing their sibling?

The busboy unknowingly disrupts the silence, packing up all the empty plates and dirty cutlery, getting the table ready for our dessert.

The lull in conversation slowly disappears, hushed whispers between everyone around me getting louder.

"Hey, Deac," Victoria says over me. "We're thinking of spending a weekend in Seattle, what do you say?"

"Well are you coming to visit Seattle, or visit me?"

"I guess we could fit you in," she teases.

"You guys want to stay with me?"

"Um," I hesitantly interrupt. "Do you guys want me to move? So you don't have to talk with me in the middle?"

"No." Deacon's voice is calm and absolute, and the hand that lands on my thigh, stilling me, is a perfect match. The move doesn't go unnoticed. Victoria looks down at his hand and then back up at him. He doesn't back down from her stare or move his hand. "You're perfectly fine where you are."

9

DEACON

I should be freaking out about my constant need to touch Julian, but right now, I'm more scared of the inquisition I know is coming from my sister.

Her posture straightens, her body stiffening in shock. Her eyes are wide, the unspoken questions written all over her face.

She isn't usually one to hold back, but the obvious clench in her jaw makes me wonder why she's biting her tongue.

"So," I drawl, bringing the conversation back. "Are you staying with me? I've got plenty of space."

"I don't think Josie would appreciate a screaming toddler in her space."

Shit. I knew there was something I forgot to tell her.

"Oh," Julian says, a little too enthusiastically. "They broke up."

"I'm sorry," I blurt out quickly. "I was waiting to see you to tell you."

Her eyes narrow in on my hand; the one that's still on Julian's jean covered thigh.

"It appears that there's a lot you still have to tell me."

And there it is. The money shot.

"Hayden," Julian calls out across the table. "I've got some questions for you about real estate. Let me pull up a chair beside you and Lia."

Both Victoria and I give Julian the side-eye. "Don't look at me like that. You two can get back to killing each other, I just have no plans to sit in between you when it happens."

He stands, his long lean body moving away, forcing space between us. I watch him make his way to Hayden and let my eyes slowly drift back to Victoria.

She hops off her seat and slides closer to me on Julian's now empty seat. "You and Josie broke up? What the fuck Deacon?"

"It's been a bad couple of months," I admit.

"Why didn't you tell me?"

"I don't want to talk about my shit," I explain. "When you and Lia call, it's the highlight of my day, and I want to keep it that way."

"Well?" She looks at me pointedly. "What happened?"

"She cheated on me." Her cheeks flare up in rage, and I put my hand up to stop her. "While I appreciate your loyalty, it wasn't all her fault."

"It's been a rough year," she says, trying to excuse the demise of my relationship. "And I didn't really like her anyway."

I should be more offended at her disdain, but it's nice not to have her glaring at me. "It would appear mom agrees with you too."

She turns to look at Mom, who's wistfully watching us, then looks back at me. "How's she been with you?"

I shrug nonchalantly. "It's all good."

"And Julian?"

"What about him?" I say indifferently.

"Really, Deacon. We're going to play this game?"

"There's no game," I say honestly. "We're just playing nice."

"That looked a bit more than just playing nice to me."

"I don't have an explanation Vic, and I don't really want to talk about it."

"He's vulnerable, Deac. Tread carefully with him."

"Carefully?" I scoff. "What the fuck do you think I'm going to do?"

My blood simmers underneath my skin, disappointed that today I managed to avoid my mother's displeasure, only to have Victoria step right in and take her place. I want to hulk out, stand up and throw fucking furniture all around the place.

I must be living in an alternate universe, the perception of myself apparently all wrong. According to everyone else, I'm a bigger asshole than I thought, clearly unable to be nice to anyone for no good reason other than wanting to.

"Calm down," she hisses, her eyes darting between me and a very concerned looking audience.

"I didn't mean anything by it."

"Don't lie to me," I spit out. "Everyone is concerned about him, because I'm clearly the monster he needs protecting from." I draw in a breath before continuing. Trying for a calmer, steadier voice. "He's Rhett's best friend. His boyfriend, and obviously everybody else's preferred family member. For Rhett, I wanted things to be better between us."

"But honestly, I don't even know why I bother." Placing my elbows on the table, I lower my head into my hands and continuously run my fingers through my hair. "I need to get back home, get out of everybody's way, and just keep to myself, like usual."

"Don't say that," she says, her expression pained. "I said I didn't mean anything by it."

"Let's just finish eating," I say, effectively cutting her off. "And then we can all get going."

The silence stretches across the whole table, and Julian returns, bravely sitting down in the middle of our war zone.

I tuck into my rice pudding, wishing I could enjoy the taste of the food I've missed so much. Wishing the day ended just as good as it had started.

I had high hopes that maybe, after a year of mourning, we could all somehow find a new common ground.

"Unca Deac. Unca Deac." Lia's voice breaks through my bleak mood. Raising my eyes to meet hers, I give her a wink when she waves at me from her father's lap. She lifts her arms up in the air, and there's no way I can deny her anything, no matter how angry I'm feeling.

Pushing off the table, I stand and walk toward her. Looking down at Hayden, I hold my hands out for her. "Can I take her outside for a bit?"

"Of course, man. Let me grab her jacket." He maneuvers her arms every which way and slips a beanie over her head. "Want me to come?"

Not really holding any animosity toward my brother-in-law, I give him a quick nod. Together with Lia's little arms wrapped tightly around my neck, we shift and angle our way through the tables.

Knowing he's going to ask if I'm okay the minute we step outside, I begin focusing all my attention on Lia. "Want to sit on my shoulders?" I coo.

"Up. Up." She bounces in my arms with every word. "Up. Up."

Ensuring she's got enough layers on to keep her warm, I take the last step over the threshold and expose us to the cool winter air. When we're out of the doorway, I turn Lia in my arms and raise her whole, chubby body into the air.

Sitting her behind my head, I make sure her legs are hanging over my shoulders, and her hands are tightly placed in mine.

"You comfy up there, Lia Lady?" Hayden asks.

"Up. Up," she shouts excitedly.

"I'll take that as a yes." Moving his gaze back down to me, his face drops in sympathy. "I know you don't want me to ask, but I'm going to do it anyway."

I let out a long sigh. "I'm okay, man."

"She's going to be beating herself up for days," Hayden tells me.

If he didn't treat my sister like an absolute queen, I would tell him to mind his own fucking business. But how do you fault a man who always has his wife's back? We've never been close, purely based on the logistics of our lives, but his love for my sister means there isn't a thing he wouldn't do for me or my family.

I have a lot of respect for him, and when he talks, I often find myself listening. He's always been a good judge of character and fair and objective in his opinions. A lot of the time, it's him who helps my sister see reason.

I know this won't be any different.

"We were bound to fight," I confess. "Tension is just too high, and it's an emotional weekend. I'll get over it soon enough."

"You don't have to get over it, Deacon," he counters. "You just need to sit with each other and talk it out."

"I'll try before I leave."

It's a promise I make to myself, because I really am sick

of being on the outs with everyone. No matter whose fault it is, or what the trigger may be, I want to go back to Seattle knowing my whole family isn't stuck in emotional purgatory. And more importantly, that I'm not responsible for it.

"I won't leave till we talk," I say a little more forcefully. "Vic said you guys were thinking of visiting and I want that." I rise and fall on the tips of my toes, while talking, keeping Lia entertained by the motion. "I know we're all really busy, but I want to make a change. I *need* to make a change."

"No matter what Victoria says or feels, she just wants whatever's best for you. So, be honest with her."

"I'm sick of being the fuck up, man."

Surprised, Hayden rears his head, obviously not expecting me to be this honest. But between him and Julian and everything else, I can't seem to live in the lie I've built around me much longer.

I'm angry. I'm hurting. I'm so fucking confused that I don't know which way I'm coming or going—and just like with Josie, if I'm not careful, everything I care about is going to slip out of my fingers.

"I don't think anyone really sees you like that but yourself, man."

"We're just always at each other's throats. I can't even remember a time it wasn't like this."

"And why are you blaming yourself for it?"

"I'm the common denominator, aren't I?" I scoff. "They're not fighting with one another."

Hayden moves closer, clapping me on the shoulder. "I wouldn't be so sure."

"Is there something you're not telling me?"

"No." He shakes his head. "It's more like something you're missing."

"Why are you talking in riddles? What's that supposed to mean?"

He doesn't get a chance to answer, because the whole family chooses that single moment to come outside. When Hayden reaches for Lia, the smug look on his face tells me he has no plans to explain himself whatsoever.

We all mill around the sidewalk, trying to work out what's next. But if the look on everybody's face gives any indication, I think the small win we all felt at being able to go out to Rhett's favorite restaurant has undoubtedly fizzled out.

Victoria stands close beside me, pressing her shoulders into me, and linking her arm through mine. "Stay for a few more days," she says, without looking directly at me. "Tomorrow we can leave Lia with mom and dad and just catch up. You and me. You, me and Hayden. Or you, Julian and me and Hayden. Just sleep on whatever this is tonight and let's try again tomorrow."

Dragging my arm out from between us, I throw it over her shoulder and hug her to me. I kiss the top of her head, knowing I will do whatever she asks.

I meant every word I said to Hayden. I want things to be different, I don't want to just run when the going gets tough. Losing Rhett was hard, but losing people who are still alive is harder.

"Sounds like a plan, but maybe…" She looks up at me, her lashes wet and long. "Maybe you could stop making Julian and I sound like a couple when you talk?"

"You're the one touching him and being nice to him," she murmurs.

She's right.

I don't have a comeback or an explanation, so I don't bite back. The man in question comes into view, both Vic and I watching him as he hugs our family goodbye, promising visits I'm almost certain he doesn't have any plans to follow through with.

When his eyes catch mine, my spine straightens, and hell if Victoria doesn't notice. Thankfully, she keeps her mouth closed, but the upturn of her lips says plenty.

He begins to head our way, and I untangle Victoria's limbs from mine. Meeting him halfway, I stop when I reach him. "I'll just say bye to everyone and we can get going, okay?"

If it wasn't for the slight nod of his head, I wouldn't be sure he'd even heard me. Determined to keep his distance, he continues to walk on by, almost acting like he doesn't know me.

I try not to take it too personally, knowing he's feeling a little raw right now. We've all been there. We're all *still* there.

I hug and kiss my grandparents and tell them I'll try my best to see them before I leave for Seattle, while I inform my parents I'm dropping Julian off and I'll meet them at home after.

By the time I reach the truck, Julian has his hands clasped together in front of his mouth, blowing warm air on them.

I quickly remove my key fob from my pocket and unlock the truck.

"Shit. I'm sorry, man," I say. "I should've given you the keys."

"Not a problem," he answers.

We both climb into the truck, and I turn it on, and switch the heat on high to try and rid us both of the chill.

"Hey," I say, noticing Julian's hunched shoulders. "Are you okay?"

A soft wistful laugh reaches my ears. "I feel like that's all we're ever saying to one another."

"Sometimes it needs to be said." I think back to all the times I should've asked the question. To Rhett. To my family. To Julian. "And sometimes we don't ask it enough."

He turns to face me, resting his back against the door, stretching the seatbelt, as if he needs to get a really good look. "Who are you?" he asks.

I quickly glance at him and return my focus to the road. "What do you mean?"

My question goes unanswered as I feel his eyes tracing over the shape of my body. I feel the intensity of his stare. The questions. The wonder. And I'm not sure how to feel about it, but there's something in his gaze that feels like want.

"Answer me this."

My ears perk up expectantly for whatever it is he's about to ask.

"You've either changed since Rhett died or was the guy I thought you were not really you at all?"

My grip tightens on the steering wheel. "It's always the heavy stuff with you isn't it?"

"Me," he responds pointedly. "Or us?"

I drag my hand down my face. "A bit of both," I tell him. "And the guy you thought I am, is me. It's the only side I really have on offer."

"Somehow, I find that a little hard to believe."

The sarcasm is on the tip of my tongue. The challenge. The impulse to argue and bite back. I shift my gaze to his, and he's expecting it, waiting for it.

Purposefully, I do the opposite, immaturely showing him he doesn't know me. Not one single version of me. No matter what he thinks.

"I want to get drunk," I announce. "Do you want to get drunk?"

"Sorry, what?" he asks confused. "Where the hell did that come from?"

"I'm sick of all the heavy. Aren't you?" I ask rhetorically. "I could do with getting rid of it for one night. I can't even tell you the last time I got messy drunk."

He twists his body, so all of him is now facing the windshield. "I'm embarrassed to say I remember my last time."

"Yeah. When?"

"When Rhett moved into my place. Our place?" He shakes his head. "You know what I mean."

"Really? That long ago?"

"He was in remission, your mom finally agreed to let him move in. We finally decided to take our relationship to the next level."

My body stiffens, and an odd sting settles in my chest. I don't want to be thinking about them having sex. "Yeah, I think I get the picture. I don't need to hear about you and my brother fucking."

"What?" he shouts, before covering his mouth in horror. "That's not what I meant."

"That's what next level means," I state.

"No." He closes his eyes and shakes his head. "That's not what I meant. I mean we had sex, but that's the night we decided to make it official."

"What do you mean, official? Haven't you always been together?"

"He really didn't tell you about us." It's a statement, not a question, and I can't work out if he's mad or shocked by the revelation.

"I didn't ask," I say, trying to relieve whatever hurt or

confusion he seems to be feeling right now. "Anything I didn't know, is all on me."

"You still want to get drunk?" he asks, making it clear we're dropping that topic for now.

"Fuck yeah," I breathe out. "Honestly, if you're not up for it, I completely understand."

He raises his hand, cutting me off. "Why don't you drop me off at home and go spend time with your family? Or you could mope around and be broody—whatever it is you do on your own," he says flippantly. "And we'll meet at The Crooked Stool at eight?"

"Broody?"

"Don't make me explain it," he huffs. "We both know broody is exactly what you are."

"Is broody a compliment?" I query.

The drive comes to an end as I pull up in his driveway. I let the truck run, keeping the heat on for both of us since Julian is in no rush to get out.

"Are you asking for one?" There's a slight lift to his mouth, and I find myself staring at his lips. They're so expressive. At any given time, they're the perfect mood indicator.

Is he flirting with me?

"Deacon," Julian calls out.

"Huh?" I drag my gaze away from his mouth and back up to his eyes. "Sorry. I didn't hear you."

He licks his lips, and my eyes move down like magnets. My skin tightens against my body, a feverish heat rushing through me.

"We still on for eight?" he asks, his voice a little breathy.

"Yes," I rush out, forcing myself to look directly at him.

This wasn't just about ridding myself of the huge anvil sitting on my chest anymore. Right now, I really just want to be around him. I want him to invade my space and push my boundaries. For the first time, the unknown is much more appealing than everything I thought I knew, and I love the way it feels.

I love that I'm feeling *something*.

The truck door opens, breaking my trance. I watch as he wordlessly hops out of the truck and keeps his back against the metal to stop it from closing.

"Broody."

"What?"

"Broody," he repeats. "It's a compliment."

10

JULIAN

Standing just out of the doorway, I rub my clammy hands up and down my jean covered thighs. Deacon is sitting at the bar, his back facing the entrance, and I'm here hiding in the background hoping not to be recognized.

It seemed like such a good idea at the time. Okay, that's a lie, it was a terrible idea. It *is* a terrible idea, but I wanted to indulge. One night. One night to let go of the heavy.

Grateful for the hours we spent apart after he dropped me off, I thought it was enough time to process the change between us. But all I really processed was the fact that I've just replaced one heap of heavy for another.

I was flirting. It was low key, but I knew what was going on in my mind. I felt the small flutter building in the pit of my stomach. I checked him out a hundred times over, like it was the first time I was truly seeing him.

He was touching some part of me every chance he got. And he was staring at my lips.

He—my best friend's brother—was staring at my lips.

He—my boyfriend's brother—was staring at my lips.

He—my boyfriend's straight brother—was staring at my lips.

He was staring at *my* lips.

Nothing about this makes sense.

But here I am. My muscles tight. My heart pounding. My body filled with warmth I know has nothing to do with the temperature inside the bar.

I should leave, not just because I'm having odd, crush-like feelings for a straight man, but because it's Deacon. There're so many lines there that shouldn't be crossed.

It's complicated and messy, and who would I be if I moved on from Rhett? What would that say about me? What would that say about what we had?

Finding courage, I take slow, apprehensive steps toward Deacon. I'm probably making a mountain out of a molehill. We can do this. We can be two guys having drinks after a long, hard day. Nothing more. Nothing less.

I only cover half the distance when beautiful, crystal blue eyes find mine. Eyes that should remind me of Rhett's, but only seem to push him farther out of my mind. They're unguarded and relaxed, his expression lazy and content; the drink in front of him potentially responsible.

His gaze darts to my feet, his stare starts low and slowly rises. From the tips of my toes, he languidly makes his way up my body. I don't know what he's looking at or what he's looking for, but my dormant nerve endings tingle from the inside out, keeping me rooted to the ground, not sure whether to move forward or take a step back.

He's doing it again. Something completely unnatural, yet he looks so natural doing it. And no matter how much internal guilt I feel, I'm enjoying it.

I'm enjoying just the idea of someone looking at me like that.

I'm regretfully enjoying the idea of *Deacon* looking at me like that.

When his gaze reaches my face, his demeanor shifts. I watch his Adam's apple bob, and his jaw tighten. He straightens his back and rubs his hands up and down his thighs, all while still looking at me.

The uncertainty between us is obvious, and I'm impressed when he doesn't turn and hide from it. It pushes me to take the last few steps. Slow and steady, I walk toward him, knowing we're both as unsure as one another. Knowing there's no way I'm going to be the one to bail. I said we could hang out. And that's what we'll do.

I take my seat on the wooden stool beside Deacon, conscious of the way his eyes never leave mine. My mouth opens to say hello, but I'm interrupted by the bartender.

"Julian. I didn't know you were coming in," Ray, one of the guys I work with says. "I didn't realize you were around this weekend. It's nice to see you, man."

"Hey Ray, how are you?"

I don't wait for his answer, choosing to turn and face Deacon instead.

"Hey," I greet, nothing but apprehension in my voice. "I see you got a head start."

He responds with a slight nod and brings the bottle of beer to his mouth. I get lost in the rise and fall of his Adam's apple as he swallows the drink; mesmerized by the veins that protrude from his neck, and the cut of his sharp jawline.

"I'm good, man," Ray answers, sliding a shot glass in front of me and reminding me of his presence. Dragging my eyes away from Deacon, I watch Ray generously fill the glass up with tequila, and hand it to me. "You need to catch up."

My eyes dart between him and Deacon. "How many have you had?"

"It's been a long day," he answers in defense.

Not one to disclose too much of my personal information at work, I discreetly respond. "I know, I was there."

Lifting the glass rim to my lips, I throw down the gold-colored liquid and feel it burn the whole way down my esophagus. I hand it back to Ray for a refill. "Thanks."

"Would you like a drink?" He's looking at Deacon and he subtly tilts his head, and that's when I realize he wants an introduction.

"Oh," I straighten my back and point between the two of them. "Ray, this is Rhett's brother."

Surprising me, Deacon holds out his hand. "Deacon."

Ray takes it and eagerly shakes it, a smile spreading across his face. "Nice to officially meet you."

I want to roll my eyes at the ridiculousness. Annoyed when the contact lingers a little too long, I rudely blurt out. "Unless I missed something, he isn't gay, Ray."

Ray's face turns a ridiculous shade of red, and I momentarily feel guilty.

"Don't worry, Ray." Deacon continues to hold on to his hand, but his eyes are deadlocked on mine. "Julian's just mad he can't get all of this."

"How much have you had to drink?" I scold. And just for good measure, I add, "Even if you did bat for my team, I still wouldn't be interested."

"I guess one brother was enough," he bites.

"Fuck you, Deacon. What's your problem?"

Unperturbed, he turns his attention back to Ray. "Can you line us up with more tequila shots? Three each sounds good right about now."

Seemingly happy to walk away from our verbal altercation, he rushes off quicker than lightning.

It's obvious everything we're feeling, or telling ourselves we're *not* feeling, is rising to the surface. Busting to come out, desperate to explode.

Ray comes back into view, lining up the shot glasses and this time placing a small plate filled with slices of lemon and two salt shakers in front of us. I'm assuming the extra effort is for Deacon.

He free pours the tequila, letting the pungent smelling alcohol overflow and drip down onto the wooden bar top.

Deacon picks one glass up and hands it to me, then grabs his own. "Drink."

I raise an eyebrow while releasing it from his hold. "I've already had one."

Challenging me, the glass touches his lips, and I'm quick to mirror his actions, throwing the drink down as quickly as he does. I hiss, clenching my eyes together, and enduring the unwelcome feeling of fire running down my throat.

Deacon doesn't miss a beat, plowing through his line of shots, watching me, as I catch up.

I reach for a slice of lemon and suck it between my teeth, hoping the sour taste will soothe the burn inside my chest. Tequila is such a bad idea.

"Need to switch to water?" Deacon asks, smirking.

God, I could punch him in the face right now.

"I know this is your plan for tonight, but tequila is the difference between a night spent having fun and a night with your head in a toilet bowl."

"Come on, it was only a few shots," he teases. "And now you're relaxed enough to lose that stick up your ass."

"Me?" I scoff. "You're the one whose moods change like the fucking wind."

"Ladies," Ray calls out, slamming two beers in front of us. "Let's not fight, yeah? This round is on me."

His embarrassment from earlier seems to have worn off, slipping back into his role as the cool and calm bartender. He gives us both a wink and moves on to another patron.

I take a sip of my beer just as Deacon says, "He seems nice. Have you ever thought of dating him?"

Pulling the bottle away from my mouth mid sip, my eyes widen at Deacon. "Tell me you're not that guy."

"What guy?"

"The guy that thinks because he's gay" —I point to Ray and then back at myself— "and I'm gay, that we should automatically go on a date."

"You mean the same way my sister tries to set me up with every 'nice girl' she knows?" He twists himself on the stool, so he's sitting perpendicular to my own body. "Maybe it came out wrong, but I was trying to ask if you'd thought about dating again."

I take a long pull of my beer before turning my head to face him. "You're going to ask me that today of all days?"

"No matter what day I ask, he's still going to be dead."

His bluntness is like a knife to the chest. "I thought you said no heavy."

He raises the beer bottle between us. "This will lighten the load."

"I have no interest in dating right now," I say honestly. "And I wouldn't even know how. Rhett and I..." I stall, knowing the alcohol is making my lips loose.

"Rhett and you what?" Deacon presses.

"Nothing. Forget it." I take another sip to silence myself, the need to talk and share surprising me. I've never felt the urge to talk about me and Rhett. Never wanted to share what I had with him, with anyone. Especially not Deacon.

Wanting to keep him talking but not about me and Rhett, I ask, "Could you date again? After Josie?"

He clicks his tongue. "It's nowhere near the same thing."

"Don't try to get out of answering," I push. "Should we be searching the bar for your next girlfriend?"

"I could do with a one-night stand, but I do not need another girlfriend."

"Oh." I shift on the stool uncomfortably, the mention of sex reminding me of how long it's been since I've had some. A hearty chuckle leaves his mouth, and my face heats up in embarrassment, worried he's read my mind. "What?"

"You should see your face right now." His eyes look behind me, and then he signals for another two beers, before bringing his focus back. "I didn't say anything scandalous. Why do you look so shocked?"

Relief at his misinterpretation has my shoulders sagging. "It just catches me off guard every time you say something so..."

"So...?"

I search my mind for the lie. "Normal."

"Normal's good isn't it?" He subtly lowers his eyes and begins picking at the wet beer label. "One step closer to civil."

"And what comes after civil?"

"Friends?" he suggests. "You don't mind having one more, do you?"

He raises his head, his blue eyes cautious, waiting for an answer that means more between the two of us than any other people in this world.

"I don't really have any," I confess. "I guess one can't hurt."

His face shifts from apprehensive to sympathetic, and I hate seeing that look on his face. Especially aimed at me.

"God," I nervously chuckle. "That sounds even more pathetic out loud."

"No, it doesn't," he says, his voice low and scratchy.

I square my shoulders, my voice stern. "You don't need to make me feel better."

"I'm not." He shakes his head vehemently. "You think nobody noticed how much you gave up for my brother? A lot more than I ever did," he adds, regret and pain evident in his voice. "Don't be so hard on yourself."

I shrug nonchalantly. "It was a no brainer."

"At the time, yes, but now?" he challenges.

"Is this what being friends with you is like?" I ask, avoiding his gaze and picking at my fingernails. "Acknowledging all the ways I'm lacking?"

I hear him expel a long breath of air, and I feel his body moving toward me. I let myself lean in to meet him, searching for that sandalwood smell that surrounds him. "You're not lacking anything."

The words come out as more of a realization than a compliment, but the small distance between us says otherwise.

Ray's curious and not-so-subtle voice interrupts us. "I see you two made up."

I'm the first one to pull away, righting myself on the stool. "Can you please get us another round of shots?" I mumble quickly.

"Coming right up," he supplies, a smug smirk aimed our way.

"Are you sure?" Deacon asks as Ray leaves.

"Yes." I gesture behind me. "I'm just going to go to the bathroom."

Deacon nods and I shoot off the stool, wasting no time

fleeing. Except I don't anticipate the effects of the alcohol and I feel myself sway.

Chuckling, Deacon wraps his hand around my wrist to steady me. "How about I ask Ray for some water too?"

I turn my head to hide the flush I can feel creeping up into my cheeks and drag my hand out of his hold. "I'll be right back," I mutter.

Concentrating on every step, I slowly and carefully walk myself to the bathroom. Not really needing to use it, I stand in front of the mirror and switch on the tap. I splash the cold water on my face, and rub my now cool hands across the nape of my neck, hoping it will help me regain my footing.

Physically.

Emotionally.

I feel so off my game, but I don't know if it's because I really haven't gone out at night in over two years, or because of Deacon. I don't even know myself right now, and standing here, hiding out in the bathroom, I can't even tell you the last time I did.

Grabbing a wad of paper towels, I dab my face and my neck, ensuring I don't walk out of here looking like a hot, sweaty mess.

I can do this. I can be out in public and enjoy myself.

I. Can. Do. This.

When I step out of the bathroom, I can see that Ray and Deacon are shooting the shit, and six full shot glasses are lined up right where I'd be sitting.

I watch Ray lean embarrassingly close to Deacon, and I hate it. I hate the sight of it, I hate that Deacon doesn't move back, and I hate that I hate it.

Every single part of me wants to walk out the door. I want to put myself out of this misery and stay indoors till Deacon goes back to Seattle; I want to slide back into my carefully constructed bubble where I didn't feel any of this stuff—where I didn't feel anything.

Deacon turns his head to face me, effectively ending his conversation with Ray. His face lights up, a soft, alluring smile turning up the corners of his lips. It's like he's actually happy to see me.

I've known him for the biggest part of my life and he's never looked at me like that. If he had, I feel like I'd remember it.

Reaching the bar, I steadily slide onto my stool that feels significantly closer to Deacon's. "What are you two gossiping about?" I ask casually.

"Nothing," Deacon says a little too quickly. "It's my turn to go to the little boys' room. When I come back, we'll do those shots."

With a dry mouth, all I can do is nod and watch him walk away.

"I bet you there's nothing little about him."

"Ray," I scold.

He hands me a cold bottle of water. "What? Like you weren't thinking the same thing?"

"He's my boyfriend's brother," I say, hoping the words are self-explanatory. "And how many times do I have to tell you he's not gay?"

"Listen." Ray leans in closer to me. "I know we don't know each other really well. You keep to yourself and we all try to give you your space, but you don't have a boyfriend anymore."

I furrow my brows at him. "How can you say that to me?"

"Because I'm not your friend. You don't want friends. So, what does it matter if I hurt your feelings? You barely talk to me anyway." He pulls a towel out of his back pocket and starts wiping down the bar. "You've had a shit run, but you could decide to come out on the other side if you wanted to."

Ray's gaze shifts between me and something further off in the distance. "So, he might not be gay, but he's definitely interested in you."

I give him a slow disbelieving head shake before raising the bottle to my lips and taking a huge gulp of water. "It doesn't work like that, Ray. You of all people should know that."

"It never works out the way it's supposed to," he says solemnly. "*You* of all people should know that."

"Like I said, I'm not interested," I say sharply. "He's my boyfriend's brother."

"Dead boyfriend," he mutters just as Deacon returns. "Dead boyfriend's brother."

Even fucking worse.

11

DEACON

Julian looks like he's seen a ghost when I return and Ray is now nowhere to be seen. I make a conscious effort not to ask if he's okay. Not because I don't care, but Julian is right. That's all we seem to say to one another, and at this point I'm feeling too buzzed and would rather make the effort to cheer him up than bring up something I don't think he wants to talk about.

"You ready for these shots?" I push three toward him and slide the lemon and salt between us. "Want to try these this time?"

Wordlessly, he raises his hand to his mouth, and licks the skin between his thumb and forefinger. Grabbing the salt shaker, he jostles it over his wet patch of skin. A small little cluster of salt sticks to him, and he wastes no time running his tongue across his hand, and letting the shot of tequila follow.

The action is completed in less than a second, but my mind is still stuck on the visual of his mouth and tongue, and the way it looked as he languidly licked the salt off his hand.

I want to watch him do it again.

"Do the rest," I hear myself say.

The request is very left field, but he doesn't even bat an eyelash.

Repeating the motions, I now watch him intently, my eyes never leaving his mouth, or the downward slope of his tongue as it scoops up the salt.

Knowing I've been staring for too long, I flick my eyes up to his, and he's staring right back at me. He's not looking at me like he's waiting for an explanation, or like he's even a little bit surprised. No... he's looking at me like he's thinking the exact same thing I am.

He throws down the last shot, and then quickly sucks on the lemon. I don't wait for an invitation or small talk before I unceremoniously drink my three designated shooters. My head is a mess, and my body is enamored by the idea of Julian's. The whole concept is foreign to me and the only answer is alcohol.

Lots and lots of alcohol.

Aggressively, I slam the last glass down, and then wipe my hand across my mouth. "I need another three."

Julian looks around for what I assume to be Ray and then back at me. "Let's get you water and you can have beer instead of tequila, because if you think I'm the kind of friend that sticks around for vomit, then you're sorely mistaken."

Unintentionally his comment is the exact levity I need to stop myself from freaking out. I still need the alcohol, but I can make it through tonight. Despite everything that's brewing underneath the surface for me, I'm having a good time—we're having a good time.

We're getting to know one another in a way I never thought we would; because I never had the desire to know anything about the man, until now.

Okay, I'll enjoy this, and worry about what it all means tomorrow.

Ray finally returns with two beers and a bottle of water. I raise an eyebrow at Julian. "Trust me, the night's still young." He claps me on the back. "When you've finished let's spice this night up a bit and play some pool."

"I don't play pool," I tell him while unscrewing the lid off the plastic bottle.

He looks at me as if I've spoken in a foreign language. "What do you mean you don't play pool?"

"It's not a big deal."

"Yes it is, everyone knows how to play pool."

"Everyone clearly" —I gesture to myself— "can't play pool."

"Ray," Julian calls out obnoxiously. "Ray."

Rounding the corner, Ray walks toward us with a clear look of concern on his face. "What's wrong? Why are you screaming?"

"Do you know how to play pool?"

He looks between us. "Are you kidding me right now? You're screaming like a banshee because you want to know if I can play pool?"

"Well, can you?" Julian asks again.

Rolling his eyes, Ray says, "Of course I can, every respectable person knows how to play pool."

"Ughh," I groan, dropping my head into my hands. "I'm losing all my street cred with you two."

"Who said you had any street cred to begin with?" Julian bites back playfully. "I can't believe Mr. Big and Broody can't play pool."

I feel myself smirk. "So, we're still stuck on broody?"

"Very much stuck on broody," he responds, while he runs his gaze up and down my body. I should be concerned by where this is heading, worried by the fallout of all these strange signals—especially for Julian.

He drags his eyes away from me and starts walking toward the pool tables. I settle beside him, matching him step for step.

"Your dad taught Rhett and me," he casually continues, like he didn't just look at me like I was his next meal. "So it's safe to say I assumed he taught you too."

"Nah," I say as nonchalantly as possible, the reminder of my past a cold bucket of ice trying to douse any positivity we may have shared. "I didn't bother. That was you and Rhett's thing."

I channel my energy into keeping my posture relaxed and the tone in my voice upbeat. I push down that familiar rush of jealousy I feel when it comes to all the ways Julian and Rhett fit with my family and I didn't.

It has no place here, and I'm desperately trying to make peace with it.

Julian tilts his head at me, his lips pressed together in a firm line. I can tell he has something he wants to say. As usual, he knows something's up.

I've spent years perfecting my lies, and moods, and masks, and in a few undisrupted hours Julian has worked them all out.

How does he always know something's up?

Thankfully he doesn't push or pry, he just nudges me as we reach the row of billiard tables. "Don't worry, tonight's as good a night as any to learn."

I look around the room and find an empty high top table surrounded by stools and claim it. "Why don't you just find someone to play with and I'll watch from here?"

He scrunches up his face. "That's the dumbest idea I've ever heard."

I shrug my shoulders and chuckle. "It's probably not *the* dumbest."

"You clearly don't know pool etiquette."

"I said I couldn't play, how is not knowing the rules a surprise to you?"

I make a show of looking at all the groups of people playing around us. "What about them?" I ask, pointing at a group of four. Two are holding cues and the others are just milling around. "Why don't you go place some quarters on their table?"

Julian's eyes widen, and I give him a quick wink. "Not a complete dumbass."

Placing his beer bottle on the tabletop, he shakes his head and makes his way across the room. One of the guys notices his arrival just as Julian pulls some coins out of his front pocket.

He places them on the cushioned exterior of the table, and I watch him make small talk with the man. When I see them both laugh, I'm inundated by a sense of both relief and jealousy. Happy the other guy isn't an asshole, and jealous that Julian is laughing without me.

Not wanting to get caught ogling Julian and every move he makes, I slide my cell out of my pocket and sip on my beer. I notice an earlier message from Victoria, just as I feel Julian's presence get closer.

She's asking if I have any ideas for what I want to do tomorrow. It's then I remember I told her I was staying. But the idea of waking up tomorrow after all this alcohol and being a functional citizen of society sounds almost impossible.

I slip the phone back in my pocket and choose to respond to her later.

"Turns out you chose a good bunch," Julian says as he reaches me. "We're going to play doubles."

I narrow my eyes at him. "I'm sorry, I just thought I heard you say doubles."

He bites the corner of his bottom lip to stop himself from smiling, while his eyes dance with humor. "I did." He puts his hand up in front of him to stop me from speaking. "But before you say anything, I won't make you play. We'll be a team, but I'll do all the hard work."

"Way to make me sound like a slacker."

"What can I say, not all superheroes wear capes."

"Oh my god, do you even hear yourself right now? Wait to see if you can even win before we start doling out all the compliments."

"Oh, I'll win."

"Won't believe it till I see it," I tease.

"You're going to owe me big time. I sure hope you can pay up."

"I'll buy you a couple of slices of greasy pizza from next door."

"And grab us some more beers?" he asks shyly, while holding out his hand for me to shake.

I take it, and let my palm press against his, enjoying his smooth skin against the calluses on my own. It takes a few beats for us to let each other go, but the thrill of knowing he was in no rush either lasts until I return with our bottles of beer.

He's animatedly talking to two of the women from the group, and I'm reluctant to disturb him. He's enjoying himself. Tonight we're rid of the heavy, just like we said, and fuck if it isn't a good look on him.

He notices me from the corner of his eye and waves me over. Both ladies turn to see who has his attention and then smile at me welcomingly. I raise my beer at them in greeting and move around them to stand beside Julian.

He takes one of the bottles out of my hold and has a quick swig. "This is Deacon," he says, pointing at me. "Deacon these lovely ladies are Denise and Keri."

"We're just going to finish up this game with our friends and the winners will play you two."

"Not a problem," I answer for the both of us.

Our new 'friends' basically hop and skip away, both of them in a fun and jovial mood.

"So who's who?" I ask, tipping my chin toward the couples.

"The two that can't keep their hands off one another are Denise and Anthony and Keri is single." He says Keri's name a little too enthusiastically. "She's pretty." He nudges me in the shoulder. "You could maybe take her home."

"To my parents' house," I quip.

"Or go to her house?"

"What about their other friend?"

"You're interested in Peter?"

"What? No. I'm just trying to get you off my case about sleeping with someone tonight."

"Oh. I thought you said you wanted to get laid."

Yeah, I'm crazy horny and I'm thinking about you in ways I shouldn't be, of course I want to get laid tonight.

"Nah, I'm good. I think I can manage keeping my dick in my pants tonight."

"Well, that's not really going to stop Keri from trying to hit on you. She already asked me if my hot friend was single."

"Hot friend, hey? I guess I don't scrub up too bad."

Julian grunts.

"What?"

"Even Ray has been trying to hit on you tonight." He avoids my gaze when he says the last part. "You scrub up just fine."

"You sound jealous," I taunt. "I'm sure if you gave Ray the time of day, he'd hit on you too."

"Yeah that's not it," he says noncommittally.

"Then?" I droll, wanting an answer.

A millisecond of time passes, and giddiness shimmies in my chest as a surprising thought crosses my mind.

Something on my face has him asking. "What?"

"You think I'm good looking," I blurt out smugly. Julian rolls his eyes at me, so I prod further, asking something that's been bothering me. "Is it because I look like Rhett?"

"Huh?"

"Do I remind you of him?" I rephrase. "Is that why you give *me* the time of day?"

"What? No." I stare at him blankly, wanting an explanation. "I mean, you're his brother and I'd like to say we've made progress. But you don't remind me of him. Not at all." Raw and honest brown eyes bore into my blue ones. "Not as much as you probably should."

I want to ask what he means, but I'm too scared to hear the truth. I'm scared to have anything rattle this tentative friendship we have blossoming between us.

Cheers from Denise and Anthony interrupt us, and Keri and Peter come over to hand us their cues.

"Hey, man," Peter greets. "I'm Peter."

"I'm Deacon."

"How good are you guys, because I hope you kick their cocky asses."

Leaning closer to Julian, I whisper in his ear. "I'm going to kill you if we lose."

"I think it will be your fault," he says through clenched teeth and a stiff smile. "You're the one that can't play."

Not leaving it to chance, I point between Keri and Peter. "Which one of you wants to take my place?"

Keri's eyes sparkle with mischief as she squeezes Peter on the shoulder. "Why don't you play, Petey. I'm going to take care of Deacon."

I hand him the cue, immediately foreshadowing the subtle let down that will eventually take place. He gives me a smirk. "Good luck with that one. She's like a dog with a bone."

Julian just laughs at me, mouthing the word 'chicken' and flapping his arms like one.

I pretend to scratch the bridge of my nose with my middle finger and he just laughs at me, his face splitting in two, his whole smile lighting up the room.

Having never been able to rid myself of the image of him lying lifeless on his bed, I get a real kick out of seeing him smile. Happiness suits him.

Keri and I are sitting in a cluster of stools, while the others become invested in the game. She doesn't waste any time, her plan of attack is in motion from the second her ass hits the seat.

"So, Julian told me you're single."

She leans in close, her arm resting on my shoulder. Normally she would be exactly my type for a one-night stand. The ultimate distraction; brunette, tight, firm body that would wrap around mine perfectly while I rammed into her recklessly.

But even with her low-cut blouse and perky tits being thrust into my face every time she gets the chance, my dick doesn't twitch. I'm not even shocked at this point.

I know what's caught my attention. He's about six feet

tall, a lean swimmer's body, and I'm staring at him like he's the second coming of Jesus Christ. Watching the way he walks around the table, taking in his every stance, his posture. I'm noticing his myriad facial expressions, the way he talks with his hands, the way he looks over at me from the corner of his eye every time Keri touches me.

"Oh my god," Keri gasps. "Are you gay?"

"What?" I intend to sound offended by her assumption, but even my subconscious sees there's no point in lying. I may not be gay, but I am unashamedly staring at Julian.

"I've been shamelessly flirting with you," Keri continues. "And you haven't even looked at me sideways, and I'm fucking hot."

I chuckle at her bluntness. "You're more than hot, babe, but I'm just not interested. Hasn't that happened to you before?"

She stands up, and maneuvers herself between my open legs, her body subtly swaying; whatever alcohol she's drinking is hitting her hard.

"Look at me," she says lazily, while waving her hands up and down her upper body. "Who wouldn't want this?"

Grabbing her hand, I drag her back to the stool, guiding her to sit back down. "Keri, you are beautiful."

"I know," she huffs, eventually sitting down.

Tucking her hair behind her ear, I place my finger underneath her chin and raise her head, till her eyes meet mine. "It's not you. It's me."

"Of course it's you," she says confidently. "But are you sure you're not gay? You and Julian aren't a thing?"

"What makes you say that?"

She raises a knowing eyebrow. "You're looking at him instead of me."

Releasing my hold on her face, I shove my hands deep into my pockets. "I guess that raises a few flags, doesn't it?"

"I don't know, does it raise yours?"

My body doubles over in laughter, her quick wit unapologetically refreshing.

"Line up, gentlemen, this one is a catch," I call out, when I've caught my breath. "She's gorgeous and she's got jokes."

"It's a pity you're hooked on your friend. I would've shown you a good time."

I almost want to drag her to the bathroom and fuck her. Fuck the idea that I'm passing up a sexy woman for Julian right out of my system.

"I'm not hooked on Julian," I lie. "He's my dead brother's boyfriend. It's complicated." I admit to a stranger. "We're trying to be friends."

"And how's it working for you?"

"It's fine," I say a little too enthusiastically. "We're out tonight and having a good time."

"Does he know you've got a thing for him?" she continues. "Because he has a thing for you. He's looked over here no less than a hundred times. Maybe I can play matchmaker," she squeals excitedly.

"How about we walk to the bar and get some water," I suggest, hoping to move her away from Julian and the possibility of him catching on to our conversation. Standing, she threads her arm through mine, getting ready to walk.

"Did someone say water?" Ray says, waltzing up to Keri and I.

"Does this place offer table service now?" I joke.

"I'm off soon and just wanted to see if you guys needed anything before I leave."

"You don't need to wait around for us," I say. "We were going to the bar anyway."

"It's all good." He turns to catch Julian's attention. "Do you guys want anything to drink before I sign off?"

Pete pipes in, answering Ray. "We're just about to kick these guys' asses so some celebratory shots on me is a must." He raises his hand for Julian to high five. "Sorry, Keri, but I've found a new doubles partner. You're officially out."

Keri nudges me in the ribs. "Seems like you may have yourself a little competition."

I tilt my head down to look at her and ask her something I know I shouldn't. "Is he gay?"

"Pete? No."

I look at her questioningly, but she just smirks. "But neither are you. Remember?"

12

JULIAN

"We'll come with you to get the drinks," Deacon says to Ray, tugging Keri to the bar with him.

She's smiling while he's rolling his eyes at her. They seem to be hitting it off, and I'm almost regretting this whole pool game idea.

Not completely though, because for the first time in forever, I had fun. It could most definitely be the buzz of the alcohol, but I don't care.

I had fun being me.

I wasn't the guy who lost his best friend. Not the guy who's in a permanent state of mourning. And not the guy who was finding himself more and more attracted to his boyfriend's straight brother.

Right now, I'm the guy with no past and no future.

I'm the guy living in the moment.

I'm the guy, that when tomorrow comes, I wish I could be.

It isn't long before Deacon and Keri return, no longer arm in arm. Deacon is responsible for the tray of shooters, while Keri walks shakily with her fingers wrapped around four bottlenecks.

He carefully places the tray on the tabletop, and we all gather around. Just as I raise the shot glass to my lips, I feel someone's hand squeeze my bicep. Putting down the drink, I look over my shoulder and see an apologetic looking Ray.

"Hey, is everything okay?" I ask him. He tilts his head to the side, and I step out of the circular formation, giving us some privacy. "What's up?"

"I just wanted to apologize before I head out for the night."

"You don't have anything to be sorry for, man."

"No, I do." He shakes his head. "I overstepped. I do it a lot."

I quickly glance over to Deacon, who's laughing with the group. "You may have had some valid points."

"Really?" he teases. "Want to be more specific?"

Playfully, I shove his shoulder. "Stop trying to get me to concede."

"Okay. Fine." he chuckles. "But maybe we can catch up outside of work sometime."

I'm about to awkwardly protest when he says, "As friends, Julian. Relax."

I run my hand across my forehead. "Yeah, of course. That would be great."

He offers me his hand to shake and I take it. When my palm touches his, he wraps his fingers around my hand and pulls me closer to him, till his mouth is close to my ear. "But if your friend decides he's into dick and you don't want him, I call dibs."

My body stills, and I can feel my teeth painfully clenching together at Ray's flippant comment. I want to snatch my hand away from his, take hold of his shirt and make him promise to keep his eyes and hands off Deacon.

But what right do I have to say that? Deacon's a big boy, he can take care of himself.

Stepping away from Ray, I don't miss the smug smile across his face, which means he didn't miss the shift in my demeanor.

Lowering my eyes away from his, I visibly swallow, trying to compose myself. Everything about this is so out of character for me. I'm not aggressive or possessive, and jealousy is not something I've ever been familiar with. But then again, with Rhett, the idea of him with someone else never even entered my mind.

We were secure. A sure thing. Inevitable.

This pull to Deacon is the complete opposite of that. It's nothing but the shell of a house standing on shaky ground.

It only needs one thing to fall apart, and any progress he and I made would turn into dust—Like it never really happened.

Ray tips his chin up at me. "I'll see you around Julian."

I don't bother responding, and he knows I have no desire to say anything in return.

Turning back to the group, I'm surprised to see Deacon standing right behind me, holding on to what I assume to be my untouched shot glass.

"How long have you been standing there?" I say defensively.

He presses his lips together in a grimace, the battle between truth or lie evident on his face. "I didn't like the way he held on to you."

Why didn't he just lie?

"Is that for me?" I ask, playing dumb and pointing at the drink.

He hands me the glass. "Congrats on the game of pool."

"Really? That's the line you're going with right now?"

"What?"

"Give me the drink, please. And maybe we can get a couple more."

I throw down the now tasteless liquid, and hope it replaces my earlier buzz with numbness. Minutes ago I was happy, and now I'm seconds away from falling apart.

I'm feeling too much, and I'm not emotionally equipped to handle it. I haven't been for a long time now.

Deacon's watching me like a hawk, but instead of asking me what's wrong, he drags the shot glass out of my hand. "Let me get you those shots while you hang out with these guys." He hooks his thumb behind him. "You're the man of the hour. Pete is determined to play with nobody else for the rest of the night."

Appreciative of his sixth sense, I slip my mask on and ease back into the raucous laughter of the group as Deacon leaves with everyone's drink order.

When he returns, I purposefully keep my distance, plying myself with enough alcohol to know I'm going to regret it tomorrow.

Somehow aware I need the space, Deacon spends his time with Keri, but his eyes track my every move, negating any physical distance between us.

Anthony and Denise get caught up making out with one another, so Pete and I play a few rounds of pool while shooting the shit.

Thankfully, Peter is a talker, and it takes little to no effort to keep the conversation focused on him. In no time I'm aware of where he was born, went to school, and that he recently got out of a five-year relationship because he felt it wasn't really going anywhere.

"You just get to a place in your life where you want to be moving forward. And she—my ex— didn't want to move forward," he explains. "She said 'later' to everything I wanted. Moving in, kids, marriage, traveling," he rattles off, while leaning on the pool cue, waiting for me to take my shot. "If it wasn't for these guys, Keri especially, I don't know how I would've survived after we broke up. And you know, it wasn't even heartache in the end. It was the realization that I gave up five years I can never get back to someone who didn't want them. Life's too short for that shit, man."

"Ain't that the truth," I mutter, as I pull my arm back and forth, the cue pushing the black ball across the table, sinking it into the left corner pocket.

"Fuck, even with all the drinking you're good at this," he compliments. "I owe you another round."

"Sounds good." Resting on the edge of the table, I finally feel the effects of the alcohol settling in my bones. I'm sluggish, every move feeling heavy and listless. I let my gaze slowly drift over to Deacon.

He's no longer watching me. He and Keri are huddled up close and deep in conversation. I feel the same wave of jealousy wash over me as earlier. Dragging my eyes away, I eagerly await Peter's return, needing more alcohol—needing it to release me from this unbearable weight on my chest.

Impatient, I push myself off the table and make my way toward the bar. I barely cover any ground when a carefree Peter rounds the corner, drinks in hand.

"I was just about to send out a search party," I joke.

"I didn't realize how busy this place gets. We hardly ever come here."

"Yeah, I only work weekday nights, and it's nothing like this," I tell him, while taking my drink out of his hands.

"You work here?" he questions.

"I didn't say that?"

He looks at me pointedly. "Come to think of it, I don't think you've said a word all night. Man, I'm sorry." he shakes his head. "Keri tells me I never let people get a word in edge-wise. I'm even worse when I'm drinking."

Relieved, I clap him on the back. "Don't sweat it, I don't have anything that interesting to say anyway."

It seems this is the moment everybody wants to crawl out of their corners and starts to mill around Peter and I. Deacon moves away from Keri and comes to stand beside me.

Only a smidgen taller than I am, he lowers his head, so his mouth is in line with my ear. "How are you feeling?"

"Is this your new way of asking if I'm okay?" I take a swig of my beer. "I have to tell you, it's pretty much the exact same thing."

"Okay," he drolls. "I have no idea what you're talking about, but I wanted to know if you were good to get going?"

"What?" I say surprised. "What about Keri? I thought it was working out."

He guffaws. "No. Not at all." He quickly raises the top of his own drink to his mouth, and I can't help but watch the way his throat moves as he swallows. "She's not my type."

I glance over at her and then back at him. I might not be attracted to her, but there's no way I could deny why other people would be. "She's not *my* type," I say. "But I'm pretty sure she's every other guy's in here."

"I'm not interested," he says matter-of-factly. "Why is that so hard to believe?"

Because as much as it fucks with my head, I need to see you with a woman so I can stop thinking about the impossible.

"Weren't you just saying earlier you wanted to get your dick wet?"

He runs his hands over his face and lets out a loud groan. "Can you please let it go, Julian? I said I'm not interested."

Both too mentally and emotionally exhausted to get into it with him, I raise my hands up in surrender. "Okay, I'm sorry. I'm letting it go."

"So, you ready to leave? I'm buzzed and I need some fucking food."

Nodding, I say, "I could eat."

"Perfect."

I tilt my chin up to our friends for the evening. "Let's say goodbye to these guys first, okay?"

"Yeah, of course."

Between the six of us there are some handshakes, cheek kisses, and one arm hugs. Pete suggests that we should catch up again for some drinks and more pool, and I explain to him that I can meet them here any time. I reiterate that my roster is usually filled with night time, weekday shifts, and that I'm almost always free every Friday, Saturday and Sunday night.

We exchange numbers, and a little bit of the giddiness I felt earlier from being out and around people returns. *Maybe the night wasn't a complete bust.*

I catch sight of Keri and Deacon exchanging goodbyes from the corner of my eye. Keri stands up, her body wobbly and intoxicated, while Deacon grips her elbow, ensuring she remains still. She rises on the tips of her toes and whispers in his ear, he leans forward to meet her, and it surprises me when he kisses her forehead.

It's not adoration or flirtatious. It's gratitude, and friendship, something that has strangely formed in a very short amount of time, and it's making me stupid angry, because in this moment I know I need to see him with someone else tonight. I need to see him with a woman so I can confirm whatever I'm feeling is just old residue of the emotions that come with sharing such important experiences with another person.

I need whatever I'm feeling to not be real, I want it to not be real. I want it to be one of those things death makes up— like when you see something that isn't there or feel things that aren't true, just to fill up the empty holes tragedy leaves behind.

But this isn't that... and the rush of relief flooding my veins, knowing Deacon's not going home with her, tells me otherwise.

Deacon looks over his shoulder and spots me watching him. He angles his head toward the door and I finish off my conversation with Peter.

Finally, I walk away from the group of people, and head toward the exit in silence. Checking my cell, I flinch at how late it is.

"Fuck, I didn't realize the time."

"You got somewhere to be?" Deacon smarts. "Or are you going to turn into a pumpkin?"

"Ha. Ha," I say sarcastically. "I didn't realize you were so funny."

"Don't worry, you'll figure it out soon enough."

"Are you still down for pizza?" I ask. "The pizza place next door?"

"Perfect."

As soon as we step into the eatery, I realize it's the last place I want to be. The smell of cooked food is strong, and the bright lights and copious amounts of drunk and loud people are making me feel very off balance.

Unknowingly, I sway, and I feel Deacon's large hand tightly grip my wrist. "Hey, lightweight. Why don't we get you home instead?"

"I'm fine. I'm fine," I repeat, tugging myself out of his hold.

He straightens his spine and takes a better look at our surroundings. "There." He points across the room. "Why don't you sit on that chair and I'll order us some food, and we can grab it to go."

Expecting us to walk in opposite directions, I'm shocked when I feel his hand on my lower back, and see him using his big frame to push people out of our way.

Thankfully the table is still free when we reach it. As soon as my ass hits the seat, I drop my head in my hands, willing the dizziness to go away. *Fuck, this went downhill quickly.*

"Here drink this." Not even realizing he'd left, a bottle of water appears in front of me. "I'm going to get us some pizza. Anything in particular?"

Unable to make my mouth move, I unscrew the bottle top and shake my head. He looks apprehensive as his gaze flicks between me and the front counter. "Are you sure you'll be okay if I leave you?"

"I'm a big boy, Deac," I manage to say. I grab my wallet out of my back pocket and hand him a twenty. "I don't need you to be my knight in shining armor."

He eyes the cash, ignoring it, and reluctantly leaves. I maneuver my seat so my back is now resting on the cool concrete wall. Closing my eyes, I let my head fall back, and try to focus on steadying my breathing.

In through the nose. Out through the mouth.

"Did you fall asleep?" a close voice asks.

Begrudgingly my eyes flick open, and he's standing there with a large pizza box in his hand. "That was really quick."

"Can you make it home? Or do you want to try to see if the food can soak it up?"

I hold my hand out for the pizza and he takes a seat in understanding. Flipping the box open, the smell of pepperoni pizza makes my stomach growl.

"This is going to go one of two ways," I warn. "I'm going to feel better after this, or one hundred times worse."

"I can take you home," he reiterates.

"Let's just enjoy the pizza," I say, ignoring him. Picking up a slice, I set it down on a paper plate in front of me. "It was your idea to get absolutely wasted, and you're not even remotely affected."

"That's probably because I slowed down while you went overboard celebrating pool wins with Peter."

"It wasn't that many."

He narrows his eyes and gestures his hand up and down my body. "Case in point."

"I told you I hadn't done this in a very long time."

"Did you have a good night?" he asks, sincerely.

Thinking back, even digesting the mixed bag of feelings I have toward Deacon, I give him a soft nod. "I think I forgot what it was like to have fun."

"You should do it more often." He takes a bite of pizza and washes it down with his own bottle of water. "You've earned it."

"How does one earn a night out?" I slur.

"You spent so many years putting yourself last."

"We've already been over this," I supply.

"We have, but I think you're forgetting that you don't have to do that anymore."

"So, what am I supposed to do, Mr. Know-it-all?"

He shrugs. "I don't think I've earned the right to give you my opinion."

"What's that supposed to mean?"

"I'm not someone who you respect or value in your life." He takes another bite of his food, his mood indifferent, like the self-deprecation is just fact. "And rightfully so, which means I don't qualify for input in life-changing decisions."

"That's not true," I reprimand.

"Which part?"

"I value you." Sobering up, I lean over to him. "If you want me to start fresh, then you have to too."

"What am I supposed to start fresh with?"

"Yourself. Stop talking about yourself like you're nobody." My voice rises, and I can feel my resolve slipping. "You don't let anybody in—by choice. And I respect that, but don't take everybody else's opinion on board when you haven't given them the whole picture."

"You basing all of this on a packet of candy corn?" he sneers.

"Fuck you, Deacon," I spit back. "Whatever you're trying isn't going to work."

Grabbing a bunch of napkins, I wipe the pizza grease off my hands, and raise my almost empty bottle of water to my lips. Finishing it off, I pile up my mess on the paper plate and rise in frustration. "Thanks for tonight, but I'm going home."

"You can hate me all you want, but I'm not letting you go home by yourself."

"Thanks, but I don't need a fucking babysitter, Deacon."

Haphazardly, I step around the plastic furniture, knocking the chair with my foot, and making the most ungraceful exit known to mankind. He isn't calling after me, but I can feel him close behind all the same.

The crowd disperses the closer I get to the exit. The moment I pass the threshold the cold air hits me hard, the perfect reprieve for the overwhelming tornado of heat inside me.

Not wanting to be a public spectacle, I veer off to the side and lean against a closed shop window.

It takes less than a second for him to see me, and somehow even less time for him to be standing right in front of me. He places his hands on the window behind me, stretching out his arms, so he's caging me in. His face peers down at mine. He's furious, a pulsing vein appearing in the middle of his forehead.

"Leave me alone, Deacon," I say dryly, my voice lying for me, while my quick and shallow breathing, and the rise and fall of my chest expose all my truths. My heart is bouncing around in my rib cage, the thump echoing in my ears.

I try to feign indifference, to ward him off, but the inferno blazing inside his eyes makes it impossible. He angles his head, lowering his mouth to my ear, his warm breath sending shivers down my spine. "What the fuck are you doing to me?"

13

DEACON

The apathy on his face morphs, first into shock, and then in anticipation. He licks his lips, and like fucking clockwork my gaze drops.

"What is it you think I'm doing to you?" he says, challenging me, his voice low and thick.

"Why do I keep staring at your lips?" It's an impossible question to ask, and one I know neither of us has the answer to. But I'm only a man, standing here, with nothing left but my vulnerability and honesty, hoping that's enough for me to wade through this clusterfuck.

"Am I supposed to answer you?" he quips.

Ignoring the taunt, I go on with my thoughts, letting the words tumble out of my mouth freely. "Does it bother you that I can't seem to take my eyes off them?"

His gaze flicks up to mine, and I watch the tip of his tongue grace his wet, plump, bottom lip. "Does it bother you?"

"Fuck you, Julian." The words are empty as I hang my head between us, force my eyes shut and whisper. "I'm going to fuck this up."

"Blame the alcohol."

I snap my head up. "What?"

"Do whatever it is you feel." He places his hands on my chest, and I feel the heat transfer between us. "And instead of it being awkward after, we'll blame it on the alcohol."

"And everything will go back to normal?" I ask, almost hopeful. *Why the fuck am I considering this?*

"You mean you'll go home and I'll be here, and we'll hate each other?" His gaze darts out of focus, as the last half of the sentence comes out croaky; almost like the words pain him. "Yeah sure."

With a mind of its own, my hand reaches for his chin, and brings his focus back to mine. "I'm an asshole, but that's not what I meant."

"Let me go home, Deacon," he says with a sigh. He wraps his fingers around my wrist. "Sleep off whatever it is you're feeling, because it'll probably be gone tomorrow."

Dropping my hand, his falls too. I take a step back and shake my head at him, laughing humorlessly. "I can't."

He straightens his stance against the glass window. "What do you mean you can't?"

"I've felt like this all weekend," I admit, rubbing my hand across the back of my neck. "And for someone who has never even glanced at another man, what I'm feeling has already lasted too long."

Feeling inundated with nausea, the confession slides out of my mouth, like vomit; with no warning, and just one big mess to clean up.

Surprising me, he steps forward with an air of confidence I didn't expect. He tilts his head up slightly, raising his eyes—filled with longing—to mine. "So do it," he says forcefully. The quick rise and fall of his chest is the only tell that I'm not alone in feeling this way. "Do. It." He enunciates.

I feel myself swaying, teetering on the thin line of indecision. Toward him? Or away from him?

"Deacon," he commands, taking a fistful of my jacket into his hands, and dragging me to him. "I want you to do it."

I let him pull me close, my eyes searching his. "Do you really?"

Pools of desire stare back at me. "More than I should."

"It could go very bad."

He snickers. "It will more than likely go very. Very. Bad."

I don't heed his warning, instead I roughly circle his wrist with my hand, gripping him tight. "I've never—"

"I don't care," he rushes out, cutting me off.

It's then I realize neither do I. Maybe after the fact. Maybe later. Maybe tomorrow. But right now, I want nothing more than to crush my whole body against his. To meld my mouth with his and find out if his lips taste as good as they look.

Throwing caution to the wind, I don't know which one of us moves first. He tugs on my clothes, pulling me to him, while my hand curls around the back of his neck, bringing him to me.

Unceremoniously I slam my mouth to his, extinguishing any second thoughts, and pressing pause on all of the confusion. I expect to be thrown off by the unfamiliarity of kissing another man, or for the trepidation that comes with the unknown to slow me down, but the gravitational pull I feel toward him is too strong.

His lips are unexpectedly soft, but his kiss is hard. It's a balancing act of push and pull, want and need, yes and no. It's a frenzied rush of frustration and desire, as we both fight for control.

Control over our bodies. Control over our minds. Control over each other.

His hands slip from between us, finding my hips, and dragging me to him. I wait for the anxiety to hit, I wait for the shock of feeling myself hardening painfully behind my pants for another man to make me want to stop.

But both the word and the notion cease to exist as my body eagerly complies. Without an inkling of hesitation, I'm cradling his stubble lined jaw in my hand, and deepening the kiss.

I sweep my tongue over the seam of his mouth, wanting more, wanting to explore. Groaning, I lean into him, pushing him against the window, sizing up the way masculinity feels underneath me.

How I can taste it with my tongue.

How I can touch it with my fingers.

How I can feel it with my body.

How come I didn't know a kiss could feel this good?

A loud cacophony of laughter spills out of the open store beside us, and I feel reality begin to settle in. I can't believe I just mauled him in public.

Reluctantly we pull apart. Foreheads pressed together, our bodies still touching, every breath between us is heavy and labored.

The sounds around us become louder, and I find the energy to drag myself away from him, and find the courage to face the consequences of what we just did.

I've given up on expecting myself to freak out, but I don't know why I didn't anticipate that he would.

His eyes dart around, looking at anything but me, while the guilt written all over his face stirs up my own. This was so much more than the straight guy kissing the gay guy. But in that moment, it was all I could think about. It was all I wanted, just to prove to myself that I wasn't going crazy. That what I was feeling wasn't all in my head.

"Julian," I start. "Julian, please look at me."

"I've got to go," he blurts out.

"Julian." I push past his personal space and grab his face with my hands. "Alcohol, remember?"

"Yeah." He nods. "I remember."

Pushing my hands off him, he steps back deeper into the alcove and takes one more pensive look at his surroundings. "I'm sorry, Deacon, but I really have to go."

"Do you want me to help you get home?" I offer.

Shaking his head, he reaches for me. With his palm resting atop my heart, he leans forward and presses a kiss to the side of my mouth. "We'll talk about it before you leave."

Highly doubt that one.

He turns to walk away, and I'm completely floored by how much seeing the back of him tears me up. How could I be so stupid? We knew it was a bad idea. We both reiterated it. Yet, I wasn't thinking about the aftermath. I wasn't thinking about anything but him and that kiss.

There's a line of drunk patrons just outside The Crooked Stool waiting for their ride. Julian joins them, standing on the end, playing around with his phone. Ignoring his request, I take large strides to reach him.

"I'm sorry, okay," I say to the back of him.

His body stiffens before he eventually offers me a subtle nod. He refuses to turn around, and I feel that rejection deeper than I ever thought possible.

I step back and lose myself in the sea of people around us, watching him from afar, waiting with him, feeling like a certifiable stalker.

It doesn't take long for him to climb into a car and drive off. I try not to focus on the dismissal and be understanding of the situation—it was naive to think either one of us would be unscathed from the get-go.

Once he's out of sight, I take it as a cue to find my own way home. Standing in the line, I run on autopilot; ordering the car, jumping in, and getting home.

I'm surprised when I arrive at my parents' place to see my father sitting on the porch, smoking a cigarette.

"Hey old man, what are you doing up?"

"Who the fuck are you calling old?"

Chuckling, I tip my chin up at him. "Can I bum a smoke?"

"One more reason for your mother to hate me," he says sarcastically. "Sure, why not?"

He lobs the small rectangular box in my direction, followed by a lighter. Sitting down on the cold porch, I pluck a stick out of the packet, and slip it in between my lips.

I flick the lighter and lean into the flame for it to catch. I take a long, unhealthy drag, enjoying the lungful of nicotine I inhale.

Fuck, I forgot how good a cigarette was after a night of drinking.

"You alright?" my father interrupts, his brow raised at the cigarette in my hand.

"Yeah," I lie. Looking away from him and back on to the empty road, I take in another drag. "Just one of those nights."

THE SOUNDS of feet shuffling and whispers make their way to my ears, filtering through and disrupting me from my slumber. I concentrate on the noises, trying to discern whether they're remnants of a dream or whether there is actually someone in my room.

When I feel a subtle dip in my bed, I turn my head to find my niece climbing up onto the bed, trying to balance herself and a bottle of milk, and Victoria, smiling and watching her.

"Well, this is a nice surprise," I say hoarsely. "I know I didn't message you back last night, but I wasn't expecting a face-to-face reminder." Pulling back the covers, I tuck Lia underneath my arm, adjust her bottle, and wrap us both like we're in a cocoon. "Not that I'm complaining seeing this cheeky thing first thing in the morning."

Victoria walks over to the end of my bed and sits on the edge of the mattress. "I had no plans to be here today, but mom reminded me she had food she needed to cook and I wasn't about to say no."

Remembering the conversation we had before we went out for dinner yesterday, I can totally understand why Vic chose not to argue.

"So, we're just having a lazy Sunday here," she continues.

Glancing down at Lia, I notice her eyes getting heavy while drinking her milk. "Why is she sleeping already, what time is it?"

"It's midday, you weirdo," she answers. "Nap time."

"I slept until midday?" I say a little too loud.

"Shhhh," Victoria hisses. "If she doesn't nap, that's on you, and you'll be on baby duty for the rest of the day."

"Relax," I say, trying to placate her. "She's not going to wake up. She'll be on her best behavior for her Uncle Deacon."

Victoria rolls her eyes, and then lowers her voice, "So, what did you do last night?" she asks, getting right to the point. "Dad said you came home late, which I'm guessing explains the sleep in."

"Yeah, Julian and I went out," I say as nonchalantly as possible. "Got drunk, made some new friends, you know the usual."

"No." She shakes her head vehemently. "No, I don't know, because none of that is the usual."

"God, you should see your face right now," I say with a soft chuckle. "Is it really that unbelievable?" *Wait till you find out I kissed him.*

"Not unbelievable," she corrects. "But very fudging"— she eyes Lia— "different."

Scrubbing a hand over my face, I groan in frustration. "Can we not do this right now? I'm hungover and Lia is sleeping."

"Fine," she concedes. "But can I at least say, even if it's different, it's nice to see you two trying to be friends."

"It is?"

"Yeah." She tucks her legs underneath her, making herself more comfortable. "I never understood why you weren't friends in the first place."

I leave the statement hanging in the air, too embarrassed to defend my reasoning. As an adult, it seems petulant and childish to have been jealous of all the attention Julian got when he was here. From my brother. From my parents.

Hindsight allows me the ability to see it wasn't on purpose, nor was it his fault. It's not like he's ever gone out of his way to be the center of attention. I realize now, he's just got that way about him. Something that makes you want to be around him.

"He and Rhett just had their own thing going. I'm older and just had other things going on."

"I get that." She grabs my foot and shakes it. "You're both

kind of loners, so it's good to see you two spending time with one another."

Scoffing, I jerk my foot out of her hold, pretending to be upset. "I can't figure out if you're insulting me or complimenting me."

"You know I like to keep your ego in check." Rising up off the bed, she points at Lia. "Are you going to go back to sleep with little miss, or grace us downstairs with your presence?"

"Don't you need someone to watch her while she sleeps?"

"Nice try, Deac. I can leave my phone in here and switch the app on that connects to Hayden's phone downstairs. The second she stirs, we'll hear about it."

"Fine," I huff. "Let me freshen up, take a shower, and I'll come down." Gently trying to shift away from Lia, I awkwardly climb out of the bed, trying not to wake her. I move her over to the middle and then build a pillow fort around her.

I feel Vic step up beside me. "I love seeing you with her."

"Is this the pregnancy hormones talking?" She swats my chest, and I loop my arm over her shoulder, giving it a little squeeze. "She's beautiful, Vic. You made the cutest kid. She better watch it though, I think this guy's about to give her some competition."

She places a hand over her subtly protruding stomach. "You think it's a boy?"

"I'd bet my kidney on it."

"You can keep your kidney, little brother. I'm going to set my phone up so it can creepily watch her, and I'll meet you downstairs."

It takes her all of five seconds to situate it on my nightstand, facing Lia at the perfect angle. The whole concept is crazy, I mean, millions of kids did just fine without their parents stalking their every move. But I'm not a parent, so what do I know?

Rummaging through my duffel, I pull out a pair of sweats, some underwear and a t-shirt. After the last few days, the thought of unwinding with everyone actually sounds appealing. Victoria and I both leave the room at the same time, and I head for the bathroom.

Finally stepping into the hot spray, I let the water cascade over me, washing away that thick coat of ick that sticks to your skin after a night filled with heavy drinking.

While rolling the tension out of my neck muscles, I grab the shower gel and begin to soap up my body. With nothing but the sound of the water hitting the floor, echoing off the tiles, I let my mind wander to where it's wanted to go since the second I woke up.

I enjoy the play-by-play in my head, reminiscing about the heat in Julian's eyes, and the warmth of his touch. I recall the taste of him on my tongue, and the electrical currents that ran through me because of him.

For him.

As expected, my dick stirs to life. Coupled with the absolute certainty that last night I was right where I needed to be for the first time in my life, my shaft thickens.

But it's the quick flash of guilt and pain that was on Julian's face after that has me leaving my erection unattended.

I shouldn't be torturing myself with this false sense of security about my sexuality and what we did, because if his reaction last night is anything to go by, it is almost definitely, never happening again.

Waiting for my body to calm down, I give myself one more once over with the soap, and quickly brush my teeth.

By the time I'm dry, dressed and making my way downstairs, I feel a little heavy in my steps. Relieved, but unsure. Relaxed, but confused.

It's an odd thing to feel the best (or the worst) of both worlds, but I figure leaving it alone for today, and letting it pan out organically sure as fuck isn't going to do any harm.

I'm not going to seek him out.

I'm not going to ask about him.

I'm going to do my fucking best to try to not even think about him.

Running my fingers through my hair, I aimlessly head into the kitchen, hoping there's something decent for breakfast because I'm famished.

A nice full plate of bacon and eggs is sure to hit the spot. Turning the corner, I'm ecstatic to see a full kitchen and extensively set up dining table. Mom is fluttering around the kitchen while Hayden and dad are sitting around the table and laughing.

It feels like old times, happier times, with the chatter and an air of comfort. It isn't till my eyes sweep around the space to find Victoria that I see the focus of my earlier thoughts sitting at the breakfast bar; doing his best not to notice me.

A week ago I would've been undoubtedly pissed he was here, infiltrating this moment, but today, I'm grateful for my family's obsessive need to have him around.

I do my best to appear ambivalent. Doing the rounds with my informal greetings, I adhere to his request to remain invisible, and casually bypass him. I don't let my eyes linger, I don't try to read his expression, and I don't try to catch a glimpse of his lips.

I don't pay him any more attention than usual, and it feels all kinds of wrong. I want to give him the space he asked for, but I also want him to know I'm not forgetting about last night anytime soon.

"Hey mom," I say when I reach the stove. A decent foot shorter than me, I crane my neck down and kiss her on the top of the head. "What's cooking?"

"Your sister has requested pancakes, bacon, and French toast."

I raise an eyebrow at her. "You sure that's going to fill you up?"

She flips me the bird. "With Lia, I was sick for the whole nine months. This time nothing I eat keeps me full."

"I was like that with both the boys," Mom pipes in. "It felt like a bottomless pit."

I point at Vic. "Told you you were having a boy."

"Everybody sit around the table, brunch is ready," my mom announces. "Food is ready."

Taking our seats, I find myself beside Julian. Vic and Hayden in front of us, and Mom and Dad on either side of the table.

It's on the tip of my tongue to ask someone to swap seats with me, but I know that will attract more attention than we both want. So I shift the chair a fraction to the side, creating some distance.

Taking my seat, I feel him staring at me. This time I can't help it. I turn my head to face him.

"What?" I challenge, a little too childishly.

Looking around apprehensively, I watch him lean over, his body as close as he can be without being obvious. "Move closer," he demands.

"Excuse me?" I hiss.

His eyes do another quick sweep around us, and he places his hand on my thigh. "I want you to move closer."

14

JULIAN

I barely even recognize myself as the words steadily leave my mouth. I got a call from Victoria this morning to see if I wanted to come over, and the answer should've been 'no'.

It was right there. My tongue sitting at the roof of my mouth ready to say the word, but I couldn't get it past my lips. The 'yes' however—that traitor—flew out quicker than I could take it back.

And here I am. Using this beautifully set table, and these extremely hospitable people to my advantage, because I'm too much of a coward to seek him out myself. If there was any way I could be in the same room as Deacon, without having to be the one to initiate it, I was going to take it.

We're locked in a stare-down after my revelation, and I know his body and mind are warring against one another just as much as mine.

His gaze moves down to my hand, and I reluctantly move it. Pretending to fix my own chair, I wait for him to re-situate his back beside mine. It's an unfair request, especially after the way I bailed after we kissed. But fuck if I'm going to be in the same room and have him pretend I don't exist.

Not now.

Not anymore.

Begrudgingly, he moves closer to me, the wooden edges of our seats now only an inch apart. I'm a little amused by how obvious his disdain is for being told what to do, and want to bask in the small victory, but I know when we're alone and we talk, he's not going to settle for anything less than the truth.

And the truth is really the last thing I want to say to him.

In that moment, when his lips were on mine, and his strong body was pressing against mine, I'd felt like I'd died and gone to heaven.

It was so much more than I anticipated. He kissed me like I was his next breath, and it was when I realized I wanted to be exactly that reality managed to sneak in and ruin the moment.

"Deacon," Elaine calls out. We both raise our heads and look at her. "Your dad says you came home late last night. I didn't know you still kept in touch with the guys from around here."

"Oh, I..." He stalls, tugging at his earlobe. "No, I don't keep in touch with them. Well, I do, but I wasn't with them. Julian and I went out last night."

Deacon reaches for the pitcher of water and pours himself a glass, while Hayden and Bill's eyes widen in shock. The smug look Victoria is aiming my way is a dead giveaway that she already knew, but it's the smile that splits Elaine's face that catches all of us off guard.

"That's such good news," she squeals in delight. "Deacon, your brother would be so grateful you're looking out for Julian for him."

Before I can process what she's said, a loud splutter erupts from Deacon's mouth, followed by a harsh coughing fit. I rush to take the glass out of his hand, while Elaine rushes to smack him on the back.

His body heaves a few times before the coughing finally subsides.

"Geez, Deacon," Elaine says. "You gave me such a fright."

"Sorry," he supplies, his voice hoarse and croaky. "It went down the wrong way."

When Elaine returns to her seat, Deacon grabs the glass of water and takes a large mouthful. His pained gaze catches mine, and I know exactly what it is that set him off.

It's the same thing that had me fleeing last night—the truth that I was really hoping to avoid just planted itself smack bang in between us, but this time there's nowhere for either of us to run to.

The hours pass, but the tension between Deacon and I never does. It ebbs and flows through us. Through every shared glance. Through our body language.

We're at an impasse. I'm not angry, and neither is he, but there's so much to be said, and even more that doesn't want to be heard. We could try and ignore it, pretend the kiss didn't happen...pretend that neither of us wants to do it again.

Thankfully Elaine's favorable mood has gained enough of everyone's attention that the discord is contained to just the two of us. And truth be told, I'd sit through this discomfort a hundred times over just to watch Deacon smiling with his family.

The living room has been transformed into a safe baby space. The furniture has been pushed to the edges of the room, and the original plush, beige-colored carpet has been decorated with a lifetime supply of toys, books, and puzzles.

Deacon is lying on his stomach aimlessly lining up puzzle pieces, while talking to Hayden. Dressed in gray sweatpants that are stretched tight over his round ass, and a black t-shirt that tightens beautifully around his shoulders and muscular arms; he's a temptation I never even saw coming.

My view of him is temporarily blocked when Vic sashays past me, and plonks her ass down on the couch beside me, holding a large mug of hot chocolate to her chest.

"You didn't want to get on the ground and roll around too?" she asks, pointing at Hayden and Deacon. *Well that's an idea my dick just paid attention to.*

 Initially they were both on the ground to play some animal game with Lia, but she's now moved on to bigger and better things, also known as sitting between her grandparents, watching her iPad, and enjoying the way they both sneakily give her candy.

"Were you as hungover as Deacon was this morning?"

"Huh?" I mumble mindlessly, too busy trying to covertly ogle her brother.

"When you guys went out?" she clarifies.

"Yeah," I answer too quickly. "So hungover."

It takes me a few seconds to realize she's no longer speaking, which isn't exactly the usual for Victoria. Cautiously, I turn to look at her, and she's just staring at me pensively.

I squirm under her gaze. "What?"

She sips the hot beverage and shakes her head at me. "Nothing."

My nerves feel like they're about to shoot out of my skin being under the microscope like this. I should get going.

Before the excuse even leaves my mouth, Victoria is on to me. "Need to go home?"

For all the times I was grateful that Vic was my surrogate sibling, this isn't one of them. She hasn't put the pieces of the puzzle together, but she isn't going to give up trying. Knowing it's useless, I still try to appear aloof and untroubled.

"You know what? I think I might." Lifting myself off the couch, I stand, and like my own personal shadow Victoria mirrors my movements.

"Julian's leaving," she purposefully calls out to the room.

Deacon's head snaps up, oblivious to our audience, and directly asks me, "You're going?"

"Yeah." I tear my gaze away from his and answer him while looking at everyone else. "I'm beat and I've got a few things I need to take care of."

"I'll walk you out," he says gruffly. Pushing himself up off the floor, Deacon doesn't bother to excuse himself from the conversation. He's a man on a mission, very much unconcerned with everybody's sudden interest in our 'friendship'.

"Sure," I squeak out awkwardly.

I offer a generic goodbye to the rest of the family, and I'm thankful for their unusual laid-back mood. It makes escape happen that much quicker.

Deacon doesn't just follow me outside, he practically stalks me. His steps so close to mine, his large body hovering, refusing to give me space.

He closes the front door behind him, and grabs my wrist before I have the chance to race down the porch steps.

"You're going to leave, just like that?" he accuses.

Clenching and unclenching my fists, I try to give my body something to focus on instead of the firm grip he has on me. I know exactly what I want to say to him, but I can't get those words out.

Not when everything around here reminds me of Rhett, not when everything around me is making me feel guilty.

"Just spit it out," he demands. "Tell me how much you regret it."

I spin on my heels, anger pulsing through me. "I can't do this here," I grit out. "Too many memories."

My arm still in his hold, he turns back to the house, opens up the front door, and drags me up the stairs. Thankfully, a few well-positioned walls stop his family from seeing us, but at this point, it's obvious Deacon doesn't care.

He leads us to his bedroom, knowing very well these four walls will keep my memories at bay. Slamming the door with such ferocity, he uses the strength of his whole body to press me up against it.

"Tell me now," he spits out. I can feel his rage match my own, his heart beating in time with mine, but his heavy-lidded eyes clarify what's really going on inside. He still wants me. He wants this. And that's what makes him mad.

"Tell me," he repeats. "I'm the straight guy, whose dick got hard for a guy for the first time in my whole life, and now you want to chicken out on me?"

He squeezes his eyes shut while trying to regulate his erratic breathing. It's naive of me to think it's only me who has issues to contend with. Kissing another man may change the whole trajectory of his life. And surely if he can face it, then so can I. Right?

He gently drops his head onto the wooden door, his

mouth by my ear. "I just want to know if you regret it," he says a little more calmly.

"No," I rush out in a whisper. Slowly, he tilts his head back to look at me, his mouth a breath away from mine. Shaking my own head, I raise a hand to cradle his jaw, letting the pad of my thumb skim back and forth across his bottom lip. "I don't regret it."

His breath hitches, and I flick my eyes up to his. "Am I confused?" I nod, answering my own question. "But, do I regret it?"

Moving forward, I angle my head, and languidly brush my lips against his. My fingers curl around his neck, bringing him closer, wanting to feel the soft press of his mouth on mine.

"Can I?" I breathe out.

"Please." His voice is strained and gravelly, anxiously anticipating my next move. Unlike last night, I set the unhurried pace. Wanting to savor the taste of him, I take control of his supple lips, and do my best to memorize them.

The shape. The feel. The taste.

When I swipe my tongue along the seam of his lips, a hum of approval rumbles in his chest. Deacon eagerly parts his mouth, and I hungrily lick the inside.

A heady groan encourages me to tangle my tongue with his, to take everything that he has on offer. I feast on the taste of all things unpredictable, revel in the familiarity of kissing a man, and bask in the newness of Deacon.

Hard and needing friction, I clutch Deacon's ass and push his pelvis against mine. Considering this is all new to him, it's a presumptuous move on my end, but when he bucks his hips, and his solid shaft grazes against mine, I have no doubt all logic was just pushed right out the window.

If possible, I feel myself get harder, as we shamelessly grind up on one another. Life ignites inside of me as I reacquaint myself with my old friends, need and want, adjusting to the thrill, succumbing to the risk.

"Fuck that feels really good," Deacon pants, his voice managing to sound like a mixture of shock and sex. "I think I'm going to come," he points out.

Searching for release, the kiss becomes sloppy and desperate; our bodies a tight bundle of unlit fireworks ready to explode. There's only one of two ways this will end, and I feel too far gone to make the right choice.

"Deacon," I pant. "I think we need to—"

"Come," he says again, his brain clearly short-circuiting at the prospect. "I need to fucking come, Julian."

Surprising me, he takes hold of my ass, and spins us so he's now backed up against the door. Covering my mouth with his, he thrusts his tongue between my lips and refuses to let me come up for air. He gives my fabric covered ass a painful squeeze, as he uses all his strength to guide my aching erection up and down his.

"I'm going to come," I blurt out, my half-hearted attempt to try to put some kind of hold on this outcome was fake and fruitless. "Shit, Deacon."

My body shudders in anticipation, my spine tingling, my balls tight and full. Fuck. I didn't know how much I missed this. I feel his body coil against mine, and I know we're both on the edge of a very dangerous cliff.

With neither of us considering the consequences, we take the leap. Crying out in relief, I bury my head in the crook of Deacon's neck as his fingers dig into my hips, and he lazily rolls his pelvis against me through his release.

Small, almost undetectable tremors race through my veins, as my spent body leans on Deacon's for support. His chest rises as mine falls, sated breaths the only sound in the room. Not wanting to be the first one to break the silence, I wait.

I wait because I don't have any words for what just happened. No words of comfort, no words of censure. Just physical proof of an unexpected connection, neither one of us can deny.

"Julian."

His voice is thick with trepidation.

"Yeah?"

"Do you need me to get you some clean clothes?"

My shoulders shake with laughter, every part of me relieved at his question. "Let me survey the damage and let you know," I tell him, finally unplastering myself from his body. "Maybe I can do a quick clean up in the bathroom and run to the car without anybody noticing me."

Stepping back, my eyes drop down to my jeans, and the fact they're black means I may be able to leave here as discreetly as I'd hoped. I look over to Deacon's sweats and notice the darkened area near his crotch.

Biting the corner of my lip, I look up at him, feeling proud. *That mess is because of me.* "I guess you enjoyed yourself then," I quip.

His eyes light up with humor as he presses his lips together to stop a smile from spreading across his face.

"Got something to say, Deacon?" I coax, knowing a witty response is on the tip of his tongue.

There's nothing but blatant lust in his eyes as they freely roam up and down my body. "I had no idea dick was so much fun."

I want to indulge in his humor, drag him to his bed and

show him just how fun it can be. But the black cloud of shame and remorse is laying a little too low, threatening to spill over and ruin the jovial mood.

"We need to talk," I announce with a sad smile.

He tucks his hands in his pockets. "Do you want me to come to your place later?"

Swallowing hard, I nod in response. Even though I feel as if I'm cheating on Rhett, or forgetting about him, I don't want to discuss this anywhere but my safe place.

"There's no rush," I inform him. "I'll be up late."

Wordlessly, I signal to the bathroom and he nods. Cleaning myself up as best I can, I wash my hands before heading back to Deacon's room. I give Rhett's room a longing glance as I pass it, wishing this wasn't so hard to work out.

Entering the room, I notice Deacon has changed into a new pair of sweats. "Want me to walk you downstairs?" he asks.

"Can you just keep an eye out?" I say, reaching for the door. "I don't really want to face your family with cum-stained jeans."

The corners of his lips turn upward. "I might be able to help you out."

Stepping out of his bedroom, we both slowly sneak down the stairs. Deacon walks ahead of me, opening the front door wide enough for me to run right through.

It feels juvenile, yet still so invigorating, like we're teenagers sneaking around. That isn't something I had or did with Rhett, and the idea of sharing something with only Deacon makes me want to see what else only he and I have in common.

He waves me off when I jump in the car, and I drive off

with a tingle on my lips, a head full of questions, and a heart full of possibilities.

Who would have ever predicted Deacon and I would've ended up here?

By the time I pull up in the driveway, the small high I felt because of Deacon has now dwindled into nothing. Walking into the house, my emotions begin their rollercoaster ride.

Dragging my feet into the bathroom, I strip out of my dirty clothes and hop into the shower, trying to compartmentalize my thoughts.

I'm simultaneously filled with dread at my lapse of judgment, and giddy with anticipation at Deacon's imminent arrival.

By the time I finish up washing and drying myself, I'm a complete mess. With a towel wrapped around my waist, I sit in the middle of my bed and drag up the one thing that usually centers me.

But as I lift up the lid of my most prized possession, I realize my lifeline might just be the one thing that helps me drown.

15

DEACON

Hopping into my truck, I place the six-pack of beer on my passenger seat and begin the drive to Julian's place. Checking the time, I decide it isn't too late to make a call I've been wanting to make all day.

The loud ringing of the phone echoes throughout my car as I wait for the call to connect.

"Hey," Wade answers, his voice booming around me. "How are you doing?"

"Not too bad," I answer honestly. "How's the shop?"

"If you can believe it, it's running even better without you."

"Haha, asshole," I say with a chuckle. "Listen, I just wanted to call quickly, and see if that offer you made before I left still stands?"

"You're gonna stay?" he asks, the surprise evident in his voice.

"I'm definitely thinking about it."

"Deac, man," he says with genuine enthusiasm. "That's great news."

"I know anything can change, but it can't hurt to try, right?"

The words hold more significance in this moment than Wade could ever know, and I feel like that simple resolution lightens the weariness that's been sitting on my shoulders since Julian and I parted ways.

With the way my days are unfolding lately, there's no way to process what the depth of *trying* really means. It's not just an arbitrary request, because *trying* to work out my feelings for my dead brother's boyfriend, is more than just a conversation; it's life changing.

But it also feels unavoidable.

Now that I've crossed a line that I didn't even know existed for us, it feels hopeless to even try and go back.

After Julian left, I casually slipped back into the living room with my family, acting like I didn't just blow my load, rubbing my dick all over another man. Every time I think about him—my hands on him, his mouth on mine, I anticipate a freak out. But the only thing I'm freaking out about is that the freak out never comes.

I am a straight man. I always have been. There isn't a time in my life where I can even recall giving another man a second glance—my attraction to Julian makes absolutely no sense. How do you know someone for more than half of your life and feel nothing, only to look at them one day, and wonder how you got by without ever noticing them before?

"So, you're sure you can get it all covered?" I ask Wade again.

"Of course," he assures me. "We'll be fine. I'll even send you daily updates if it makes you feel better."

I chuckle, because he knows me well. Daily updates would make me feel better. I don't like spending time away from the shop, unless it's an absolute necessity.

And while this isn't even remotely close to what I would classify as urgent, it feels pretty damn important.

"I look forward to them," I remark. "You know if I don't hear from you in a few days I'll be blowing up your cell, anyway."

"Looking forward to it. Now get off the phone and enjoy your time with your family."

"All right, man. I'll speak to you soon."

The end of the conversation comes just as I park in front of Julian's place. Pressing the end button on my steering wheel, I switch off the ignition and wonder if I should've called before coming over.

We've both had the same cell number for as long as I can remember, an exchange made on the off chance of a family emergency that required us to contact one another. Thankfully that moment never came, but it also means I've never needed to call or text him, and this makes me more reluctant to start doing it now.

Jittery, I head to his front door, and nervously rap my knuckles on the solid wood. Before I've even pulled my hand back, the door swings open.

A smug smile spreads across my face. "Couldn't wait to see me, huh?"

He grins back, and I'm stunned by the way my body reacts to his relaxed mood. He looks comfortable now in lounge pants that sit low on his hips and a well-fitted t-shirt. "I thought you were my food."

Clicking my tongue, I lower my eyes and hide my widening smile. It's on the tip of my tongue to tease and suggestively say that I wouldn't mind being *his* food, but I hold back. If he was a woman, we'd already be onto our fifth or sixth exchange of sexual innuendos, the comfort of my sexuality usually encouraging. But with Julian, I tread carefully, because I'm out of my element on every single level.

Instead, I raise my hand holding the six-pack of beer. "I brought drinks."

"You didn't have to do that."

He reaches for the bottles, but I jerk my arm away. "Depends, is there enough food for me? Because if there isn't? I'll keep these and you can eat by yourself."

He offers me a bemused smile. "There's enough food."

"Then I guess I can put these in the fridge then?"

Stepping out of the doorway, Julian gestures for me to come in. Passing him, I amble toward the kitchen. Making myself at home, I open the fridge and place the bottles on the spare space on the top shelf.

Closing the door, my eyes snag on an important looking letter, being held up with a magnet. "When did you get this?" I ask without a second thought, my fingers tugging at the edge, and pulling it off the fridge.

I feel him behind me, his chest brushing up against my back. "Friday?" he questions. "The day I saw you at the cemetery," he clarifies.

I count the days in my head, and turn to face him. *Has it really only been three days?*

Leaning on the fridge, I offer us some space and jut the piece of paper between us. "You didn't say anything."

Snatching the letter from me, he leans over and hangs it back up. "When would you have liked me to slip it in? Before or after you used all your energy to ignore me?"

Dropping my chin to my chest, I try to hide the shame I feel at how I've treated him. Peering up to look at him, I catch his expectant gaze.

"I was jealous," I say under my breath, unsure of whether I really want to admit to this with him.

"Of me?" he asks incredulously.

"It's complicated," I sigh.

Long lean fingers grip my chin, tilting my head up. "*Everything* about this is complicated. Tell me," he urges.

Like a cliched scene in a movie, the sound of someone knocking interrupts us, but Julian doesn't rush to open it. "This isn't finished," he warns. "I want to hear what you have to say."

I nod as his hand drops from my chin. When he walks away, I grab two bottles of beer, like we agreed upon, and trudge through his house. Placing the bottles down, I shrug out of my jacket, the house warm enough to be wearing a t-shirt. Once I throw it over the nearest piece of furniture, I drop down to sit around the square shaped coffee table in the middle of his modest living room.

When he returns, he's got his hands full with plates and food filled containers. "You ordered that much Thai food for one person?" I ask, stretching my arms up to take some of the load.

"I knew you'd get here eventually."

"Confident much?"

He lowers himself down to the floor, sitting with his legs crossed and neatly tucked underneath the table. "More like hopeful," he says honestly.

We sit in relaxed silence as we both plate up our food. I open up both our beers and place his closer to him.

I've almost cleaned my plate when he interrupts the lull. "Tell me why you were jealous?"

"This is going to make me sound ridiculous," I admit.

He nudges my leg with his, but keeps his eyes on mine. "Probably."

Focusing on my plate, I move my food around in circles with my fork. Making piles and shapes with the leftovers, I give my mind something to absentmindedly concentrate on, instead of fixating on the awkward words that are about to leave my mouth.

"You just fit in," I blurt out. "It wasn't like you tried too hard, or you were excessive and over the top, wanting everyone's attention." I chance a sneak peek at his face, and he's watching me thoughtfully. "Maybe it was just a case of middle child syndrome. Victoria was the only girl, so I never felt the comparison with her. And with Rhett, he was just effortlessly better. At everything and anything."

"And me?" He hesitates.

"You got their attention, in ways I never did," I confess quietly. "Their pride. Their smiles. Their laughter. They couldn't get enough of fussing over you, and as an adult, I know how stupid and pathetic it sounds, but it bugged me for a really long time. And then it just felt like too much time had passed to change the way I felt."

"Deacon." I flick my gaze up to his and catch his empathetic smile. "Surely you know why they were like that toward me?"

I look at him confused.

"They felt sorry for me," he states. "My parents were dead, my grandmother died, and the Andersons were just placeholder parents. Your mom and dad are too good to not be nice."

It's logical and makes perfect sense because Bill and Elaine Sutton *are* good people, but none of that matters in my brain. Because it still doesn't change that my mother's good nature and need for perfection constantly made me feel like I wasn't enough.

"I know that," I tell him. "But it doesn't change anything up here." I tap two fingers to my temples. "You were the icing on the cake, and I resented you simply because I could," I say truthfully. He gives me an encouraging nod, so I find myself wanting to tell him more. "Growing up, it was like Rhett could do no wrong, I was his older brother, but mom wanted me to learn from him. But, no matter what I did, I always got a reprimand, a side comment of how I could do better or do more. After Rhett got diagnosed with cancer, I gave up on trying. It became easier to stay away, because Mom—rightfully so—became a wreck."

"I was alive and her perfect son wasn't," I exclaim, my voice cracking a little at the end. I pick up my beer and draw back as much of the cold liquid down my throat as I can. My heart is hammering in my chest, disbelief swimming in my stomach at how I can't stop talking.

I feel him scoot a little closer, the place where the corners of the table and our elbows meet, now touching. "And how do you feel now?"

"Honestly?" He nods at me. "I feel like I'm going to spend my whole life trying to make up for something that wasn't my fault."

"Rhett always wanted to tell her, you know?"

My throat tightens, and I try to push away the reactive feeling of jealousy and listen to Julian talk with my head instead of my heart. There's always going to be things he and Rhett shared, just like now there will be things only he and I share.

"What do you mean?" I ask.

"You didn't imagine it, and he would always grumble at why she couldn't just let up."

Overcome with emotion, I bury my head in my hands and digest his revelation. His words validate years of inadequacy, years of feeling unbelievably misunderstood.

A strong hand squeezes my shoulder, and I tilt my head to meet his gaze. There's a fine line between sympathy and pity, and I'm glad I only see the former staring back at me. Sympathy I can deal with, pity is just embarrassing.

"But this weekend has been good for you guys, hasn't it?" he asks, hopeful.

"It has," I tell him truthfully. "It's been better than I anticipated."

Wanting to take the spotlight off me, I clear my throat and steer us back to an earlier conversation. "The eviction notice said you need to be out of here by the end of the year."

He drags his hand off me and folds his arms, resting them on the table. "I haven't really had a moment to digest it. Between the anniversary and everything else." There's emphasis on the words 'everything else', with a heavy dose of accusation, but I don't bother arguing, because he's right. It has been one heck of a weekend.

"Are you okay with moving out?" I query.

"I don't really have a choice," he quips.

"That's not what I meant," I huff. "I mean leaving *this* place."

He doesn't answer straight away, taking a sip of his beer instead. When he places it back on the table, he asks. "Do you ever feel guilty?"

All the time.

"You're going to have to be a bit more specific," I retort, even though I'm almost certain I know where this is heading.

"Say the owners weren't selling the house at the end of the year, and I just wanted to move out. Does that mean I'm moving on? Forgetting him?"

Call me conceited, but I feel very responsible about his line of thinking. I'm also painfully aware that maybe my idea of staying and pursuing this in any form is a really bad idea.

Pushing aside our physical connection, and some new developments in my sexuality, I choose to give him advice as a friend, because first and foremost, that's what I want to be to him.

"The most important thing to remember is you're never going to forget him," I tell him. "It's impossible. But if you don't feel ready to move on, then don't."

I wait for him to acknowledge that he understands what I'm saying. Hoping that he hears the sincerity in my voice. I may like the way his lips meld against mine, and under any other circumstances, I would be chomping at the bit to explore what this meant for me and how far it could go.

But that's not the case here. He's who he is and I'm who I am, and I don't want to, nor would I ever be somebody's replacement.

Not being good enough, that's a hard limit for me.

If he wants to move on, he has to do it for him, and only if he's ready.

"You don't have to move on to move forward, Julian."

It takes a few long beats before his russet-colored eyes meet mine. They look at me, searching, almost like I might have all the answers. I don't, not even *some* of the answers, but I do know for a fact my brother would be turning in his grave knowing Julian's life was at a standstill because of him.

"Are you finished?" he asks, At first I think he means have I finished talking, but when he points at my plate, I concede on the conversation change.

"Yeah, I am." I scrape my leftovers into an empty container and then grab Julian's plate. "Let me clean up, it's the least I can do."

He doesn't argue, and I'm grateful for the momentary

distance.

I find my way around the kitchen pretty easily, disposing of our scraps and refrigerating the leftovers. After rinsing the plates, I look over to Julian, who's now moved to his two-seater couch, picking at a beer label, while lost in thought.

Drying my hands on my sweats, I lean back on the kitchen counter and just watch him. It's creepy and weird, but I don't stop. I stare at him long and hard. He's got his back to me, his shoulders hunched in defeat; one leg stretched out across the couch, and the other hanging over the edge.

He's carrying the world on his shoulders, and no matter what he says or how cool he plays it, his body gives him away. I don't want to be the one who adds to that, do I?

He must notice I haven't returned, because he spins his head around to look for me. His gaze lands on me, and I don't make an effort to move. I don't know why, but my stubborn streak decides to appear, and I don't want to be the one who initiates what little or big move comes next.

When the silence becomes deafening, I hear him say. "Are you going to stand there all night?"

I stay quiet.

He sighs at my defiance. "Can you come here, please?"

Swallowing hard, I bite the bullet and stride over to him. When I reach the couch, he grabs my hand and pulls me down to sit.

With his legs open wide, I find myself situated between them. It's close, so I attempt to shift myself back, so I'm facing him, but it does little to counter the proximity.

Bent at the knee, one of my legs rests on top of his. My body doesn't jerk at the small contact. Come to think of it, I don't know if it ever did. But I'm slowly learning, it doesn't matter how little or how much, it always wants more.

He releases my hand, only to place both of his on my cheeks. He holds me still, so I have nowhere else to look.

Pools of raw, unfiltered, anguish stare back at me, and it feels like a razor blade to the heart.

"Whatever explanation you think you owe me, you don't," I say forcefully.

He vehemently shakes his head, and I see the determination harden his gaze. He's going to slice himself open regardless of what I say.

"Never in a million years did I ever think I would kiss you." His eyes drop down to my lips. "Or that I would even want to." He looks back up at me, offering up the saddest smile. "Or that *you* would want to be kissing me."

I want to interject and say the joke's on both of us, but I know this monologue is more about Julian getting it off his chest than him needing reassurance from me.

"You're a great kisser," he compliments, and I don't even bother holding back my laugh. "But afterward," he clears his throat. "Afterward, I just feel so—"

"Guilty," I finish off for him.

His hands drop into his lap in defeat. I catch them, give them a squeeze and bring them up to my lips. My movements are based on instinct, and instinct alone, as I hold his examining gaze, and kiss each of his fingers, before lowering them between us.

"You have nothing to feel guilty for," I say, wringing his fingers between mine. "I know you're his. I know you're still mourning. I *know* better," I persist. "So, let me wear that guilt, okay?"

"And what if I want more?" he asks. "You going to blame yourself for that too?"

"Julian," I huff. "I'm trying here."

Uncurling my fingers from his, I try to pull my hands

away, but he clutches on to them, his eyes daring me to pull away. "You don't think I'm trying?" His voice is like lava, nothing but thick heat. He leans in, his hands trailing up my arms as he moves closer.

"You don't think I'm trying to forget how you feel against me? How you taste? How perfect your goddamn mouth is?"

My body burns with every confession he sets free, and I hate him for it. I hate him for feeling the same and I hate him for making it almost impossible to walk away. I hate him as I throw myself at him, because I know with absolute certainty I don't hate him at all.

His mouth captures mine, as if he's done nothing but wait for me to kiss him. I swallow his low groan as his hands circle my biceps, and he begins pushing me back down onto the couch. I fall with abandon, taking him with me, wanting to feel the heavy weight of his body pressed into mine.

Hands slip under my t-shirt, and the skin to skin contact makes me gasp.

"Is that okay?" Julian asks. My tongue is thick, my voice is tight, so I just grab the back of his head and slam his lips to mine once more.

The kiss is fueled with pain and passion as he spills his secrets into my mouth, and my tongue greedily hoards them for safekeeping.

The regret. The guilt. The shame.

I kiss him hard enough to forget them. I kiss him hard enough so he'll remember me.

With every swipe of his tongue, I feel understood.

With every swipe of his tongue, I feel a little less lost.

With every swipe of his tongue, I feel tethered to a man I can't have.

And with that last tantalizing swipe of my tongue against his, I know I'll never be alone again.

16

JULIAN

It's Thursday night and I'm wiping down the bar top for the hundredth time. Tonight has been slow. So painfully slow. I've been left alone with nothing but my thoughts for the third day in a row, and I'm about ready to gouge my own eyes out in frustration.

If I thought my life was lonely and monotonous before, spending the weekend around people, letting myself laugh, smile, and feel has only emphasized just how depressing the way I'm living really is.

If I'm not careful, I'm going to wake up one day and I'll be a forty-year-old man who has nothing to live for, nothing to die for and absolutely nothing to lose.

Is that really how I want my life to go? No passion? No drive?

And then there's this thing with Deacon. He may be the wrong man for me, but am I going to be able to be with *anyone* in the future?

I almost sigh in relief when I see Bill saunter into the place, hoping the mindless conversation with him will get me out of my own head. Even just a little.

He slides onto the stool and I don't even waste time with small talk. I hand him both a finger of whiskey and a bottle of beer.

"On me," I announce.

He picks up the whiskey glass and throws it down in one mouthful. "A man can't say no when it's free, can he?"

Slamming it on the wooden bar, he swaps his empty cup for his full bottle. "How have you been, son?" he asks.

"Not bad," I say while puttering with the limes and lemons on the bar for the hundredth time tonight. "You?"

"Better than I've been in a while," he declares, with a smile. Despite my own issues, it warms my heart to hear him happy. "The house feels a little empty now, but having you all over on the weekend sparked a bit of a spring into Elaine's step. I wouldn't say she's a new person, but more like the old her than she's been in a while."

Grabbing the bottle of whiskey off the ledge behind me, and a clean glass, I pour us both a shot. Raising the drink in the air, I make a toast. "To happy drinking."

He lets out a raspy chuckle and clinks his glass with mine. "It must be nice having Deacon home too," I add, nonchalantly.

He tilts his head, looking perplexed. "Deacon went home early Monday morning."

Like a punch to the gut, I pretend the words mean nothing to me at all. I hide away the hurt and embarrassment that we shared hard truths, and soft touches and none of that warranted even a semblance of a goodbye. That *I* didn't warrant one.

After we managed to pry our lips off one another, I felt the guilt and blame going backward and forward like a tennis match between us. We made a conscious effort to ignore it, even if we didn't say it out loud.

We'd laid down on the couch, his arm draped across my body, like we'd done it a million times before. The television was on, the conversation was light; and for a moment in time, we were just two people enjoying each other's company.

Not so surprisingly I fell asleep. His body was like the perfect cushion, and my body wanted to take advantage of it. The only problem was, when I woke up, I had a blanket covering me, and he was gone.

It was very reminiscent of the night he held me, two days after Rhett's funeral, except this time I thought we were different and he just needed space. I didn't think he would actually leave.

Well, what did you expect him to do? You told him you felt guilty.

I try to push the errant, rational thought out of my mind, because I think the kissing after that declaration negates the issue. *Doesn't it?*

And why did he leave when I specifically recall him saying he was staying, because he wanted to work things out with his family, and he wouldn't put a time limit on how long it was going to take.

"I'm pretty sure he's coming back for Thanksgiving," Bill informs me, probably noticing the distress on my face.

Shaking my annoyance off, I ask. "How do you think things went between him and Elaine this weekend?"

"I think that's why I'm so fucking happy," Bill exclaims. "It was so effortless. Even when he said goodbye, I didn't feel panicked that she may have pushed him far enough that he might not want to come back."

I'm relieved. For Bill and his family. For Deacon.

"That's great news, Bill," I say sincerely. "You guys deserve something to look forward to."

As I stack the empty tumblers, a beefy hand lands on my forearm. "Everything okay, Bill?"

"I actually came here to talk to you about something." I raise an eyebrow in question. "Deacon may have mentioned you need to move out of your place soon."

That motherfucker.

"It's no big deal," I brush off.

"Well." He clears his throat. "I wanted to make sure you know our place is always open to you. Permanently or temporarily. Our doors are always open while you get on your feet."

Begrudgingly, I smile. "Thank you, Bill. I appreciate the offer. It means a lot."

And it does, but it doesn't mean I have to take him up on it.

I steer clear of Bill after our conversation, and it doesn't take him too long to notice my annoyance, and call it a night.

The last two hours of my shift drag even slower than the first four. By the time I get home, I'm on my last nerve, ready to explode with anger and frustration. Grabbing a beer from the fridge, I shove the door closed a little too hard in irritation.

How dare he share my business with them?

By the time my beer is empty, I've thought about it long enough to know I'm not mad he told his parents I needed to move. I'm just mad at him. Period.

Dragging my cell out of my pocket, I drop onto my couch, kick my feet up on the coffee table and click on the messages icon.

I scroll through my contacts and click on his number. It opens up an empty message box, and it hits me that I've never texted him. I haven't ever called him either. *Is this even his number anymore?*

Fueled by adrenaline, I quickly type out a message.

Me: I can't believe you told your parents I was getting evicted.

The message is more of a lead in to what's really bothering me, needing an outlet but feeling a little too wrung out to lay it all on the table from the get-go.

Not wanting to stay up all night staring at the phone, I power it down and head for the shower.

By the time I've finished my nightly routine and jumped into bed, curiosity gets the better of me and I turn my phone on. It's already past one a.m., and I've set my expectations for a response very low.

I tell myself I don't care if he doesn't respond, but when my stomach erupts in flutters at the succession of messages that show up on my screen, there's no denying how disappointed I would've been if he didn't acknowledge me.

Sliding on one of the notifications, I watch the screen light up with a barrage of texts.

Deacon: Was it a secret?

Deacon: They would've found out anyway.

Deacon: What's the big deal?

Deacon: Why would you text me if you're not going to answer me?

Noticing the time stamp, I realize he wasted no time responding, and his last message was sent half an hour after the rest. I'm not going to lie, I find his impatience extremely satisfying.

Me: The big deal is I'm not their charity case.

Deacon: Caring and charity are not the same thing.

Me: What do you "care"? You didn't even tell me you were leaving.

Before I have the good sense to turn my phone off, it vibrates in my hand. Stubbornly, I decide I'm not going to answer.

The ringing lasts longer than usual, and I just place it down on the mattress and wait for him to give up. He doesn't.

Eventually, I decide to put him out of his misery and answer.

"Yeah," I answer.

"Well, hello to you too."

His voice is hoarse and tired, putting a halt to my smartass comeback. I wonder if my first message initially woke him up. "What time do you get up for work?" I ask him, my concern evident.

"Shop opens up at seven," he answers gruffly.

"You should get to bed," I suggest.

I hear some movement on the other side of the phone. "Did you work tonight?"

"I got home not that long ago," I tell him.

Propping another pillow behind my head, I try to find a comfortable position, while waiting for him to pick up his turn of the conversation. The line is filled with nothing but our alternating breaths, laced with nervousness, neither one of us rushing to say anything.

Glad to be in bed and off my feet, my eyes grow heavy, enjoying the quiet.

Just as I can feel myself slipping under, I hear a low, but very audible. "I'm sorry."

I keep my eyes closed, and stay silent, because I really don't have anything to say. Beyond the anger and the confusion, I know how impossible this is for both of us.

But, unfortunately, his apology doesn't dull the twinge of pain I've felt inside my chest all night. I wish I could predict the future, or shake a magic eight ball so I can ask if any of this is worth it and have it tell me 'The answer is yes.'

Instead of elaborating or expanding on something we have no control over, he asks me. "How did you know I told my parents about your place?" he asks.

"Your dad came in for his usual weekly drink and let me know that if I needed help he was there," I answer. "But it was more like a 'you can always move in with us' type of thing."

"My dad comes in for a usual weekly drink?" He sounds concerned, and I cringe at my loose lips.

Mulling it over, I decide on being honest, it's not like the man is hiding an alcohol addiction. "He's been coming one night a week since Rhett died."

"Fuck. I feel like I should've known that," he scolds himself.

"You couldn't have known that. I don't even think your mom knows that," I pacify. "And to be honest, I really think he just used it as an excuse to check up on me."

"Is that why you got defensive about the house thing?" he asks cautiously.

Rubbing a hand over my tired face, I sigh into the empty room. "I think I'm having a small existential crisis."

"Sounds serious," he retorts, injecting humor in his voice. "Anything I can do to help?"

"You've done plenty, thanks," I joke. When I hear a deep chuckle through the phone, I'm glad he took the comment with the lightheartedness in which I meant it.

"Let's not focus on how fucked up things are over here in my head," I say dismissively. "Your dad may have mentioned you left on a good note with your mom."

"I did. I was certain this weekend was going to be this huge blowup, but she surprised me. It was nice to actually not want to say goodbye." I hear him yawn before asking. "Is that normal?"

"I have no point of reference on what's normal or not, but I do know what you mean, and I'm glad you got that. I know how much it means to you."

"I'll be back for Thanksgiving," he slips in casually. I mentally count how many days till Thanksgiving, and then berate myself for acting like a teenage girl with a high school crush. "I don't know if I'll be able to stay more than two days because of work," he adds. "But I'll try."

The sentiment buries itself in the dark, dusty corners of my bruised up heart, because I hear what he doesn't say. *I'm not cutting it short for you. If I could stay, I would.*

"You should get to bed," I suggest. "I didn't mean to text you so late, and wake you. I was actually certain I had the wrong number."

"One would have to sleep to be woken up," he informs me.

"Why aren't you sleeping?"

"It might have something to do with that existential crisis."

"Aren't we a pair," I snicker.

"You get to sleep all day though, right?" he clarifies.

"Yeah," I muster. "No complaints here."

"What about you?" I find myself asking. "Tell me about your shop."

"What do you want to know?"

"Whatever you want to tell me," I quip.

"Umm," he muses. "How much do you know?"

"About cars?"

"No." He laughs. "About my business."

"Is this like a quiz on how much I paid attention over the years?"

"I never thought of that," he says, his voice full of excitement. "Would you win or lose?"

"You're serious, aren't you? Are you going to answer questions about me?"

"You want me to tell you how much I know about you?"

"Definitely," I enthuse. "What's good for me is good for you. Albeit I don't think there's much—"

He cuts me off. "You were going to apply to college after school to become a high school teacher."

Startled, I sit up, the blanket falling to my waist, shock making it impossible for me to sit still. "How did you know that?"

"It's your turn," he challenges, ignoring my question. When there's nothing but silence coming out of my mouth, he adds. "I'm feeling a little heartbroken at your shock."

I choke out a laugh. "I'm sorry, I just really am shocked. I didn't think anyone but Rhett knew that."

"What can I say? I pay attention," he boasts. "Now let's see what you know."

"Ummm. Let me think," I deliberate. "Oh, I know," I say more to myself. "When you were sixteen, you came home absolutely totaled from a seniors' party you were invited to."

"How did you know that?" I can't help the smile that dances across my face, knowing it's my turn to shock him.

"I also know that you vomited all over your date that night," I tease. "What was her name? Yasmin was it?"

"No fucking way you know that," he bellows. "Nobody knows that."

Laughing, my body languidly falls back onto the pile of pillows. "I totally won that round."

"Fuck that, you did not win."

"One thing I didn't know was how much of a sore loser you were," I taunt.

"Bullshit," he mumbles.

"Don't worry, Deacon," I soothe. "Your secrets are safe with me."

"You might be the only person who knows them all," he responds.

The mood shifts and I feel the change between us squeezing my heart. It's warm and honest, and effortless; and it's growing roots. Hooking themselves around my veins, making themselves comfortable. Making themselves somewhat at home.

"You ready to call it a night?" I prompt, selfishly wanting to go to sleep feeling the exact way I feel in this moment.

"I can only try," he says. He's silent for a few seconds before he adds, "Are we good? You're not still pissed off at me?"

"No." I chuckle. "I'd say we sorted it out."

"I'll speak to you later?" The inflection in his voice indicates he's very much asking me a question.

Do I want to talk to him when he's not here?

"Yeah," I answer sincerely. "I'll definitely speak to you later."

17

DEACON

It's the weekend before Thanksgiving and Wade and I have dedicated every free hour we have to the shop. We get extremely busy around this time of year, everyone wanting their car in working order so they can make the long trips to visit family all around the country.

To reward ourselves, we take four consecutive days off. It's probably the longest time we close the shop, with the exception of Christmastime. We usually finish half day on Christmas Eve and open back up on January second.

Most other bosses would use their status to their advantage and take as much time off to spend with their family, but since I never felt the need to, I was always eager to come back, leaving Wade to enjoy those luxuries.

Tonight we're both holed up in the office getting through the never ending list of admin duties. In case it wasn't obvious, he and I are insufferable control freaks.

We could easily hire an accounts person to take care of it, and at some point, probably very soon, we will, but for now, we'd rather share the load between us.

"So, it's been close to two weeks since you came back

from your parents' place, and you still haven't told me why you came back early."

"Ughhh," I groan. "I thought I told you to let this go. There's no underlying reason."

"Bullshit," he coughs.

"And you're super cheerful lately, so you obviously didn't have a blowup with them," he continues.

"I'm not super cheerful," I argue.

"Dude, do you know how long it'd been since I'd seen you smile?"

I look up at him from the stack of papers I'd been viewing, perplexed at his statement. His voice is serious, grave even, and I'm shocked. I laugh. I smile. "That's not true."

"I've known you for ten years, Deacon," he says. "And you've always been a broody motherfucker, so fucking spill."

The word broody immediately reminds me of Julian, and that has my lips turning up. Wade jolts out of his seat, pointing and yelling at me. "That's it, right there. Caught in the fucking act. What's behind that cheesy ass smile on your face?"

Resting my elbow on the arm of my office chair, I rub my hand over my mouth, covering my widening smile. His reaction is ridiculous, yet extremely entertaining.

I wish he was wrong in his observation, but he isn't. He knows me better than I know myself sometimes, and I'd be lying to both of us if I said I hadn't noticed my mood change. I know when it started. I know the reason. But I don't have a single idea on how I'm supposed to tell my best friend that I'm fucking giddy thanks to my dead brother's boyfriend.

Wade walks from his end of the office space to mine and turns the chair that sits on the opposite side of my desk. With the back of it facing me, he sits down, resting his chin on the top of the chair.

"I'm not moving from this spot till you tell me."

"We're really doing this?" I ask.

"Fuck yeah, we are. If you're happy I want to know why and who to fucking thank."

"You make it sound like I'm fucking miserable," I chide. "You know my brother died right?"

"Bro," he says, slowly shaking his head. "That was a terrible thing sure, but you're different lately, and what I'm talking about comes from here." He curls his hands into a fist and taps it over his heart. "When you're really happy, you feel it right *there*."

I feel my chest expanding with warmth at Wade's explanation, because I know what he's talking about. Like my heart was a deflated balloon that's now, slowly, getting fuller every day.

Small tufts of air, infusions of life, that are sneaking up on me every time I speak to Julian. Since the night he called, we talk and text at all hours. Early. Late. For something insignificant, and for things that are important.

I want to say we're friends, and for some people, that much communication is normal for friends, but for this surly, closed off bastard, this means something. This means *more* than something.

"It's a guy," I blurt out.

I've got to give it to Wade, because his face doesn't falter, not even for a second. I know he's got nothing against gay people, so that isn't my issue, but seeing as I, his best friend, have never shown any interest in the same sex, I was expecting some kind of shock from him.

He's thoughtfully quiet, and I hold off on telling him who it is, because I'm not ready to hear his opinion on it. I don't want to be told I may have found something that's making me happy, only to hear later it's not mine to have.

Throwing my hands up in the air in frustration, I yell, "Really? You're not going to say anything?"

"Like I said," he starts. "You're happy, so the rest doesn't matter."

"Like fuck it doesn't matter. You're not even going to ask me who it is? Or how it started?"

He narrows his eyes at me. "Should I be asking who it is and how it started?"

I push my chair back and eagerly stand, needing to move. With my fingers pulling and pinching at my bottom lip, I pace up and down the length of our office.

It's crazy how telling him who it is feels more daunting than telling him I'm into another man.

Turning to face him, I meet his curious gaze. "It's Julian," I say carefully.

This time he does flinch. It's subtle and only for a moment, but I don't miss it. His face scrunches up. "Are you guys, like, together now?"

"What?" I run a hand through my hair. "No, it's not like that."

Sighing, I sit back down and steeple my fingers over my nose. *What the fuck is it like?*

"What's it like then?" he prods.

Lowering my arms, I cross them over my chest. "Honestly, I don't know."

"Break it down for me." Intentional or not, his tone is petulant, and it pisses me off.

"Don't talk to me like an idiot," I say through clenched teeth. "I was happy not to tell you—"

"Fine," he interjects. "You're right. I just don't know how you went from barely giving the guy the time of day, to this."

"One minute we were bickering and the next we weren't." I swallow hard. "I've spoken to him almost every day since I left Montana, and I'm not sure what to do with that."

"Is it Rhett? Do you guys talk about him and maybe that's why you feel close?" It's a fair question, but I bristle anyway. Not because there's any truth to it, or I don't want to answer it, but because lately it makes me feel jealous of my own brother.

And that's not something I enjoy feeling.

I shake my head at him. "We don't spend a lot of time talking about him in the way you think we would. It's not just a verbal homage to my dead brother every evening."

"I didn't say that, I'm just trying to understand it with you." He scratches at his temple. "So, you're not just friends."

"I think that's what we're trying to be," I confirm. "But I don't text you any chance I get, or wait for you to call me at one in the morning when you get home from work," I say sheepishly.

This earns me a bark of laughter. "I guess you got it bad then," he teases. "And like, physically, you're attracted to him?" A flush of embarrassment settles on Wade's cheeks, and I can't help but cackle at his awkwardness.

"Are you asking if my dick likes dick?"

"This is so fucking weird," he mutters. "But yes, that's ultimately what I'm asking."

"Well then, yes, my dick *definitely* likes *his* dick," I say with a very practiced straight face.

Wade pinches the bridge of his nose and groans. "This is what I get for trying to have a meaningful conversation with you." Rising up from his seat, he spins it back around and tucks it under the edge of the desk. He raises his hands above his head and stretches out his body as if he's been sitting down for too long. When he's done, he walks back to his desk and begins packing up. He slings his backpack over his shoulder and then walks to the exit. "I just have one question before I go home and bleach my eyes so I can unsee your dick in my mind."

I nod with a smirk. "Sure."

"Why are you trying to be 'just friends' with him if you think it could be more?"

"Isn't it obvious?" I huff. The blank look on Wade's face says otherwise, so I spell it out for him. "He was my dead brother's boyfriend."

IT'S midnight and I've just finished locking up the house and throwing my duffel bag in the back seat of my truck.

Jumping in the truck, I place my travel mug of coffee in the cup holder, stick my car charger into my phone, all prepared to make the trip back to Montana for Thanksgiving.

It's been a little over two weeks since I was there last, and the unanticipated urge to return consumes me. There's no denying it has nothing to do with my newfound peace treaty with my mother, and everything to do with my newfound fascination with Julian.

In the smallest amount of time I'm sharing and feeling things I've never felt for another person, not even Josie in the whole five years we were together. There was always something missing between us, and now I'm forever racking my brain trying to work out what it was.

Is it because she's a woman? Or is it because she isn't Julian?

I try not to play the comparison game too much, or spend too much time trying to theorize why he and I connect, because it really just leaves me with more questions than I started with.

We've kept in contact every day, our conversations deep, our text messages funny. I can't remember the last time anybody was ever this interested in things I have to say.

He listens. With an open heart and an open mind, it's impossible not to bask in that type of attention. And none of that even comes close to what it's like hearing him talk. Hearing his thoughts, his ideas, what's important in *his* world.

It also means I've been privy to how much of himself he's holding back. This I know is synonymous with Rhett, something I know he has to work out in his own time and by himself, but it's painful to witness. Julian Reid has a lot to offer this world, I just don't think he's figured it out yet.

For two weeks we've been straddling the line between friendship and intimacy, and it honestly feels like purgatory. While I'm infatuated by the ease in which our relationship is developing, there's also a profound ache in my chest from how much I actually miss being around him. Wanting to be around anyone is new to me; craving that invasion of space and time.

I would love to see his facial expressions when he's talking, see the light in his eyes when he's excited, the smile on his face when he's happy.

The weekend we spent together feels like a cluster of stolen moments that I have thought about more times than I can count. It felt good, and exciting, and not at all foreign in the way it should have, and I want to try to have more than that. I want the freedom to test the waters, to explore the depths of our physical connection.

But what I want above all of that is to know with certainty that he wants all that stuff as much as I do. I'm worried that when we come face to face Julian will realize it was the distance that made him feel so relaxed.

With me in another state he doesn't have to worry about me being in his space or the guilt he said he feels at the temptation of wanting someone else. It's a safe distance to attach yourself to someone without the commitment. *Could he really want that?*

I'm about two and a half hours into my drive when my phone rings. I check the digital clock on the dashboard and notice Julian's calling a little later than usual. I told him I'd be up and driving tonight, and he said he would call me after work and keep me company.

"Hello," I answer, barely able to contain my smile.

"Hey," he greets, sounding both tired and relaxed. "Are you already driving?"

"Yeah, I'm about to round up to my third hour. What about you? How was work?"

A low groan comes through the phone. "I'm glad it's over. When people don't have to go to work the next day, they drink like it's their job," he complains. "It's so busy and messy."

"I don't know how you do it, I couldn't handle inter-acting with that many people," I say.

"It's the only reason I work there," he states.

"What do you mean?"

I hear a loud sigh leave his mouth, as well as the sound of a door opening and closing. *He's stalling.* A mixture of other noises fills up the empty void, and I'm almost tempted to tell him to forget I even asked when he finally speaks up.

"I didn't leave the house, or speak to anyone for six weeks after Rhett died." His confession sits in the silence, percolating between us. His voice lowers significantly. "I was in a pretty bad way."

I don't have to imagine what 'bad way' means. I saw it that night with my own two eyes, and to think he was some version of that for six long weeks, all alone, has me clenching my hands around the steering wheel.

Seeing him like that, knowing how he was, I berate myself for not telling someone to check up on him more regularly and selfishly a part of my mind wanders off somewhere completely unexpected. *Can I compete with the depth of his grief? Am I just something like the bar to make his days a little more bearable?*

"I had quit the bar when Rhett was nearing the end, but I eventually managed to lug myself out of bed and ask Steven, the manager, for my job back."

I know there's more to the story, but I don't push, because what he's revealed is enough, and I don't want to think of him hurting like that. It hurts *me* to think of him hurting like that.

"I'm glad you got yourself out of bed," I say softly.

"Me too."

The quiet lingers longer than is comfortable, and I'm almost certain he's fallen asleep.

"Julian," I whisper.

"Yeah."

"You should go to sleep."

"No," he protests through a yawn. "It's my favorite time of the day."

"The early morning?"

"No," he says gruffly, and I imagine him shaking his head on the other side of the phone. "Talking to you."

I don't tell him that it's mine too, that my favorite part about all of this is that when the rest of the world is asleep, it's our time. Just the two of us.

Unaffected, uninterrupted, real time with one another.

"I wonder if you'll still feel that way when I ask you if you've thought any more about where you're going to move?"

I bite my lip in anticipation of his answer, because over the past two weeks this has been the biggest point of contention between us. He's living in denial, hoping for a miracle, while I'm here quietly hoping he'll let me help him.

"Do we have to talk about this?" he whines.

"Do me a favor," I say. "Are you in bed?"

"Are you trying to get me naked?" he smarts.

"The first time won't be over the phone." *Did I just say that?* "Fuck, I didn't mean it," I stammer. "It just came out."

"You want to see me naked?" he teases, the humor evident in his voice.

Keeping my eyes focused on the dark, long road ahead, I take a deep breath. It's crazy that my mind has just adjusted, the thoughts easily steering themselves down the rabbit hole. "The idea of it doesn't make me any more uncomfortable than if you had a pussy."

"So eloquent." He chuckles.

"Are you trying to get out of talking about moving out of your place?"

"Just answer this question," he says firmly. "And then I'll answer whatever it is you want to know about my living arrangements."

"Does it freak you out?"

"Does it freak *you* out?" I counter.

"Deacon, I've had my whole life to get used to being attracted to men."

"I'm not attracted to men," I say boldly. "I'm only attracted to you."

18

JULIAN

My heart is in my throat as I lay on my couch. The clothes I wore to work, now dirty, still on my body, and my black combat boots still on my feet.

I'm only attracted to you.

His confidence is like a fucking aphrodisiac. Like a drug injected straight into my veins, pumping blood around my body, literally bringing me back to life.

He may have rendered me speechless, but every part of me is aware of him. Thinks about him. Dreams about him. Just wants *him*.

"Does it freak you out?" I hear him ask.

Freak me out? No. Am I fucking scared? Shitless. But I don't answer with my insecurities. I don't want to give them time. I don't want to give them air. I don't want them.

Instead, for the first time in a very long time, I dangerously think with my dick.

"I bet we'd have a lot of fun teaching you."

I hear a sharp intake of breath, quickly followed by, "Fuck you, I don't want to get hard when I'm driving."

I snicker into the phone and rub my hand over my own hardening cock. "Ask me what you wanted to ask me about moving."

"You want me to try and form coherent thoughts now?"

"Unless you want me to hang up and go jack off in the shower, then yeah, let's get this back to safe territory."

"Jesus," he mutters, before I hear him murmur, "A is for apple, b is for bear, c is for cat."

"What are you doing?" I exclaim.

"I'm trying to get rid of this stiffy. It can't stay up if I'm singing the alphabet."

"Is that a fact?" I sputter through a laugh.

"It's been known to work a time or two," he says, his voice pained.

"Okay. Okay, how about I go have a shower and call you back? Give you time to get your thoughts back on the road."

"Don't touch yourself in the shower," he commands.

I click my tongue. "Bossy and broody, huh?"

"You have no idea."

I bite my bottom lip to keep the unintelligible moan that wants to jump out of my mouth at bay. "I'm going to hang up and shower real quick," I announce. "Don't miss me too much."

"I'll try not to," he says playfully.

"Drive safely," I say, before hanging up.

Pushing myself up off the couch, I begin undoing the buttons on my shirt and jeans, leaving a trail of clothes behind me as I head into my bedroom, and straight for the shower. It's a really quick wash as I'm eager to get back on the phone with Deacon, and I don't want to be tempted to touch myself, even if he'll never really know.

By the time I'm dry and dressed, I'm climbing into bed with the phone to my ear waiting for Deacon to pick up.

"Hey," I greet.

"Hey."

"How's the drive going?"

"Let's just say I've never once wanted to replace my car ride with a plane ride until now."

I smile to myself. "I'm flattered," I tell him. "How long have you got left?"

"About another seven hours," he huffs. "I usually stop for an hour when I hit the halfway mark. Have a power nap, refill my coffee, and top up the gas."

"Don't worry," I appease. "I'll keep you company."

"Are you in bed?" he asks.

"Yes," I answer warily, worried we're about to repeat the last half an hour, and thinking I can't withstand it a second time.

"Then you're not going to keep anyone company. You'll be asleep in less than forty-five minutes."

"You want to bet on it?" I taunt.

"No," he says sternly. "I just want to know if you've looked at places to stay when you have to move out."

"Why are you so hellbent on this?" I argue.

"The better question is why aren't you? Where are you going to live?"

I imagine the vein in his forehead protruding because of his exasperation. I'm not purposefully trying to be vague or appear indifferent, but there's so much to think about, and so much of it has barely anything to do with the fact that I'm moving houses.

It's just forcing me to take a long, hard look at the way I'm living, and I can't help but be a little disappointed in the shell of a man I've become. Do I want to move this whole house, sad memories and all, into a new building and just continue to work nights in something so uninspiring?

"Close your eyes," he demands.

"What? Why?"

"Just trust me."

And because I do trust him I lay on the flat of my back and close my eyes. "They're closed," I inform him.

"Now, just imagine yourself somewhere," he instructs. "Anywhere, really, but what would you be doing? What would your days be filled with? Your nights? What do the four walls around you look like?"

A lump forms in my throat as he continues to rattle off all the hypothetical scenarios he wants me to conjure up.

They're simple requests, but they're poignant.

As if he's listened to all my unspoken insecurities and found a way for me to embrace them.

He guides me. Encourages me. Until the visual he wanted me to create sits in beautiful, unfiltered focus behind my eyelids.

"Deacon," I choke out.

"Don't say anything," he says softly. My eyes burn with emotion as he whispers, "The world is waiting for you."

MY BODY WAKES up with a startle, my eyes blinking repeatedly as I try to remember why I feel out of sorts. And then it hits me. Skating my hand around my mattress, I finally find my phone underneath one of my many pillows and stick it in front of my face.

Fuck. I don't even remember falling asleep. There're a few notifications from Deacon, the last one four hours ago.

Deacon: Sleep well.

Deacon: Just reached Spring Gulch to refuel.

Deacon: On the last leg. See you soon.

Scrubbing a hand over my face, I mentally calculate how long he's got left in his drive and then tap his name on the screen and bring my cell to my ear.

"Morning, sunshine," he says gleefully.

"Fuck, you're chirpy this morning," I respond groggily.

"Coffee and energy drinks will do that to a guy. How'd you sleep?"

"Good. I think. I'm sorry I fell asleep."

"Lucky we didn't bet on it," he gloats.

"Shut up."

"What do you have planned this morning?"

"I have to get up at some point. What time is your mom expecting us?" I say without thinking. "Everyone," I correct quickly. "What time is she expecting *everyone*?"

Amused, Deacon has the nerve to chuckle at my wording. "She's expecting us anytime after two, but you know she wouldn't care what time you showed up."

"I've got a few things to do around here first," I inform him. "Then I'll head over."

He doesn't ask what I'm doing or mention seeing one another before he heads to his parents' place, and I try not to let it bother me.

My focus for this morning is to start the day off better than I did last year. Being so close to Rhett's death meant the day went by in a blur, and while I don't have some attachment to the holiday, I am using it as a marker to do better. Be better, for myself.

I don't ever want to be that person I was after he died, especially when deep down I know this time around, I have a few extra things to be grateful for.

"Can you send me a text before you leave your place?" he asks.

"Umm. Sure."

There's an awkward pause that's never been there before, and it's unsettling. What changed between last night and this morning?

I don't know if it's because there's something he wants to say, or because there's something he doesn't.

"Okay, I'm going to get back to the drive," he says stiffly. "I'll speak to you soon?"

"Yeah," I answer numbly. "Bye."

I don't bother to wait for a response, ending the call and tossing the cell back onto the mattress. I'm not going to let that throw me off my game this morning. We can work it out later, or we won't. Either way, I've got shit to do.

Throwing the blankets off, I storm through the house a little more frustrated than necessary. I take my time eating breakfast, getting through some laundry and busying myself tidying up shit around the place.

A little over an hour and a half later I drive myself to the cemetery. I usually go once a week, no specific day or time.

Since Deacon went back to Seattle, I contemplated not going, feeling a strong pang of remorse at my growing feelings for Rhett's brother. But there's no use denying them, they're very much here to stay, and keeping my distance from one of the few places that has brought me comfort isn't going to change a single thing between Deacon and me.

The weather is freezing, the sky is overcast, and the wind blistering. I tug the zipper of my jacket up all the way to my chin and fist my hands into the warm pockets.

When I reach the marble headstone, a loud snicker involuntarily leaves my mouth. *When the fuck did he get here?*

Walking closer, I grab the bag of candy corn and shove it into my jacket. So, he came here first? What am I going to do, begrudge him for visiting his brother?

We're such a fucking mess.

Closing my eyes, I tilt my head up to the heavens and breathe in the frigid air. "You really need to help me out here," I say to nobody.

I think of the conversations Rhett and I had before he died, how many times he told me to move forward and keep living. I know that's why he wrote the letters, to give me the little push. But I'm not built to go back there, to imagine him alive and having to write those words.

And I don't want to read them and then wonder if it would all stand if he knew it was Deacon who had me wanting to move forward. Would he want all those things for me if he knew it was Deacon holding my hand? If it was Deacon pushing me to flirt with happiness and be seduced by the idea of a life without loneliness?

Crouching beside the headstone, I lightly touch the picture embedded in the marble.

"I just need to know you understand," I say to the photo, my voice low and pleading. "Tell me I'm doing the right thing."

Obviously, the answer doesn't come, but the splatter of big, heavy raindrops against my head is enough for me to take as a sign that someone heard me. Rain like this is unheard of this time of year, Montana usually dry at the best of times.

Standing, I throw my hands over my head as the rain gets heavier and make the quick dash to my car. By the time I'm inside, ninety percent of my clothes are soaked through, but thankfully there's a tuft of lingering warmth in the car from the heater.

Unzipping my jacket, I shrug out of it, hanging the sopping material on the back of my passenger seat. I blast the heat on, hoping it eases the chill about to settle into my bones.

When my body temperature regulates, I finally manage to get my hands and legs working enough to leave the cemetery. I drive as fast as I can without being too reckless in the rain, my plan to head straight to the Sutton house now thwarted by my need to change into new clothes.

The rain pounds against my windshield, the wipers unable to keep up, as I hit every single red light. When I finally arrive home, I grab my parka, throw it over my head, and race to get inside.

Slamming the door shut, I'm surprised when there's a knock only seconds after I've closed it.

Annoyed I'm still in my wet clothes, I swing the door open. "Can I—"

The words become lodged in my throat as my mouth drops and my eyes widen when I come face-to-face with a saturated Deacon. "What are you doing here?" I stammer stupidly.

Beads of water fall down his face, running down his long lashes, falling off the tip of his nose, and landing on his slightly parted lips.

My gaze lingers on every feature of his face, wanting to catch the droplets with my mouth and taste the rain off his skin with my tongue.

His breathing is heavy, the sound shaky and nervous. Sea blue eyes stare at me, a mixture of truth, fear, and longing on display. His heart's in his eyes and I can feel the significance in my gut.

This man never takes off his mask. I've spent years looking at the face of indifference, but this, lately... It's blinding.

Him, here, for me. It's an opening. Small steps. An invitation.

"You think after the last two weeks, and the longest

twelve hours of my fucking life," he says hoarsely, "you weren't the first person I wanted to see?"

I'm stunned into silence. After the very impersonal way we ended our last conversation, I didn't expect him to show up here, raw need written all over his face.

"You didn't say anything," I croak out.

He runs his fingers through his wet hair and lowers his eyes nervously. "I wanted to surprise you."

Hating the sudden apprehension and hesitancy, I step out into the cold, forcefully grab his chin, and raise his eyes to mine. "I'm surprised." There's no space between us now. His eyes unable to hide his hunger. His breath fanning my lips, the end of his nose touching mine. "Everything about you surprises me."

He's pushing us inside before I even utter the last word. He slams the door behind him, and I slam him up against the hard wood, ignoring the discomfort of our clothes, unable to think of anything else but his mouth on mine. Needing the connection. Needing the taste. Needing *him*.

Rough and urgent, we meet in a brutal collision. He tastes like coffee and Deacon as his lips greet mine while my tongue welcomes his. Starved for one another, there's no time for soft and tender. I use all my weight to lean into him. I'm met with a hard chest and an even harder dick, grinding against mine. His strength meets my force, and it's everything I love about being with a man.

My lips move down across his stubbly jaw, running up and down his neck and back to his mouth. "Let's get you out of these wet clothes," I murmur against his skin.

My eager fingers fumble with the layers, irritation tempting me to just rip them off his body. The heavy jacket finally comes off, followed by a black and white hoody. He's got a white wife beater underneath and I pull my head back to look up at him in frustration.

"What?" he says smugly. "It's fucking winter, it's cold."

My hands slip underneath the material, pushing it up his torso as I enjoy the feel of his bare skin against mine. His body is like a work of art; hard planes, deep lines and... nipple piercings?

"You had these under here the whole fucking time?" I say incredulously, my mouth nipping at his earlobe while I roll the new found metal in between my fingers.

"I didn't realize advertising them would get this kind of reaction."

Impatient, I bunch the material up to Deacon's neck, and he raises his arms in the air for me to take it all the way off.

Throwing it on the floor, I look at his hands in the air. "Keep them up there," I demand.

He raises an eyebrow, and I cock my head at him in challenge. Offering me the sexiest smirk, he does as I've asked and then captures my lips with his own.

When I suck on his tongue, his hips buck into mine. Lowering one of my arms between us, I cup his shaft with my hand and stroke him through his pants.

"Fuuuuck," he rasps.

My mouth eats up every delicious groan before resuming my exploration of his now half-naked body. I make my way down his throat, skim across his collarbone, and lower my head to one of his nipples.

My tongue swirls around the silver barbell while my hand continues to deliciously torture his thick, hard cock. I switch my attention to the other one when I feel a hand in my hair, pushing my head closer.

I peer up at him, the view of his control slipping enough to make me want to stick my own hand down my pants.

"Like that?" I tease.

"You've got no fucking idea," he pants.

My mouth continues to trail down his abs, the light smattering of his hair ghosting across my lips. By the time I reach his waistband, I'm on my knees looking up at him.

His chest is heaving in anticipation, his eyes glazed over with desire, his body trembling with need—he's a goddamned vision.

Despite every single molecule inside my body wanting my mouth on his cock, I stop to give him time to think about it.

"We don't have to go any further," I tell him. "I know it's different—"

Wordlessly, his hand lands on the top of my head, tilting it back, so I'm looking right up at him.

"I'm not questioning this," he says. "Not one single fucking part of it."

I give him a subtle nod, keeping my eyes on his. We stare at each other as my hands undo the tie on his sweats and drag them down his thighs. He's wearing black cotton boxer briefs that can barely contain the bulge he's sporting.

Without even thinking, I press my mouth to his hard shaft, lightly running my teeth over the material, my gaze refusing to waver from his.

I both feel and watch his stomach tighten when I pull the fabric down to meet his pants. His hard cock springs out, skin tight around the crown, the heady erection slapping against his stomach.

It's impressive. In perfect proportion to the rest of his built body, his dick is the fucking icing on the cake.

Desperate to see every single one of his reactions, I watch him as I wrap a hand around his thick girth and stick my tongue out to swirl the head of his cock.

I hear a thud as his head drops back onto the door, and an unmissable hiss leaves his mouth when I spear my tongue into his leaking slit.

"Fuck," he breathes out. "Do that again."

Knowing I could never deny him his request, I repeatedly slide my tongue over the top of him, a new drop of pre-come forming, ready for me to collect, after every swipe.

When I feel fingers press into my scalp, I go in for the kill and cover his whole length with my mouth.

He reactively thrusts, hitting the back of my throat. I momentarily gag and he tries to pull out.

"Shit. Sorry," he says huskily.

Grabbing his ass cheeks, I stop him from moving back and urge him to push farther into my mouth. It only takes a few seconds for his hands to find their way back into my hair, guiding me, just the way he likes it.

I greedily suck on him. Hungry for him. Hungry for this, *with him*.

When my hand cradles his balls, unintelligible words fill the room and his grip on my hair tightens. I continue to roll them in my palms while bobbing up and down his length.

"Fuck, you're really good at that," he says, his hips now pistoning in my mouth.

My dick aches for attention, getting harder with every sound he makes. Every thrust of his enjoyment goes straight down into my own heavy balls.

"Tell me you want me to blow down your fucking throat," he says, his voice like gravel. "Because if you're not into that, you need to get off. Like five seconds ago."

I fist the base of him, stroking his hot skin, jacking him off while keeping his crown enveloped in my eager mouth.

As if his body is warning me, he thickens against my tongue, and I feel him begin to tremble beneath his skin.

"Oh fuck," he shouts, as the first spurt of salty liquid drenches my tongue. "Oh fuck, oh fuck, oh fuck."

I feel his whole body sag against the front door, his hold on my hair loosening as he continues to empty himself inside my mouth.

Looking up at him, I lick up the remnants of his release from the head of his dick, enjoying the way his body shudders with every soft, lingering swipe of my tongue.

He's watching me with lazy, sated eyes, half-naked, with his pants almost near his ankles, and his dick spent.

I did that.

My lust-filled pulse continues to ratchet underneath my skin, and my dick relentlessly throbs for this man before me. I lower my hand to my stiff cock, but a commanding voice stops me.

"Don't fucking touch what's mine."

19

DEACON

Julian stills, his hooded eyes staring back at me, his hand resting on his junk. He looks fucking delectable on his knees for me, more than I thought possible for another man.

Haphazardly, I pull my underwear and pants back up my legs and then extend a hand out for Julian to take.

Helping him rise, I wait till we come face-to-face before taking his chin in my hand and bringing his mouth to mine.

I dip my tongue between his lips a few times. "How do I taste?"

"You're trying to kill me, aren't you?" he says in between kisses.

"Who said anything about killing?" I cup my hand around his hard cock. "I'm just trying to return the favor."

Deftly, I unbutton his jeans and waste no time sticking my hand between his skin and his waistband. When my fingers circle his length, he closes his eyes in delicious anguish, and I relish the unfamiliarity.

I've only ever felt my own dick, so this is definitely new,

but the one thing that has my heart pounding inside my chest is that it doesn't feel wrong.

It feels damn near perfect, and that's what scares me.

"I'm gonna come, Deacon," he says, his voice full of indecision.

"Is that not the goal?" I tease. He drops his head to my shoulder, searching for restraint. So I ease up on him. "I'll take it slow."

Pulling my hands out of his pants, I'm surprised he makes a strangled noise at the loss of me. Gripping the edge of his polo shirt, I lift it off over his head, then grip his hips, using them to guide him to the door.

We shuffle through the randomly discarded clothes surrounding us in the doorway, and I inwardly chuckle at the fact we didn't make it farther into the house.

Turning him, I wait for his back to face my front, and then I speak right into his ear. "Put your hands up and don't move."

He shudders, and I feel my cock stir at his anticipation. He raises his arms, and my eyes take in the way his back muscles flex with every move.

My hands gravitate to his skin, wanting to take my own personal tour. I drag my fingertips down his spine, enjoying the minute pebbles that form under my touch.

Stepping closer, I nuzzle my head into the crook of his neck, my tongue licking his skin while my naked torso presses against his.

I move my lips across the span of his shoulder as my arms slip around his waist, and my fingers hook into the waistband of his underwear. My body is slightly broader than Julian's, allowing me to look over his shoulder, which gives me a perfect view of my hands freeing his heavy cock from the confining material.

I feel his body rise and fall with every shortened breath as I circle his dick with my hand; the power I hold over him in this moment hardening my own cock completely.

His tip glistens with pre-come and I can't help but roll my thumb over his crown. "How do you think you taste?" I taunt. I bring my thumb up to his mouth, and his tongue circles the sticky digit, the same way he teased my cock. "Do you taste as good as me?"

He turns his head to me, capturing my mouth with his, wordlessly inviting me to taste him myself. It's a hint of sweet and sour, and our tongues do a delighted dance, wanting nothing more than to devour and dominate.

Julian grabs my hand and pushes it back onto his cock.

"Hard," he rushes out against my mouth. "Squeeze me hard."

My grip tightens as I begin to firmly stroke him. My fist moves up and down while my tongue moves in and out.

Pulling us apart, I look down at our connection, mesmerized by the contrast of his soft skin and the thick, solid feel of his hard shaft. I get lost watching Julian move his hips, rocking them for friction, fervently fucking my fist.

"Ah fuck," he groans, letting his head fall back on my shoulder. "Please, don't stop."

I latch my mouth onto his shoulder, sucking his skin while moving my hand faster; desperate to see him unhinged.

It only takes a few more strokes for his body to convulse in my arms and drench my hand with his orgasm. I loosen my mouth's hold on him, gently licking instead of sucking, holding him as he slowly comes down from his high.

I wrap my free arm around his torso, my hand landing directly over his heart. Julian surprises me when he covers my hand with his.

We both stand there, the beat of his heart like a constant between us. Basking in the afterglow of finally feeling you're exactly where you were always supposed to be.

We're here, together, alive, and against all odds, we could make one another happy.

"Come to Seattle with me," I say while resting my chin on top of his shoulder.

"Is that your orgasm talking?"

"No." I awkwardly disentangle myself from him, picking up a shirt and wiping my hands on it. "Can we clean up first?" I ask. "Then you can hear me out."

"That's probably the best idea," he muses, tucking himself back into his pants. "Do you want to jump in the shower with me?"

My eyes dart around the house, and I see little pieces of Rhett lying around; on the shelves, in a photo, probably in the bathroom and the bedroom too.

I hate that I'm jealous of my own brother right now, but unless I want to make this awkward and make Julian think I regret what just happened, I need to steer clear of anything that has the potential to sour my mood.

"I'll just wait for you to go first," I tell him.

He raises an eyebrow at me. "Okay."

"Do you want to show me where your washer and dryer are so I can stick these clothes in there?"

He takes the dirty shirt out of my hands and picks up the rest of the clothes around us. "How about you have a shower first, and I'll take care of everything out here. You can use my bathroom or the guest one. There're towels in both."

"Can you do me a favor?" I ask. Julian nods. "Can you get my bag out of my truck, so I can grab clean clothes?"

"Of course."

I gesture to the hallway. "I'm going to jump in, I won't be

long." Before I walk away, I grab Julian by the back of the neck and press my lips firmly to his. "Thank you for the orgasm."

He laughs and then kisses me back "You're more than welcome."

Just as I'm about to walk off Julian calls out, "Deacon."

"Yeah?"

"Take your pants and underwear off so I can wash them."

"If you want to see me naked, all you have to do is ask," I tease.

Dropping my clothes to the floor, I step out of them and give them to Julian. "I owe you."

"I'll be sure to think of something really good," he quips.

Naked and laughing, I'm feeling comfortable about the mood between us. If we can keep this up, he'll hear me out about coming to Seattle.

Once I reach the bathroom, I make quick work of the shower, soaping my body and brushing my teeth with a lick of toothpaste on my finger.

I drag the towel off the rack and dry my body before wrapping the plush fabric around my waist.

Opening the bathroom door, I'm surprised to see Julian on the other side holding my duffel. "I was just going to drop this in here for you."

Taking the bag off him, I lean in for a kiss. "Come to Seattle."

He rolls his eyes playfully and then pinches my nipple. "So I can bring you clean clothes?"

"Ouch." I rub my chest. "It could work in my favor."

"It's my turn to shower," he tells me. "I won't be long."

When he leaves, I continue getting dressed. Not wanting

to sit around in stuffy Thanksgiving clothes just yet, I put on my makeshift pajamas—sweats and a t-shirt—and head to the living room.

My eyes gravitate to something sitting in the middle of his coffee table.

I pick up the candy corn packet and realize we both had the same idea this morning.

Sitting down on the couch, I rest my elbows on my knees, and fidget with the rectangular packet while thinking of where to go from here.

I want whatever this is with Julian, and I don't want to walk away from it unless it's my only option. But as my fingers fiddle with one of the very few connections I have with my dead brother, I realize some things, no matter how much you want them, aren't yours to have.

I hear a door click shut and feet softly padding against wooden floors. Looking toward the hallway, I see Julian dressed in fresh jeans and a V-neck sweater, toweling off his wet hair.

He looks at my occupied hands, his stare lasts a few seconds too long, but I don't call him out on it. His eyes then shift to my clothes and then, finally, to me. "Did I miss the change in plans?" he asks casually. "Don't we have somewhere to be?"

"Come to Seattle," I say to him for the third time.

"Deacon," he says with a sigh.

Dropping the candy on the table, I grab his hand, pulling him down to me. I hold him as he lands on my lap, and then I lean us both backward till we're lying across the couch; my arms are wrapped around him, and his head is nestled comfortably in the crook of my elbow.

He brings my forearm up to his lips, skimming them across my skin as he listens to me talk. "I'm not asking you to come to Seattle for me," I start. It's a half-hearted lie, but it isn't my whole motivation for suggesting it, so I'm not going to base my whole argument on it.

"But you should come for you," I suggest. "Check out a job, a place to live." I press my lips on the top of his head. "You could enroll in college maybe? Think about getting that degree you've always wanted."

"And you'll be there," he says. It's not a question, more matter of fact. A statement I hope really is his deciding factor.

"Could you take time off work?" I hedge. "Spend a week or so with me and check out the city for yourself."

"You want that?"

I squeeze him to me tighter, inhaling the fresh, soapy scent of his hair and skin.

"If I don't lay it all out on the table with you now," I tell him honestly, taking advantage of the fact that he can't see my face, "I'm going to regret it. And I don't want to regret shit anymore."

"Tell me then," he probes. "Lay it all out."

"I just want to see if this thing between us can work." I pause and soften my voice. "And I don't think we can do that here."

"Here?" he echoes.

"This is your space with Rhett, and it's not like an ex-boyfriend. He's dead, and I feel like I'm desecrating everything you two had together by being here as anything more than his brother," I rush out. "I don't want that. I don't want to feel like that. And I don't want to be the reason you feel like that."

He turns in my arms, emotion-filled eyes looking up at me, and I'm certain there's nothing but raw vulnerability staring right back at him.

"Do you think this thing between us can work?" he asks.

I slide myself down the couch, so our faces are parallel. I brush my knuckles along his clean-shaven jaw and let my thumb memorize the shape and feel of his mouth.

"I think if I'm going to have to see you at every family occasion for the foreseeable future, sitting opposite me at the dinner table, smiling and laughing. Knowing what it feels like to kiss you."

Softly, I press my lips to his.

"To touch you," I say hoarsely before kissing him softly, again. "To know what it's like to watch you fly high with pleasure from just my hand."

The memory alone of his hard cock spilling all over my hands has me urgently fusing my mouth to his. When Julian's arm and leg hook over my body, I know he's envisioning it too.

"If I'm going to do all that," I breathe out against his swollen lips, "then I need to know with absolute certainty that you and I gave it everything we had to try and make it work."

My heart is thrashing around my ribcage as we wordlessly hold one another's gaze. Everything that I can say has been said. There's nothing I haven't revealed to Julian.

From the beginning, I've been like a sinner at confession, cracking my heart open for him while my flaws, fears, and insecurities spill out between us.

And this is no different.

Seemingly wanting to get the upper hand, Julian pushes against me. Rolling me onto my back, his large body hovers over mine. "I'll come with you to Seattle," he concedes. "I'll speak to my manager, and if that works out, I'll drive back with you."

"You will?"

"Under one condition," he counters.

I nod. "Anything."

"Always be honest with me, okay?" My face must show my confusion, as he runs his index finger between my brows, softening the evidence of my puzzlement at his request. "Just like that. If we're going to work, you have to be honest." He lowers his mouth to mine and gently kisses me. "Always." Once. "Exactly." Twice. "Like." Three times. "That."

Like I ever had a fucking choice.

THANKSGIVING, so far, has gone off without a hitch.

After a make out session on Julian's couch and an impromptu nap, we both sheepishly showed up to my parents' place a few hours late.

Even though we made the effort to come in separate cars, so as not to appear like we had been together, the timing and the look on our faces probably suggested otherwise.

Thankfully, my family, except Victoria, is fairly good at sweeping things under the carpet, and for once, this works just fine for me.

It's not that I don't want to share what's happening between us with my family; as I explained to Julian, there are so many layers they'll need to process, and I'm not ready for the questions and queries to ruin how we feel *right now*.

So, at this moment, I'm literally shooting the shit with my family, counting down the painstakingly long minutes till Julian and I can get the fuck out of here.

It turns out being in the same room as Julian and not being able to touch him is more of a problem than I anticipated. I don't do public displays of affection, or at least, I have never felt the need to, until now.

And it's not like I *need* to be kissing him and hugging him, or even holding his hand; it's the simple knowledge of knowing that if I *wanted* to do those things at any given moment, I could.

We share secret looks and touches on the sly all while listening to Victoria juggle talking about her pregnancy and entertaining Lia. Mom and my grandmother fuss over the food in the kitchen, and my grandfather sleeps in the living room with the television on.

It's a typical Thanksgiving Day, but it's the most normal get together this family has had in a while. My stomach flutters with excitement that maybe a good type of change is in the cards for all of us.

"Okay," Victoria says with a raised voice. "I know this is cliché, but I really want to go around the table and say the things we're grateful for this year."

Vic is cautious with her request, looking around at the seven sets of eyes staring back at her. "I'll start," Hayden says, always being the perfect husband. "I'm thankful for my beautiful wife."

Victoria blows him a kiss. "I'm thankful for my amazing daughter. That she's happy and healthy. I'm thankful for the imminent arrival of my son."

"Hold on," I interrupt. "Did you find out it was a boy?"

"No," Vic shouts at a laughing Hayden. "He thinks if he just keeps putting it out there the universe will have no choice but to listen."

"Well, it can't hurt to try," my dad interjects, backing Hayden and his crazy notion up.

"Since you agree with his dumb theory," Vic says to our father, "you can go next."

He clears his throat. "I'm thankful that you're all happy and healthy. It's been a long time since I've seen my family smile, and for that I'm thankful."

"Here. Here," my grandfather shouts, raising his bottle of beer and taking a sip.

Per my sister's request, we all take a turn. Julian's firm hand discreetly slides over my thigh when Victoria points at him like she's a game show host. "Now, what are you grateful for?"

"I'm thankful to you guys. For always being my family, especially after." I watch everyone's face around the table soften at his honesty. "And this year, I'm thankful for the future."

My fingers intertwine with his, squeezing them, assuring him I heard the words he wasn't able to say. I read between the lines, and I'm thankful too. I'm thankful that despite the odds being against us and the obstacles we still have to face, he and I somehow made it here.

20

JULIAN

Deacon and I were less than an hour away from arriving at his place, and I'd be lying if I didn't say the knots in my stomach were bordering on painful.

The last twenty-four hours were both chaotic and exciting; the high of doing something different fueling me while the fear of not being home in my routine tried to cripple me.

It's not that I didn't want to go with Deacon, because I did.

I do.

I want to see this side of him. I want to see the man he hides from his family. I want to see him in all the places he feels most like himself.

After leaving Bill and Elaine's house last night, both of us were trembling with an immeasurable amount of need. We were thirsty for one another. Greedy for touch, hungry for a taste. The flood gates had opened, and we couldn't stop the flow of desire between us, no matter how hard we tried.

The couch became our haven because Deacon refused

to be together anywhere else in the house, and I hated that part of me was relieved he'd made that decision for us.

The move, whether it was to Seattle or just another place here in Billings, was the right move for me; it was the right move for *us*. But that didn't mean any part of it would be easy.

It didn't matter that my heart was beating to a new sound, because my guilt still sat in a wooden box in my bedroom, and I was running out of ways to defend its existence.

I wasn't holding on to it as a souvenir, I wasn't holding on to it to commemorate his memory. I was holding on to it because I didn't know how to let it go.

I knew and loved Rhett for longer than I knew the people who were my own blood. I didn't know how to just switch him off. And it's not because Deacon would expect that of me, it's because I want him to know what's between me and him is *only* between *me* and *him*.

We spent the night on the couch at my place and left Montana with the sun rising behind us. With the intention to stay a little over a week, I argued with Deacon that I would drive my own car up. But he was adamant my 'rusty piece of metal' wouldn't make the twelve-hour drive.

Seeing that his opinion on the matter did hold a lot of weight, I grudgingly gave in and agreed to fly back when the time came.

My bank account would feel the hit, but the whole move was going to require me using some of the money I'd been keeping in savings, so I may as well get used to the idea.

"Earth to Julian." A hand squeezes my thigh, and I realize this mustn't be the first time he's tried to get my attention.

"Huh? Sorry. Did you say something?"

"Are you chickening out on me?"

My head snaps up at his question. "No," I say with certainty. "I want to spend this time with you, please don't doubt that."

His insecurities hurt me just as much as they hurt him. The idea that he would think himself to be anything less than the wonderful man he is pains me.

He's more than he or anybody else gives him credit for, and I've made it my mission to make sure he sees the man I see.

"I've never left Montana," I say, sharing my thoughts. "Twenty-seven years old and I haven't done anything more today than the day I was born."

"Besides the fact that that is completely false, you've got your whole life ahead of you. Plenty of time to do whatever you want to do." We stop at a traffic light and Deacon moves his hand to the back of my neck. "I didn't want you to just come here for me," he reveals. "I can be a selfish mother-fucker, but that's not what this is. I want you to see what's out there." He pulls my head to him, kissing me on the temple. "If you want to spend a week at a hotel and the days exploring by yourself, I can respect that."

I turn my head to face him and capture his mouth. "Your version of chivalry, or whatever this is, has been duly noted but is also not welcome here," I tell him. "You're stuck with me. Don't try to back out now."

"I would never." Someone honks at him from behind and he flips his finger at them in the rearview mirror and takes off driving.

"Why didn't you ask me what I came up with the other night? When you asked me to close my eyes?" I ask curiously.

He sneaks a peek at me while driving and then takes

hold of my hand and brings it to his lips to kiss it. "It was never about me knowing. I just wanted you to be able to see what I see for you."

Emotion gets stuck in my throat; how did I ever think this man was indifferent and unfeeling? Love pours out of him, like he's been waiting his whole life to shower someone with it.

My hand finds its way to his thigh, caressing his body through his clothes. "How long till we get to your place?" My voice is low and thick and hoarse, clearly showing my intention.

Words aren't enough for me right now. They don't capture the moment; they don't single out quite the right feelings. I need to touch him and I need him to touch me.

I need him to know that his instinct to know what *I* need, is something I've missed in my life. Independence lies to you, tells you you're doing fine on your own. But alone never felt so lonely until right now. Until I knew what it was like to have a man like Deacon *want* to take care of me.

He threads his fingers through mine and brings my hand dangerously close to his groin. "This drive has been long," he muses. My hand is guided higher. "And hard."

I want to snicker at his obvious boyish jokes, but the need sizzling inside me is too much for me to think of anything else.

As he moves my hand directly over his hardening cock, I hear him say, "We're here."

I reluctantly drag my eyes away from his dick and take in our surroundings.

Entering an underground garage, he turns into one of the first empty parking spots. The sign that says 'residents only' confirms this is indeed where he lives.

"Ready?" he asks me, his eyes flicking between me and my hand on his erection.

Not wasting a single second, I tear myself away from him and hop out of the truck.

Collecting my bag from the back seat, I impatiently wait for Deacon to lead the way.

After grabbing his own duffel, he slips his hand in mine and leads us to the entrance. It's ridiculous how my heart exerts itself over the action.

We walk into a waiting elevator in silence, the sexual tension buzzing, the anticipation increasing. In less than two minutes, it stops on the fifth floor, and he ushers me to a chocolate colored, walnut door with the number 502 stuck in the middle.

"This is me."

Deacon makes quick work of the lock. Walking in first, he flicks some switches on a panel beside the door jamb and then holds the door open, gesturing for me to come inside.

The second the entryway is closed, Deacon takes my bag and unceremoniously drops it on the floor with his. His arms wrap around my waist, his hands slipping under my clothes, and his lips press to my neck.

Tingles work their way up my spine at his touch, but the space in front of me demands my attention.

It's Deacon's space.

"This is your place?" I ask incredulously.

The tone in my voice distracts him enough to stop kissing my shoulder. "Yeah. Why?"

My eyes dart around the open plan living space. It's tidy and masculine and so much more suited to Deacon than any place I've ever seen him.

The whole apartment is lined with charcoal hardwood floors. The living room area has an off-white rug covering the space and a light gray sectional around the edges. It's both cozy and spacious and the perfect contrast to the plethora of steel and wood that decorates his kitchen.

A large bookshelf sits in the corner of the room, reminding me of the one I touched at his parents' place.

"It's perfect," I manage to say.

I can feel him shrug behind me. "It's just an apartment."

I turn in his arms, unsure if I'm going to say the right words, but knowing, deep in my bones, he needs to hear it anyway.

"You should be proud of yourself, Deacon."

Blue eyes shine at me with gratitude, and I respond with a gentle kiss.

"Can you show me your bedroom?" I ask playfully.

"You want the grand tour?" he teases.

"Definitely."

Instead of small, evenly paced steps, he tugs at my arm, dragging me down a hallway.

"This is the guest bathroom," he says flippantly. "And this is the guest bedroom."

We arrive at the last door in the narrow hallway and Deacon releases my hand and rushes through it. "And this," he waves his arm across the span of the room, "is the only place that matters."

His bedroom is as minimalist as the rest of the place, the gray color scheme continuing on the comforter and pillows.

A king-size bed sits in the middle, and there's a night stand on each side. A walk-in closet and an en suite complete the setup, giving it a warm yet sophisticated feel.

My eyes take in every surface in the room, lingering on the bed and then looking back at Deacon.

The air crackles between us. Between the time we've spent missing one another and the difficult hours we've endured to get right here, the lure of a bed is the only thing we need to set each other on fire.

Deacon's now a few feet away from me. He looks tired from the drive, but the need in his eyes burns as bright as the sun.

There's a slight shake in my hands as I begin to remove my clothing. There's always going to be things we need to talk about and reasons we should slow things down, but none of that exists right now. I have unfettered access to this broken beauty of a man, and nothing is going to stop me from being as close to him as I possibly can.

When I've got nothing left on but my pants, Deacon takes my actions as his own personal cue. After toeing off my shoes and stripping off my socks, I step into Deacon's personal space, enjoying the show.

The shape of his long, thick cock presses beautifully against the fabric of his sweats.

I reach for it and he hisses. His ability to be turned on by me—turned on by another man—without a single care in the world blows my mind.

He's unmistakably hard for *me*. He's never done any of this with anybody else but *me*, and I want to ride that high and never come down.

One hand now cups his cock, rubbing my palm up and down his length while the other does the exact same thing to my own dick.

"Take them off," Deacon demands.

Wanting to see him in all his glory first, I clumsily pull down his pants and boxers, and he pushes them to the floor, quickly stepping out of them.

When his gaze returns to mine, he smirks. "I meant take yours off."

With my fingers now circled around him, I lazily jerk

him a few times. "Sorry, as you can see, my hands are rather busy."

Big hands grip onto my waistband, roughly dragging the layers of material over my ass, freeing my shaft and letting the offending sweats drop to the floor.

Without hesitation, his hand mirrors mine, and the contact is all the invitation I need to crash my mouth to his. With teeth and tongues, the kiss is harsh and unyielding as we both continue to stroke each other into oblivion. When I need more, I push him toward the bed, hovering till he falls back. "Get in the middle," I rasp.

He wastes no time adhering to my command, laying there stark naked, cock in hand, pumping himself with a delicious rhythm.

Crawling onto the bed, I stop when I'm on all fours between his widely spread legs. I lock eyes with him and remove his hand from his shaft, placing it beside him and giving him a silent order not to touch himself.

I lower my mouth to the defined dip in his abdominal muscles, licking and kissing his skin. I completely ignore his dick, and the strangled groan that sounds from the back of Deacon's throat tells me he isn't pleased.

Tracing the details of his body with my tongue, I move up his torso, giving extra attention to his nipples.

"Don't ever take these out," I say in between licks. "They drive me fucking wild."

"Drive *you* wild?" he pants. "I'm about to lose my goddamned mind if you don't touch me soon."

I make my way higher, biting his neck, and sucking on his earlobes. When my cock grazes his, his hips buck off the bed, desperate for friction.

"Easy, baby," I whisper. Slipping my hand between us, I circle a hand around us both. "I got you."

We're both dripping with pre-come and the moisture turns the already delicious grind against one another into an erotic dream.

I make my way to his mouth as my hand strokes us faster. My tongue plunges into his mouth, catching the hoarse cry that slips between his lips.

My balls begin to tighten, and I know there's only so long I'll be able to hold on. Pulling away from Deacon, I'm now straddling his body, both of us blessed with the perfect view of our arousal.

Deacon's hand joins mine, and the added extra pressure is enough to light up every single one of my nerve endings.

Heavy lidded eyes meet mine, and we both divide our attention between our faces and the salacious mess we're making with our cocks. My legs are on his, our hands around us, his eyes smoldering, and our bodies close to combustion.

Our strokes become fast and frantic as nothing but moans and groans fill the air around us. Every muscle in my body clamps up as I use my other hand to roll our balls around together.

The sensation seems to tip Deacon over the edge as he grunts through his release. "Fuuuuuuck."

He arches his back, his corded throat bending beautifully as his head presses back into the pillow, and creamy streams of come decorate his perfectly sculpted stomach.

It's a picture worth a thousand fucking words, and all I need for my orgasm to quickly follow. A loud shout erupts from my mouth while our dicks pulsate in my hand, and my come surges out, desperate to sit pretty with his.

Exhaustion rips through me, my head hanging between my shoulders, my hand pressed into the mattress, doing its best to hold up my weak, sated body.

"Holy fuck," Deacon says. I lift my head up to look at him. He's alternating between drawing on his stomach with our come and licking the taste off his fingers.

I shake my head with a chuckle and cautiously climb off him. "Towels in your bathroom?" I ask.

"Yeah. You'll see them as soon as you walk in. Can't miss them."

My legs lose their Jell-O-like feeling with every step. Inside his en suite, I wash my hands and run two face cloths under the warm water. I clean myself first, leaving the towel behind, and then head back to Deacon with the other.

He's exactly like I left him, still fascinated with our mess. "Do you think you've stared at it enough?" I tease.

"Come here," he says.

When I sit beside him, he holds up two fingers to my mouth. I raise an eyebrow at him. "Is this a requirement?"

"You saying you don't want to taste us?"

"Us, huh?" Grabbing his wrist, I bring his hand to my mouth and indecently suck on his fingers. "Good?"

He sits up on his elbows and kisses me. "Perfect."

When his body sinks back to the bed, I take my time cleaning him, enjoying that I can.

It's not just the orgasms, it's all the little things. The before and afters and everything else in between.

Rising off the bed, I quickly discard the towel and come back to find the blankets pulled back, and Deacon, still naked, waiting for me to join him.

I slip in and he brings the covers up and over our bodies. He curls his front to my back, his lips on my shoulder, his arm resting on my waist. We're skin to skin, and it's exceptionally comfortable.

"Does any of this bother you?" I question.

"Does any of what bother me?"

"The two dicks? The nakedness?"

I feel him smile on my skin. He slides his hand from my waist to my chest, purposefully placing it right above my heart. "It's about what's in here," he explains, tapping his fingers on my pec. "That's what called to me, and that's the only thing that matters."

21

DEACON

"So he's staying with you?" Wade asks while we work on a car together. It's Tuesday afternoon, and the first time we've been able to exchange more than a few words since I returned after the long weekend.

While he was utilizing the consecutive days off to visit two families, I was too busy with Julian. Being in Seattle with him was like being caught in a fresh gust of wind. It woke you up, it made you aware, it forced you to pay attention.

And I could clearly see everything I had been missing out on. All those missing pieces were no longer missing, because I'd found them in Julian.

I almost don't recognize myself. The smiling. The laughing. The all-around happiness. It's foreign, and that's probably the worst part about all this, because it shouldn't have been. Before Rhett's death, even growing up, I should remember feeling this way.

But I don't. Almost like I never have.

The version of living I was doing was clearly living alone and being miserable. Having Julian in my space, in my bed

—now *that* was living. I was so fucking alive, I felt it everywhere.

"For a little over a week, yeah," I answer.

"And after the week?"

I cautiously raise my head up from under the hood of the car, looking at Wade with confusion.

"And after the week, he's going back home?" Irritation mars his features. "So, what exactly are you doing here?"

I look around the workshop. "Working?"

"I can see that," he drolls. "But why are you here and not with him?"

Slowly, I bring my head all the way out from underneath the hood and stand, facing Wade who's cleaning an engine over by the work bench. "I just wanted to help you catch up, and I'm giving him a bit of time to explore Seattle, discover things he likes, reasons he could live here."

"And none of that includes you?"

"What's with the twenty questions?" I ask defensively.

"Nothing." He raises his hands in mock surrender. "I'm just trying to figure out why you're not doing those things with him. Spending the week with him before he leaves again."

"I want him to like this place because *he* likes it," I explain. "Not because I'm here—I don't want him to move just for me. I don't want to smother him."

"That's the dumbest shit I've ever heard," he mutters, shaking his head. "Are you going to watch him get an apartment too? Both of you living separately because you're too worried your feelings will scare him, so you didn't open your fucking mouth?"

"Who said anything about moving in together?" I argue. "Isn't that a bit fast?"

He throws a wrench onto the bench in anger and wipes

his greasy hands on a towel. "You're head over heels for a *guy* for fuck's sake, what does fast even mean at this point?"

"I'm not head—"

Wade raises his hand, silencing me. "Don't you even bother finishing that sentence. I know what love is. *I'm* in love. You can pretend you're not, or ignore it if it makes you feel better about it, but you are most definitely in love with him."

Not wanting to explore his observation any further, I give Wade my back and resume my work under the hood of the car. It's not that I hadn't considered falling in love with Julian as a possibility, it was more the wonder of when it had actually happened.

"So, is he at least enjoying his days 'exploring'?" Wade probes. "Do you think he'll stay?"

"He's been looking at colleges and job opportunities," I tell him. "They're fairly permanent types of searches, don't you think?" Wade offers a small smile. "What?" I ask defensively. "I just want him to be putting himself first, you know?"

I air one of my biggest fears, the worry that Julian will put me first, and he'll merge into my life without specifying his needs and wants. And that bothers me. I know the circumstances were different, but that's what he's done with his whole life. More specifically, when Rhett got sick.

Julian became whoever Rhett or his sickness required him to be, and that's not going to work for us. I want him to be the man he's always been meant to be.

"I do know," Wade agrees. "What type of jobs is he looking for?"

"He's sticking to bartending for now," I inform. "The hours are usually flexible for students and he's got years of experience."

"Are you telling your family?"

The question feels like it came out of left field, but in reality, it's exactly what one would expect we'd do. My gut tells me it will be a shock; whether it's because he's a man or because it's Julian, I'm not sure.

They didn't freak out that Rhett was gay, but I know the fact I've only ever been with women may affect their reaction.

"Eventually," I answer ambivalently. "Probably Christmas, and only because I can't be around them all again and keep it to myself. Thanksgiving was hard enough."

"Deac." I flick my gaze to his, and he's got a sad smile on his face. "Don't let them fuck this up for you, okay?"

"What do you mean?"

"Just remember exactly how you're feeling right now, in Seattle, with him, and that dopey ass grin on your face. And don't let them take that feeling away from you."

My stomach flutters with a mixture of nervousness and fear at Wade's warning. I know better than to feel like I can predict anybody's reactions, but I'm really hoping Julian is what makes the difference this time.

"Thanks, man," I say sincerely.

"For what?"

I give him a shrug. "For just fucking rolling with it."

"That's what brothers are for."

And we really are brothers. So much more than friends. There isn't anything I wouldn't do for Wade and he for me.

"So," I start. "Does Christy still want to go to Pike Place Market on Saturdays?"

"Always, why?"

"Can we come?" I ask sheepishly.

"Oh shiiit. Can you be dick whipped instead of pussy whipped?" he muses. "Because that's so you right now."

I throw the greasy shammy cloth at him. "You're a fuckwit."

He catches it, throwing it back. "Told you closing up on Saturdays was a good idea. We will only go on one condition," he goads.

"I'm listening."

"Take the rest of the week off, and then we can double date on the weekend and show him what he's missing. Just enough to bring him back to you."

"You're nauseatingly romantic, you know that, right?"

He claps his hands and cheers animatedly. "Nothing but the best for my boy."

I'D BEEN MULLING over my conversation with Wade all day, and by the time I'd made it home to Julian surprising me with dinner, I knew there was one thing he was absolutely right about.

"You know you could live here," I blurt out while we're sitting side by side, eating at the breakfast bar.

Julian eyes me warily. "Am I supposed to know what this is about?"

"If you move to Seattle, you'd move in here," I clarify. "You wouldn't need to look for your own place."

"Is this because I cooked for you?" His eyes dance with humor. "You want me to be your housewife?"

Fighting off a smile, I put down my cutlery. "It's a nice fucking selling point, sure, but even if we ate takeout every night, we would still be having this conversation."

"Can I think about it?"

"Of course." I nod. "You can think about it and not even take me up on the offer, but I wanted to make sure you knew. And while we're telling each other things," I continue, "you don't have to cook either. I can do it, or we can order in or go out even."

"I haven't cooked in a while," he reminds me. "I forgot how much I liked doing it." He raises his beer. "So in the spirit of finding myself, I made us dinner."

"You're a good cook," I compliment.

"You don't have to butter me up, Deac. I'm pretty sure I've made up my mind anyway," he says absentmindedly, continuing to eat his food.

"And?"

His face splits into a huge grin as he sings, "I'll never tell."

We both laugh, the level of comfort between us never ceasing to amaze me. We continue to talk through the rest of the meal, nothing too light, nothing too heavy.

When we're finished, I collect the empty dishes and walk around the counter to the sink.

"I don't mind cleaning up," Julian says.

"Don't you even think about it," I warn. "Go sit down, find a movie or something, and I'll join you when I'm done."

Julian reluctantly complies while I enjoy the view of him sprawled across *my* couch while I clean up after *our* dinner.

He fits in. Like he's always belonged, and I know, even after only a handful of days, my place will feel empty without him.

When I finish up in the kitchen, I dry my hands and join Julian.

Taking a seat on the rug, I keep my back up against the furniture; one of my legs straight, the other bent at the knee. Warm fingers slide up and down the length of my neck. "I would've made room for you," Julian says.

"I'm fine right here," I insist, enjoying how he's touching me. "Did you pick anything to watch?"

"No." He hands me the remote over my shoulder. "I figured it's your place, and you can choose."

I tug the control out of his grip and begin flicking through the different streaming services. "That feels like a cop out because you don't want to be left making the final decision."

He chuckles. "What can I say? I'm trying to make a good impression and I don't need you to judge my TV choices."

"Chicken," I mutter.

I keep searching for something that could potentially interest us both when Julian shifts behind me. He's sitting up now, his legs on either side of my body, and his hands massaging my shoulders.

My eyes fall closed at his touch.

His hands knead me like dough, releasing the tension, relieving the pressure, working the knots. I let my head roll back, lazily opening my eyes to look at him. "You're really good at this."

He kisses the tip of my nose. "It's really just an excuse to touch you," he admits.

"You know you can touch me any time you want."

His hands slide over my shoulders and down to my pecs, his fingers teasing my nipples. As if they have a direct line to my groin, my cock responds almost immediately.

His lips press against my forehead, reverently moving and kissing every inch of my face. It's so soft and delicate, I'm almost worried.

"Are you okay?" I ask before he finally lands his mouth on mine.

He doesn't answer, he just keeps kissing me. I want to shove away the sudden sliver of doubt burying itself between us. Grabbing his face, I still his movements and move out from under his touch.

I rise off the floor, squeeze Julian's shoulders, and push him back onto the couch, draping my body over his.

"What is it?" I probe.

"What's what?"

Pressing the issue, I throw his own words back at him. "This honesty thing works both ways, doesn't it?"

He chews on his bottom lip, thinking before he speaks. "I'm just so happy right now, here with you."

My whole body deflates on a relieved sigh. "You're happy?"

He gives me a small nod. *Thank fuck.*

"That's not what I thought you were going to say," I reply honestly.

He runs his fingers from my temple down my jaw. "I'm just trying to savor you."

"I'm not going anywhere."

"But I am."

But you're coming back.

I refrain from arguing with him, and I pretend those three words don't feel like a slap to the face, because I made myself a promise: Julian needs to do what Julian needs to do, and I will accept wherever that road takes him.

It's not an easy choice, but it's the right one. For both him and me.

Julian's hands are still touching me. My cheeks, my neck, my back, my hair. While we just stare at one another, with nothing but truth and unspoken feelings of love between us.

I revel in the knowledge that he doesn't seem to want the distance any more than I do. I can live with that right now. I can work with that.

"I know how quick the week will go," he discloses. "And I know how much I'm going to miss you when I get back home."

"Well, lucky for you," I say playfully, "I'm not going to work for the rest of the week."

"You're not?" There's a glimmer of excitement in his eyes, and I thank the heavens for having a friend like Wade to kick my ass when I need it. "You didn't have to do that," he backtracks. "I would've been fine entertaining myself."

I press my hips into his jokingly. "Why? When I could entertain you so much better."

A smile breaks out on his face, and I capture his bottom lip with my teeth. "Could I interest you in some dick on dick time?"

He throws his head back in laughter, and it's that perfect reminder that he *is* happy.

Julian tsks. "Dick has turned you greedy."

"No." I smirk. "*Your* dick has turned me greedy."

"Wait, wait, wait," he says, pushing me up off him. "I want to show you what I did today, before we get carried away."

Leaning back on the couch, my arms spread across the back of it, I watch him walk into my bedroom and come back with a page full of writing. When he sits back down, he wordlessly hands me the piece of paper.

My eyes scan what's in front of me, and my heart skips a beat. It's a list of colleges. Some I recognize, some I don't; all of them here in Seattle.

I clear my throat, trying to school my voice. "Should I be getting my hopes up?"

"They're all the schools that have good teaching programs," he supplies. "There's a lot I have to take into account—namely money," he admits. "But I want you to know I really want this to work."

Turning to look at him, I slide my hand to cup his face, my thumb grazing his cheek. I believe him. I believe his efforts are made from the purest place, with the most honest intentions. But I'm scared. I'm scared that when he leaves here and goes back to the shell of a life he had with *him*, all the effort in the world isn't going to be enough to bring him back to this life with *me*.

22

JULIAN

The days were flying by and I was doing everything in my mere mortal power to try and slow them down. Spoiler alert, nothing was working.

It had been a beautiful glimpse into what my life could be like without the constant reminder of what I was leaving behind.

When we were here, we were so much more than two people connected by grief. I was me and he was him, and we were individuals who laughed at the same jokes, enjoyed the same movies, and argued about food.

I was contemplating a future, and not just with reference to Deacon. My head was clearer than it had ever been, my lungs could breathe and my heart was so full, there was nothing left for it to do but fucking explode.

It is going to kill me to go back to Montana, and that only made the decision for me to come back the right one.

I hadn't told Deacon yet, because I knew how protective he was about the idea of me doing what *I* needed to do and not being swayed by what *we* were doing.

And while school and a new job were very persuasive

reasons to stay here, the only one that mattered was Deacon. The only thing that swayed me to Seattle was him, and I didn't have one good reason to stay away.

I knew I was going to have to contend with how I was going to pack the last twenty years of my life into a few cardboard boxes, but that wasn't Deacon's problem, it was mine.

And it wasn't something I wanted to think about now anyway.

Today we were spending the day with Deacon's friend and business partner, and it felt like a big deal. The last and only time I'd ever seen Wade was at Rhett's funeral, where I was the grieving boyfriend. And now, I am the boyfriend.

Fuck. Is that what we are?

Boyfriend seems like such an immature word for the lives we've lived before one another. Two insufficient syllables to describe the depth of the connection between us.

Yet, it's somehow the only word that makes sense.

Rubbing my hands together, I bring them up to my mouth and try to blow hot air into them, hoping it will warm me up. Deacon and I are standing side by side right underneath the huge ruby red Pike Place Market sign waiting for his friends, Wade and Christy, to arrive, and it's probably the coldest I've ever felt in my life.

I don't know whether to blame the cold or the nerves, but, either way, my bones are quivering beneath my skin.

Deacon is standing with his hands buried inside his coat pockets, laughing at me. "Come on," he scoffs. "It's not even that bad."

"Shut up," I quip. "You're only warm because of those beefy muscles of yours. They add extra pounds to your body."

He looks down at his arms and then back at me. "Stop your whining, you love these beefy muscles."

"I can't believe there're so many people here and it's still this cold."

"Come here," Deacon calls. He tugs on my jacket and pulls me close to him. He covers my clasped hands with his and brings them to his mouth, blowing on them.

It's not any different to what I was doing, but the gesture is enough to weaken my knees.

It's then that I hear a loud voice call out Deacon's name. I expect him to move away, or drop my hands, and when he does neither of those things, I try to do it for him.

His friends need some time to get used to seeing him with a man, don't they?

Pinning me with a look that's filled with irritation, he squeezes my hands and moves them back to his mouth. "I'm not that type of guy," he says before continuing to try and warm me up.

I don't get a chance to say anything to him because, grinning from ear to ear, Wade and Christy have arrived.

They're an attractive couple. Wade has the same build as Deacon, but his skin is tanned, and his hair and eyes border on black. Christy's tall and has red hair and forest green eyes. She's wrapped up in a colorful array of ponchos and scarves to keep the cold at bay; the perfect marriage of pretty and petite.

"Oh my God," she squeals. "I think we picked the coldest day in history to leave the house." She holds out her hand, "Hi, I'm Christy, it's so nice to meet you."

Genuine in her greeting, it's impossible not to smile back and introduce myself. "Hey, I'm Julian, it's nice to meet you too."

She shimmies over to give Deacon, who still hasn't let go of my hand, a one-armed hug and a kiss on the cheek. So I bite the bullet and smile at Wade, because this is kind of like the first time I'm meeting him.

"Hey," he enthuses. "It's good to see you again, man."

"Yeah, you too." We shake hands, but it's still somewhat awkward. "Thanks for letting us crash your day."

"Anything for Deac." There's a serious timbre to his voice, and it's not hard to read between the lines. Deacon is important to Wade.

They're family.

The one Deacon chose.

His opinion of all of this matters. And while he doesn't seem to be perturbed by me or us being together, it doesn't mean he isn't wary of me potentially breaking Deacon's heart.

He has every right to be; I come with a lot of baggage. We both do, but I'm not going to give him the satisfaction of telling him he's right. Instead, I slap on a confident smile and squeeze Deacon's hand.

"We were thinking we could walk around a bit before our reservations at twelve," I say cheerfully.

"Yes," Christy exclaims while nudging Wade. "Let's go see people throw raw fish at other people."

That's enough to get him to crack a smile, and the four of us walk around the marketplace checking out all the different stalls. When we come across a lady who knits homemade beanies, scarves, blankets, and gloves, Deacon stops us.

"What are you doing?" I ask, watching Christy and Wade get lost in the crowd.

"Do you have gloves that will fit him?" He raises our joined hands to the older lady manning the stall.

"Yes," she claps. "I've got the perfect ones. Let me rummage around and find them."

"We're getting gloves?" I tug at his hand, bringing him closer to me.

"No, you're getting gloves."

The sweet lady returns with both a brown and a gray pair. "Try these on," she instructs. "And tell me which ones you want."

"Thank you," Deacon says, handing her a twenty and taking the gray set off her. Directing his attention back to me, he says, "Put your hands up."

His kindness has rendered me speechless. It's effortless, like taking care of me is as natural to him as breathing. I've never had that before. When my family died, I took care of myself. When Rhett was sick, all I did was take care of him. I put both hands up in front of my chest, my fingers spread apart, and I watch him take care of me.

Deacon sinks his teeth into his bottom lip, concentrating as he slides the warm, thick material over each of my long digits. He tugs at the ends, making sure they fit.

He drags his gaze up from my hands to my eyes. "Wiggle your fingers around," he orders. "How do they feel?"

Not caring who's around, I grab his face and bring it to me. "You bought me gloves."

It's not a question, or even a statement, it's a fucking revelation. *I think I'm in love with you.*

"You bought me gloves," I repeat.

His face splits into a beautiful smile. "Why do you keep repeating that?" he asks. "Yes. I bought you gloves. If you're going to live here, your hands need to be warm in winter."

I gently brush my mouth over his. "You. Bought. Me. Gloves."

"Hey, love birds," a deep voice interrupts. "We're going to be late to our lunch reservation."

Slowly, I pull myself away from Deacon and nervously

turn to Christy and Wade. They're both smiling, and I've never been more relieved in my life.

He bought me gloves and his friends don't care he's dating me. Maybe everything really is going to be okay.

"You can suck face later," Wade adds. "I'm fucking starving."

Sheepishly, Deacon and I walk behind them as they lead us to the eatery they chose for lunch.

"Do you promise to suck my face later?" Deacon says into my ear.

"If you promise to never stop buying me gloves, I promise to suck anything you want me to."

He chuckles. "What's with you and the fucking gloves?"

I think I'm in love with you.

"Stop asking questions and show me what's so good about this marketplace. Aren't you supposed to be trying to convince me to stay?" I taunt.

"Is that a challenge? Because you're gonna regret it."

I jokingly slap his ass. "Try me."

THE REST of the afternoon went off without a hitch. Deacon and Wade were in their element, ribbing on one another, talking about their business and things they had planned, and reminiscing on how far they've come.

Together, they opened up the memory vault, and like an eager student, I stored every piece of new information, just so I could paint an even more detailed picture of the man Deacon Sutton is.

It was like being in the Twilight Zone.

While he was ultimately the Deacon I always knew, the man in front of me is the one I'm falling in love with.

He'd touched me every chance he got this afternoon. Public be damned, he couldn't get enough. I knew it was different for him because Wade would stare for a little bit too long every time it happened. Not in disgust or even disappointment, but in amazement.

I don't even know if Deacon realizes how tight he's still holding on to me now. We're in the elevator, waiting for it to stop on his floor, and his hand is squeezing the life out of mine.

The good mood from lunch is nowhere to be found, both of us somber, stuck in our own heads, thinking about my inevitable departure that's just around the corner.

The walk into the apartment is silent, the weight of the goodbye is like a thousand tons of stone sitting on my shoulders. The space is dark, the winter siphoning the sun out of the room much earlier than usual.

"Deacon," my voice croaks.

"Mhmm."

He's no longer holding my hand, but pacing around the room. He's not looking at me. He either can't or he won't, but it doesn't matter, because they both hurt all the same.

"Deacon," I say, my voice a little firmer. He freezes but still doesn't turn around. "Deacon, look at me."

Several long seconds pass before he speaks. "I had one of the best days of my life today and all we did was eat with my friends and talk shit."

"And buy me gloves," I add.

I think I'm falling in love with you.

"Yes," he exclaims, spinning on his heels, taking large strides towards me. His large calloused hands grab my face with restrained strength, and his blue eyes shimmer with all the love I feel in my chest. "And buy you gloves, you fucking weirdo."

I'm not sure which one of us moves first. Fueled by love and goodbyes, our lips collide in desperation.

It's hungry and feral and every bit as rough and raw as we're both feeling.

"Please come back," he pleads through our kisses. "I know I said—"

I cut him off, bruising his lips. Searing him with my touch, so even when I'm not here he never doubts how much I love kissing him. The lengths I would go to to be able to do it for as long as he'll let me.

"Trust me," I murmur. "Trust me with your heart. Trust in us."

Deacon groans as he deepens the kiss. It's punishing and heady, masking the fear I feel trembling beneath his skin.

Wanting to reassure him, I walk him back down the hallway, our lips still glued together. By the time we pass the bedroom's threshold he's tugging my clothes loose, itching to get at my skin.

"You're wearing too many fucking clothes," he grunts. "Fucking winter."

A strained chuckle leaves my mouth as he pushes me onto the bed and begins stripping me naked.

By the time his hands are at the buttons on my jeans, my cock is thick, hard, and ready to explode.

"Wait," I breathe out. "Deac, wait."

He snaps his head up. "What is it?"

"Go to my bag." His eyes narrow. "Just do it," I say shakily. "You'll work it out."

He stomps into the walk-in closet, and I lazily stroke my dick over my jeans, anxious for his return.

I need the release, I need to feel him, and I need it soon.

"Are you sure?" His voice is lust and gravel as he walks in holding the bottle of lube and the box of condoms I bought earlier this week. We hadn't discussed *this* specifically, but we'd both spent the week familiarizing ourselves with one another enough to know what's next.

But I want this. I want to give myself to him in every way I can. I can't yet give him my words, but I'll be damned if I walk away from him this time without giving him my body.

"Yes."

My breath hitches, causing him to cock his head at me. "Are you sure?"

"Do you want me to take care of it myself?" I challenge, unbuttoning my jeans, lowering my boxers, and pulling my leaking cock out. It's the only motivation he needs, because he's pouncing on me like a crazed animal, swatting my hands away from my shaft, and dragging the heavy denim down the length of my legs.

Completely naked, his eyes roam the expanse of my body.

Staring back at nothing but a wildfire of desire, I'm certain any trepidation is now forgotten, one hundred percent replaced with only carnal need.

Climbing over me, he lowers his head till we're a single breath apart. His tongue slips out between his lips, and then painstakingly slowly he explores the shape of my mouth.

"Tell me what you want me to do," he says. "I want to do this right."

"I've never done this," I confess.

"What?"

"No." I shake my head, realizing he's misunderstood what I meant.

Swallowing hard, I hold on to his biceps to keep him somewhat close to me. "Nobody's been inside me before."

I watch his face morph from shock, to surprise, to understanding. But it's the last look of undeniable possession that steals my breath away.

He crushes his mouth to mine. Licking me. Kissing me. Effortlessly driving me to the brink of insanity. When he sucks my tongue and wraps his fingers around my dick, a needy whimper echoes around the room.

"Deacon," I cry out. "Don't fucking tease me."

He pries himself away from me and starts stripping out of his own clothes. "Get in the middle of the bed," he instructs. "Lay on your stomach."

Exhilaration swims in my veins as I heed his request. When I hear the cap of the lube bottle open my eyes immediately dart behind me.

Deacon is a mass of muscle and man; his cock thick, hard and angry.

I watch him place one knee up on the bed, lean forward, and crawl over me. He's on all fours above me, and I almost have to tuck my hands underneath my body to refrain from touching him.

Lips press to the back of my neck, kissing me softly, kissing me slowly.

Lost in his touch, my body shivers when an unexpected pool of cool liquid lands just below my nape.

Fingers dance down my backbone, smearing the lube down the length of my back, drawing circles around every single knob in my spine. When he reaches the top of my crease, my ass clenches in anticipation, but the touch never comes.

Instead, I feel another cold dollop land on my skin, this time the cold leveling out the heat flaring in my veins. He repeats the same motions: up, down, and around.

Each time he slides the lube a little bit lower, slipping it a little farther. By the sixth time, my cock is throbbing, my balls aching.

I whine embarrassingly into the pillow while trying to grind my hips into the mattress.

Deacon grips my hips to still me. "Don't even think about it."

"Please," I beg.

"We're just getting to the good part," he taunts.

When I feel a fresh round of liquid at the base of my spine instead of the top, my breath hitches. Instead of working his way up, Deacon's fingers slip inside my crease. He's got one hand stretching my ass cheek while the fingers on his other hand are covered with lube and grazing up and down my taint.

Just like he did to my back, he's running his fingers up and down, circling my hole and back up; making sure to do it over and over again.

Eventually, he takes pity on my squirming body, and I feel his thick digit slowly breach my opening. It's a slow, slick slide, the very pinnacle of pleasure and pain, and we're just getting started.

"Fuck. That's tight," Deacon growls. "You okay?"

"Mhmm," I manage. "I want to feel you move. Get deeper."

Spurred on by my request, Deacon's finger thrusts in and out of my hole. When the tip of his finger grazes my prostate, a loud shout escapes my mouth at the same time Deacon groans. "Fuck. I felt that. Let me do it again."

Enthralled by his new discovery, Deacon repeatedly hits the spot, working out the perfect angle, the perfect curl of his finger, and the right amount of pressure to make me come.

But I don't want to. Not yet.

"Deacon." I turn my head to look at him. "Give me another finger, and then I'll be ready for you."

"Are you sure?"

Absolutely not, but I'm not blowing my load without you being inside me.

Feeling bold, I raise my hips, stick my ass in his face, and stretch my cheeks myself. The image is self-explanatory, and as two fingers press at my entrance, I know Deacon is finally on the same page.

When they both slide in my whole body convulses. I have to lower my hand between the mattress and my body to grip the base of my cock to try and stave off the orgasm that's threatening to crash through me.

Deacon alternates between scissoring his fingers and brushing them against my prostate. The combination is maddening; the pressure and the intensity of the fullness only leaving me desperate for more.

"You ready, baby?" Deacon asks hoarsely.

We lock eyes, and the sight of him squeezing his shaft and looking as unhinged as I feel is the only answer he needs.

"Get on your back," he demands. "I want you to remember my face when I fuck you. So you know exactly who you're walking away from, and the man you better fucking come back to."

23

DEACON

The words are gruff and possessive, and completely out of character, but as thoughts of ravishing his body race through my mind I can barely stop the words *mine mine mine* from spilling out of my mouth.

As shameful as it makes me feel I don't care about, nor do I want to think about, anything he did or who he did it with before this moment. Because this, right now, is ours, and I'm not going to let anyone, alive or dead, take it away.

Julian surprises me when he sits up and scoots to the edge of the bed. Grabbing the condom off the mattress, he slips the foil packet into his mouth, tearing off the top and pulling the rubber out. Warm fingers circle my rigid cock, and the tip of his tongue peeks out to lick my wet crown.

"Fuck," I hiss.

"Just wanted a quick taste before I got this on you," he says nonchalantly, like he didn't just try to tease me over the edge before I even got inside of him.

He rolls on the condom, and even with the barrier between us, having his hands on my shaft pokes holes at my already dwindling control.

"Want me to lube you up?" he quips.

I give his shoulder a little push. "If you touch me any more than what you're doing, this night is going to be over a lot quicker than either one of us wants." I tip my chin up at him. "But you can watch me do it."

His eyes drop to my dick, and I offer him a little show with an upward stroke of my hand, preparing myself for him.

When his tongue darts out to lick his upper lip I climb up on the bed, stalking toward him. Forcing him to the middle I hover over him and slam my lips to his. His arms circle my neck while his mouth feasts on mine, keeping me in place, keeping me close.

Lowering my hand between us I rub, tease, and jack his stiff length. Wet and sticky, Julian's arousal covers my hands. Sliding my fingers past his tight balls I prod and prep his slick hole.

Reluctantly, I drag my lips away from his and pull back, wanting to look at him properly and make sure he's certain this is what he wants.

His face is flushed. Pink cheeks, parted lips, and a slight sheen of sweat forming on his hairline, I continue to drag my digits in and out of him, ghosting his prostate. "Ready for me?"

His whole body bears down on my fingers. "I want *you*, Deacon," he breathes out, and the layered meaning slips right between my rib cage and deliciously pierces my heart.

He whimpers at the loss of my fingers, and his neediness makes my dick impossibly harder. Sitting back on my haunches, I take hold of Julian's thigh, spreading him out with one hand and I slowly guide my sheathed up cock to his ass.

My heart stops, and the tightness in my chest only

increases as my crown presses against his hole. Never in a million years did I envision this, but now, with his body exposed, vulnerable, and all mine, I don't know how anything else ever felt right before this. Before *him*.

Wanting to see every moment as it plays out on his face, I focus my gaze on him and begin to push in. It feels almost impossible. He's tight and my dick refuses to stop thickening at just the thought of being inside him.

On instinct, his body clenches, trying to stop the intrusion, and I begin to try and slide back out.

"No," Julian rasps, reaching for my hip. "Stay."

Blowing out a ragged breath, I slowly sink in farther, now feeling myself breach the tight ring of muscle that was so desperate to keep me out.

My body shudders as I hold his thighs up to my chest and slowly pull my hips back slightly. The angle. The grip on my cock. Everything about this is exquisite torture as I gently begin to move myself in and out of him.

"How's that?" I ask, my body finding a sweet rhythm. "Feel me?"

Hooded, lust-filled eyes beam at me. "Everywhere," he answers. "I feel you *everywhere*."

My breath hitches, my heart sputters, and my body responds the only way it knows how. My movements become a little more needy, a little more desperate, a little more frantic.

"Fuck," I grunt out. "I can't stop," I admit. "How do you ever expect me to stop this? Stop you?" High on fucking sex and euphoria, my heart spills from my lips, falling on us in waves of heat and heaviness.

"It's right there, baby," I confess. "Like a fucking neon sign across my heart."

Three words I won't say first. Three words I want to say first.

"Please," Julian begs, wrapping one hand around himself and the other sitting directly on top of his heart. "Please," he repeats. "Show me."

Consumed by lust and love and pure wanton need, my body ruthlessly slams against his—*showing him*. With every thrust I'm branding him, taunting him. Daring him to forget this. Daring him to go back home and fucking forget *me.*

Julian's hand moves faster with every inch of me his body swallows. Tipping his head back with a loud, deep, satisfied groan, his teeth sink into his swollen bottom lip, and we both climb to the edge of the cliff in search of the fall.

"Come with me," I demand.

"Yes," he shouts, and with all the synchronicity of our unspoken words, unspoken feelings, and unspoken fears, we plummet. "Yes." Hard. "Yes." Loud. "Yes." And forever changed.

Heavy breathing fills the air, blue eyes questioning brown ones, brown eyes answering blue ones. Both physically and emotionally drained, I carefully drag myself out of Julian, watching him momentarily wince at both the pain and the loss.

"You okay?" I ask, my voice hoarse.

His lazy smile answers before he does. "Never better. "

I offer Julian my hand. "Shower?"

Wordlessly, he takes it and, together, we head for the bathroom; bodies dragging, minds quiet.

Under the hot spray, we stand in silence, washing each other, memorizing each other, loving each other.

When the soap runs off my skin Julian's lips join the drops of water that beat down on my body. He presses delicate, meticulous kisses to every part of my skin his mouth can reach. My face, my chest, my back, my legs. Over and over again.

The lump in my throat and expansion of my heart keeps me silent, because in this moment, feeling him love me is just as good as hearing it.

When he finally melds his mouth to mine, I let my timid, fearful heart kiss for me. I kiss him till my heart has made its way into *his* chest, and then some. I kiss him till he's breathless. I kiss him till all he can see is me.

Me and him.

Him and me.

Me and you.

You and me.

"Come on," I whisper. "Let's get you to bed."

Dry, exhausted, and naked, we both slip between the blankets. Lethargic limbs wrap around one another, both of us trying to still time. To stall the inevitable.

"We're going to be okay," Julian says into the darkness.

"You told me to trust you," I tell him. "To trust *us*."

He squeezes me tighter, and I squeeze him back, burying my head in his neck, tilting my mouth to his ear. "That's the only reason I'm letting you walk away from me tomorrow."

"HEY, MAN," Wade greets with a smile.

I widen my front door and gesture for him to come inside. "Did I miss something? Why are you here?"

He raises a six pack of beer. "I thought we could watch some football highlights and shoot the shit."

I narrow my eyebrows at him. "I'm still not following.

Don't people usually wait for an invitation to come to someone's apartment?"

He strides in, heading to the kitchen. "Not when the person whose place it is is potentially crying into their cup of coffee."

"Can you speak in fucking English, before I kick you out for real?"

Placing the beer bottles on the counter he pulls one out of the holder, twists the lid off, and takes a swig. "I'm checking up on you, you broody motherfucker."

"Firstly, you're supposed to offer me the first beer." I counter, irritated. "Secondly, don't call me broody."

"Touchy much?" He opens the second bottle and walks it to me. "People don't get to choose their insults from their friends."

"It's not an insult," I argue, taking the drink off him and dropping onto the couch. *It's a compliment.*

"What the actual fuck are you even talking about now?" Wade exclaims.

"Nothing," I mutter. "Have you checked up on me enough? Am I doing fine by your standards?"

"Well…" He brings the rim of his bottle to his mouth, and looks around the room pensively. "You're not sitting on the couch crying and stuffing your face with ice cream, so that's a plus."

I almost choke on my beer, quickly putting it on the coffee table and hacking up a lung. When I can concentrate back on Wade I glare at him.

"I like a bit of dick now, but I didn't grow a fucking vagina."

He shrugs, unperturbed. "I'm just checking."

Jumping off the kitchen stool he rounds the couch and sits beside me. "Seriously, though, are you okay?"

"It's been a handful of hours," I deadpan. "He just went home, it's not like he threw me out of his life."

"So, it's a visit?"

"Hopefully," I answer with as much positivity as I can muster.

"Do you believe him?"

"I do," I insist. "I believe he wants this as much as I do. But I'm fucking scared shitless that he's going to walk into that house alone, and he's not going to be able to leave Rhett behind."

I feel like a piece of shit for even saying those words, despite their truth. They're the crux of every single insecurity I have, and I don't want him to forget my brother or anything they shared—that isn't what this is about. It's just wanting to be enough for now. For his future. For his *more*.

I couldn't compete with my brother when he was alive, and I can't possibly compete with him now that he's dead.

"I'm just going to wait," I tell Wade. "Christmas is only three weeks away. It's not going to kill me to show a bit of patience. He has to move out of that place regardless, and I know that in itself isn't going to be an easy feat for him."

"It's going to be okay," he states. "I don't know what I expected yesterday when the four of us went out, but honestly..." He pauses, his eyes drop to the floor and back up again. "I don't mean any disrespect when I say this, and I don't know what it was like for him and your brother or what they looked like together. But the two of you..."

"The two of us, what?"

"You look made for each other, man."

I feel the ridiculous, uninhibited smile stretch across my face and flick my best friend on the leg. "And you think I grew the vagina."

"Ouch, you fucker." He rubs his leg. "I was being nice."

He is, and what he said is more than nice. It echoes thoughts and feelings that don't feel comfortable for me to bring into the light of day just yet.

"Thank you," I say. "Thank you for being a pain in my ass and checking up on me."

Nodding, he slips his hand into his pocket and pulls out a small, black, velvet box. "There may have been another reason I wanted to come over."

"Are you fucking kidding me?" I shout excitedly. I shoot up off the couch and pluck the box out of his fingers. Opening it up, I see a shiny, white gold band with a large, square halo diamond perfectly perched on top of it. It's elegant and romantic and perfect for Christy.

"When are you going to propose?" I pry.

He shrugs. "Probably Christmas."

"Have you thought of how?" He gives me a smug smile, and I chuckle. "Of course you have, you romantic fucker."

"I was actually hoping you'd be my best man," he says, more seriously.

"She's got to say yes first, you cocky motherfucker," I joke. "But yeah, man." I nod, the emotion of everything we've shared along the years with each other hitting me hard. "I'd be honored."

"Hey." Julian answers the phone, and I feel the distance between us immediately. His voice is reserved and uncomfortable, and I hate not knowing if it's me or if it's something else.

When he landed, we texted a bit back and forth, but agreed to just talk later tonight when he'd settled back in. And now that nighttime is here I'm wondering if we should've just stuck to text, where the truth is easier to hide and the lie is easier to tell.

"How are you?" I ask awkwardly. "How's it feel being back?"

I flinch at my own question, because it wasn't my intention to ask. Because I'm not sure I want his answer.

"Different," he responds.

Good different or bad different?

"I miss you," he says cautiously.

The tension in my body drains at the declaration. It's dumb, because deep down I know he's still thinking about me; I know he hasn't forgotten about me, but I can't help but crave that acknowledgement with the physical distance between us.

"I miss you too."

There's a beat of silence so I blurt out the first thing that comes to me. "Wade's going to propose to Christy. He came over today to show me the ring and ask me to be his best man."

"Oh my God," Julian says in shock. "That's amazing. They're perfect together," he rambles. "I can just imagine Christy when he pops the question. I don't think I've ever seen two people so smitten with one another."

"It's true," I agree. "I can't wait to hear how he's going to ask her."

"So, are you going to be his best man?"

"Of course," I exclaim. "I'm actually pretty pumped he asked me."

"You'd be a great best man," he compliments.

"Thanks."

The conversation moves from wedding talk to things that happened in the airport and on the plane, to just random shit that really has no major significance to either one of us, but we can't seem to stop.

It's avoidance of the highest form, and I'm just hoping and praying it's not going to be like this till I get back to Montana for Christmas. I tell myself the last time we were apart things were different. We were different.

Now, the stakes are high. Maybe too high for Julian.

"I'm going to get to bed," Julian says.

"Are you okay?" I ask.

"Mhmm."

"Julian," I say sternly. "Just tell me. Whatever it is, even if it's about us. If something's wrong, I want to know."

"Nothing's wrong." He sighs. "I just...I have to go," he clips.

Feeling so far removed from the conversation and the man on the other end of the line I close my eyes and count to ten.

"Call me if you need me," I tell him.

"I will."

"Or text me," I add. "Just don't shut me out okay?"

"That's the last thing I want to do," he says apologetically.

If you say so.

"Goodnight, Deacon."

"Night."

If I was waiting for him to delay the goodbye or even save the conversation, neither happened. Looking up at the ceiling, I spin my phone in between my fingers. I told Wade tonight I would be patient, and that's what I have to shut up and do.

No matter how many times he tries to keep me in the dark, I have to trust him. Trust us.

Swiping at my screen, I open up a text message to Julian.

Me: I know being back there is hard. I'm sorry, and it's not my intention to make it harder. If I could take the burden off you, I would. Please know that.

The phone stays silent for entirely too long, and ten minutes later when the message comes through, I wish the quiet had lasted a little bit longer.

Julian: I'm scared. If I tell you the truth, you'll be upset. If I keep it to myself, you'll still be upset.

Me: Try me.

Julian: The next three weeks are going to be tough for me, and I can't guarantee that every time we speak it isn't going to go exactly like tonight.

My stomach feels the kick of his words, hard and fast.

Me: I can come and help you.

Julian: I wish it were that easy.

Me: Let me.

Julian: You can't.

Me: How can I help?

Julian: Trust me. Trust us.

24

JULIAN

S tepping out of the shower, I hear a knock at my door.

"Shit." *I wasn't expecting anyone for another hour.* Quickly drying myself, I clumsily throw on a t-shirt and step into my sweats.

"I'm coming," I call out. When I swing the door open, I find a short, older man on the other side of the door.

"Are you Julian?" he asks.

"Yes," I respond. "Are you Lou?"

"Yeah, I'm here for your couch." I look out the door and see his truck with a trailer attached in my driveway.

"It's all here ready for you." I gesture inside. "Do you need help carrying it out?"

"No, I'm fine. My son is in the truck. I brought him along to help," he explains. "He can put those quarterback muscles to work."

Chuckling, I open the door as wide as it will go and wait for his son to climb out of the truck.

Since returning from Seattle I've been diligent in emptying the house, cleaning the house, making sure it's pretty much left the exact same way I found it all those years ago. I initially thought it would take the whole three weeks till Christmas, but as I hit the middle of the second week, I realize the only thing I've got left is the one thing I've been avoiding.

My emotions haven't seemed to acknowledge the deadline, and as every day passes, I delay the inevitable. My chest tightens in panic at the thought of having to go through Rhett's belongings. There isn't much. Between hospice and often returning to his parents' place when he was doing chemo, the stuff that's left here is more significant to the two of us.

Which ultimately means it's harder for me.

The thought of having to part with any of it—potentially throw it out—makes me nervous. I know his family would love to have some of it, and while I wish I were comfortable with the idea of Elaine, Bill, and Victoria coming here and taking what they want, I'm not.

I'm too possessive of this moment. Too scared to break, and, quite frankly, a little bit worried I won't. I don't need an audience to witness the most bittersweet moment of my life.

The guilt to Rhett for moving forward. The guilt to Deacon for looking back.

I've been going over the last year, namely the last couple of weeks, in my head, and wondering if it's too soon to feel this way with Deacon. But when I think of the alternative; think of walking away from him, it hurts.

A life without him would hurt me, and grief isn't supposed to feel like a punishment.

I haven't been able to sleep in my bedroom since I returned. Instead, I sleep on the couch by myself, every night, in a desperate attempt to feel closer to him.

The reality is, it has been nothing but torture and borderline masochistic, because I can't even hold a functional conversation with him. I rush off the phone every time we speak. Scared to say too much, scared to hurt his feelings. Most of the time, I cowardly resort to text messages, giving just enough information so he won't feel like calling.

I know I need to tell him my plans. That he is a part of my plans. But I need to let go of my past first. I need to let myself out of this voluntary exile I started after Rhett died, and I haven't figured out how to do that yet.

Logically, I know I have to move out of this place regardless, but knowing where my next steps will be has my subconscious roaring at me, questioning my love, questioning my loyalty.

"Seems like you've cleaned the place out," Lou says, interrupting me from my thoughts. He waves over to his son to hurry up, and then looks back at me. "If he can get his head out of his phone, he'll be here before the year ticks over."

I watch his mountain of a teenage son trudge up to the house. I'm almost certain a kid that size can carry the couch himself. My eyes dart between Lou and his son, perplexed by their size difference.

"I know," he says, calling me out. "I don't know how he got that big either."

When the son reaches us, I move out of their way and quietly watch them take my reminder of Deacon.

Other than my bed, it's one of the last things to go, officially emptying out my living room area. My kitchen is all packed up, apart from some basic essentials, and my bathrooms are pretty much cleaned out.

After Lou and his son tie the couch down to the trailer I find myself aimlessly walking into my bedroom. My eyes gravitate to the wooden box in the middle of the bed and the piles of Rhett's belongings that are scattered all over the room. It's been untouched since I got home.

The routine I held on to for so long, forgotten, the box is no longer my anchor, holding me still, keeping me sane. Now it feels more like a noose, and I hate that.

Pacing the room I run my fingers through my hair, pulling at the strands repeatedly. I just need someone to tell me what to do.

I can't form a single coherent, logical thought when dealing with any of this. I don't know up from down, right from wrong, or good or bad. Without a second thought, I pull my cell out of my pocket and tap on Deacon's name in my contacts.

"Hey," he answers. He sounds surprised I called, and that makes me feel a million times worse. "How are you?"

"You're coming Christmas Eve, right?" I blurt out. "You're coming to see me?"

There's a slight hint of panic in my voice and I feel myself slowly unraveling because of the uncertainty.

"Yeah, baby," he soothes, clearly noticing my distress. "I'll be there to see you. First thing."

My heart races inside my chest as I climb up on the bed, sitting cross legged in front of the letters.

"Did Rhett write you letters?" I ask Deacon.

My question shocks him into silence. His brother is the one thing we've never talked about. He's our elephant in the room.

"One," he eventually supplies. "He wrote me one."

"Did you read it?"

"Have you read yours?" he asks, deflecting the question. "Is this what your question is about?"

"You know I have letters?" I exclaim.

"I assumed that was what was in the box I brought over," he replies. "You haven't read them?"

His response reminds me of a question I've always wanted to ask him. "How come you came over that night?"

"My mom told me to, and..." I hear heavy breathing on the other side of the phone. "I told myself I did it for Rhett. To take care of you, for him."

For a split second, I wonder why the thought hadn't occurred to me. The possibility that all his niceness came from a place of pity and responsibility.

"What do you mean you told yourself?"

"I think I felt it then," he confesses. "I couldn't leave your house without making sure you were okay, and deep down inside, I know I did it for me."

"Julian," he adds. "I didn't lay on your bed and wrap my arms around you for my brother."

Closing my eyes, I hold the phone to my ear and let my body free fall on the bed. "How did you know?"

"I didn't. Not always," he clarifies. "But around you I run on instinct and feelings, and for a long time it didn't necessarily make sense."

"And now?"

"It's the only thing that makes sense." I let his words seep into the pores of my skin, but when I don't answer he continues talking. "I don't like being away from you. I don't like that you're struggling, and I don't like that you won't talk to me, so now I'm going to talk to you, and you're going to listen."

My pulse quickens at the steady, commanding timbre in his voice.

"It's naive of us to think that your life with him didn't exist. He's my brother, we can't just ignore it. Ignore he existed. Ignore that you loved him first." His voice shakes with his last statement, and my heart knows how hard this is for him to say. "I'm not perfect. And sometimes I'm irrationally jealous of my own brother, but that was a problem long before you came along.

"But despite all that, he was my brother, and I know, with every fiber of my being, he would want nothing more than for you to be happy. With someone or on your own, here or halfway across the world. Just. Be. Happy."

"I want to be," I admit. "I just feel like I'm saying good-bye, and I don't want to."

"The way you feel about him and the choice you make to move forward are not mutually exclusive," he explains. "Missing him doesn't mean you have to be miserable, and being happy doesn't mean you've forgotten about him."

"When did you get so wise?" I try for humor, but my throat feels too thick from emotion.

"You've given me a lot of thinking time."

"I'm sorry."

"Don't be," he says with sincerity. "If we never talk about this we'll never move forward." He pauses. "And I'm still holding on to hope that you and I are moving forward."

We are.

"W—" I don't even get the one syllable word out.

"That wasn't an opening for you to answer me," he says. "You wanted time and that time isn't up. But on Christmas Eve, I'm coming for you. None of this limbo shit we're in."

I smile to myself. "You've got yourself a deal."

"Good. Now tell me what you've been doing since you left."

I do. I tell him about how quick it was to pack up most of the house, and the enjoyment I got out of selling the things I didn't need, and how a man named Lou and his house-sized son came to pick up the couch.

Our couch.

It's amazing what honest communication can achieve; the huge distance between us becoming very much non-existent. Deacon would dismiss his strength, but I know not every man who's lived in their brother's shadow would man up the way he did.

To put his truths on the table, for my benefit. To put my needs and worries above his own is just another one of the multitude of reasons as to why I love him.

And I do.

The hows and whys don't matter to me anymore. All I know is I'm irrefutably in love with Deacon Sutton, and for the first time in a long time, the idea of that doesn't scare me.

I feel hope.

I feel promise.

From the boy who lost his way, not once, not twice, but three times, I finally feel like I'm home.

I CHECK the time and estimate that it's another fifteen minutes till Deacon gets here. For the past week, we've fallen back into an easy and familiar routine of late night/early morning phone calls and all-day texting.

It will be a welcome change to be in each other's space again. To touch him. To hold him. To love him.

Every part of me misses him, and I can't wait to tell him we'll never have to miss one another like this again.

Like clockwork, the knock on the other side of my door sounds. I look around the mostly empty room and make sure everything is in order.

Racing to the door, I swing it open, my face already splitting into a smile based on nothing but pure anticipation.

When he comes into view, the look on his face is as elated as mine. I jump into his arms because seeing him in the flesh and not being held by him is a wrong that I waste no time rectifying.

He catches me with ease, squeezing me, ensuring I'm real.

"Fuck, I missed you," he murmurs into my shoulder. "Please tell me we never have to do that again."

I cling to him as tight as I possibly can, my arms protectively wrapped around his body. I drop kisses wherever I can, and when my mouth is directly by his ear I whisper, "We never have to do that again."

He whips his head back, his arms still around me, nothing but his heart and all the hope in the world in his eyes. "Are you saying what I think you're saying?"

I give him a teasing grin. "What do you think I'm saying?"

"You better not be fucking with me right now."

"Close your eyes," I demand. "And no peeking."

Taking a step back I run my hands down his shoulders, down the length of his arms, and entwine my fingers with his. Walking backward, I drag him into the house until we're standing in front of my surprise.

Letting go of his hands I move behind him, circling his waist with my arms. "You can open them now."

Because I can't see him, I wait for his body or mouth to give his reaction away. I don't have to wait too long, because he spins around, grabbing my face, his eyes wide. "Really?"

I look behind him to the group of boxes, each individually labeled with a 'Seattle Bound' sticker I had made, and then back at Deacon. "Not obvious enough for you?"

Deacon's resounding answer is in the form of a brutal yet breathtaking kiss. It's weeks of built up emotion; our original glass half empty now more than full. It's over-flowing with love and commitment and forever and always.

When our tongues tangle the heat between us rises exponentially. Weeks of distance and abstinence have my body feeling like there's nothing but waves and currents of high voltage electricity running through me.

Breathlessly I pull away from Deacon, needing to get the single most important task of my whole entire life crossed off my checklist.

"I love you," I exhale, my body deflating in a monu-mental wave of relief. No other three words in the English language have ever held this much weight and pressure over me. And finally, I've been given the most perfect moment to give them wings to fly.

"I love you," I repeat with even more conviction. "I love you, and I don't want one more second to pass without you knowing how I feel about you."

Taking deep, heavy breaths, Deacon closes his eyes and rests his forehead against mine. "It feels like I've waited so long to hear you say those words to me."

He presses his lips to mine, quick and forceful. "I feel like I've waited even longer to be able to say them back to you."

Opening his eyes he keeps his gaze locked with mine, his hands still resting on my cheeks. "I am so ridiculously in love with you."

My heart bursts like a ball of confetti inside my chest, the smile on my face evidence that this is the happiest I can ever remember being.

A throaty chuckle slips through his lips while he shakes

his head softly. "I can't believe how good I feel now that I've said it."

"God, me too," I groan.

"Now," Deacon starts, kissing the corner of my mouth. "I just need to hear you say it while I'm inside you and this will go down as my favorite Christmas ever."

"Yeah. About that?" He looks at me quizzically. "I literally have no furniture."

He finally takes the time to look beyond the boxes. "Not even a fucking chair you can ride me on?"

I bark out a laugh. "While you get an A for creativity, and the visual is highly motivating, I really don't even have a chair. The landlord needed the key by tonight, so I've got to pack my car up with the boxes, drop the key at the realtor, and then check into the hotel I managed to book."

"You fucker," Deacon says. "You could've led with 'I booked a hotel room.'"

"Well, I figured sleeping in your childhood bedroom, with your parents in the house, wasn't really an option."

His face scrunches up in anguish at the mention of Elaine and Bill. "We're going to tell them, aren't we? Tomorrow?"

I cock my head at him. "Are you asking me if I want to tell them? Or asking me if I don't want to tell them?"

"I'm asking if you have any preference."

"Do you?" I counter.

"I'm nervous," he admits. "But they didn't really care when Rhett came out, so maybe this will be kind of like that."

"You think they'll care that it's you and me together?" I say, voicing my only fear.

"They love you," Deacon reassures me. "I don't doubt they'll be shocked, but you're coming to Seattle with me and they're going to put two and two together because of that, anyway. Maybe we should go this evening so there isn't a whole Sutton family audience," he suggests. He grabs the collar of my shirt and pulls me to him. "Then we can head off to the hotel, and I can fuck you into Christmas day." He presses another brief yet potent kiss against my lips. "Collect on my Christmas present."

"What's my Christmas present?" I ask jokingly.

Deacon nips at my earlobe and lowers his voice. "Me. It's always going to be me."

25

DEACON

When Julian and I finally manage to stop teasing one another the heat and banter is replaced with a more serious, worrisome mood.

I'd been so transfixed by the news that Julian was coming back to Seattle with me it took a little too long to remember what that actually meant.

He was leaving the house that had held his heart for so long. And even though he seemed completely enraptured with the excitement of his move there was no way I wasn't going to ask how he felt before he walked out of here for the last time.

"I'm going to pack the boxes into my truck," I tell him. "Just take your time with whatever else you need to do."

"You can put them in my car," he says.

I give him an exasperated look. "You are not driving this car to Seattle."

"I need a car, Deacon."

"I'm well aware of that, but this one is not it." He glares

at me, and it triggers an idea. "Okay, if you want this car to come with us, then you have to let me drive it home."

"What?" he shouts.

"You heard me. I'm driving it."

"I'm not going to win this argument, am I?" he says on a sigh.

Shamelessly, I shake my head. "Unlikely."

Julian walks up to me, placing a hand on my shoulder. "I know you're only doing this because you're worried about me driving it, and I love you for it, I really do. But please don't make this a thing."

Ignoring his request I just use my selective hearing to focus on the only part of that sentence I wanted to hear again.

"Say it again," I interrupt.

He narrows his eyes at me. "What?"

"Tell me you love me."

Julian bites his bottom lip, stifling his smile. "How bad do you want to hear it?"

"I'll let you drive if you say it."

"Really?"

"Probably not."

"Dick," he mutters with a smile. "But I love you."

Offering him a quick kiss, I drag my keys out of my back pocket. "Let me give you some privacy. Tell me if you need anything"

He latches onto my wrist, stopping me. "I'm fine, I promise. We'll do the boxes, then I've got something I want to show you before we go."

It doesn't take too long and all the boxes that are coming with us are securely stored and covered in the bed of my truck. When I step back through the front door Julian is waiting for me with the same wooden box that changed my life all those months ago.

Warily I walk over to him and tip my chin toward the box. "Did you end up reading those?"

He shakes his head at me. "I think what you said to me that night last week was the perfect summation of exactly what's in these."

"How do you know?"

"Because, just like you pointed out, I know him. I forgot that along the way, and you reminded me of that." One of his hands begins to mindlessly trace the patterned wood while he continues, "There would have been no conditions placed on the happiness he wanted for me. So, I made a conscious effort to stop putting conditions on myself."

Unshed tears pool in the corner of Julian's eyes, and I use all my self-control not to rush in, wipe his tears, and fall into the default, protective mode he seems to trigger. "So, what do you want to do with the box?" I ask, sensing that's what this is really about.

"I don't know how we're going to swing it, but do you think we can try and bury it next to him?"

In three large steps, I'm standing directly in front of him, cradling his face and swiping my thumbs underneath his eyes. "For you, I'll try."

He leans into me, kissing me softly. Thanking me. Loving me. The whole exchange is a place I never thought we'd ever make it to, but as we both remember the essence of the strongest, most courageous man we ever knew, we allow ourselves to accept that maybe this was his plan all along.

Needing to lug around two cars to each of our stops, we both drive to the realtor so Julian can drop off the key. And then I follow him as we head to the cemetery. The weather is cold, the wind bitter, but the warmth emanating from my chest is enough to soothe me from the inside out.

As I wrap my arms around his waist and rest my chin on his shoulder none of this feels wrong. I'm not ashamed of my feelings, of what I want, and what I have. And in a unusual twist of maturity, I realize my brother died knowing what it was like to love and be loved by a great man, and that alone is something I will always be indebted to Julian for.

"I think the toolbox in my car might have something we can use to dig up the grass," I offer.

Julian lifts the lid and pulls out two mini spades. He hands me one. "Help me?"

Kissing his temple, I take one of the tools off him and release my hold on his body. Wordlessly we decide on the grass behind his head stone and begin digging. The earth is a little harder and more claylike than I would've preferred for this, but with dry winters it's an unrealistic expectation that the dirt will move easily.

In silence we dig, and we dig, and we dig. When it seems that we've made enough space, Julian raises the box to his lips, closes his eyes, and kisses the wood. I watch him with wonder, gratitude, and appreciation. He's so peaceful and whole and happy, and he's mine.

Finished, I stand and hold my hand out to Julian, helping him up off his knees. We both climb into our respective vehicles and prepare for what's next. One monumental thing down, one more to go.

Forty minutes later, we both park curbside in front of my parents' place. Giving them a heads-up would've alerted them to something being wrong and potentially made them worry. Neither of those reactions are conducive to the conversation we need to have with them.

"Are we ready?" I ask Julian as we meet at the bottom of the porch steps.

"Ready as we'll ever be." He slips his hand into mine, giving it a squeeze. "I love you, baby."

I turn my head and he does the same, our lips meeting for a quick peck. "I love you too."

With lazy smiles, we both face the front door, only to be met with my wide-eyed mother, looking at us like she's seen a ghost.

I feel my face fall, and I imagine Julian's looks much the same. She looks mortified. Absolutely disgusted. I don't know which one of us is squeezing harder, but if Julian breaks my fingers it would be a welcome relief from the chill in her stare.

Reluctantly we both trudge up the stairs, holding our heads high despite my mother's intimidation tactics. When we reach the top, I clear my throat and greet her. "Hey, Mom. Is Dad home? We want to talk to you both."

Her eyes dart down to our joined hands and she points at them. "What's this?"

"Can we come inside?" My voice is thick, and I sound weak and choked up. I fucking hate being a grown man and reverting to this.

"Julian," she snaps. "What's this? Why are you holding his hand?"

"Elaine," he says calmly. "Deacon and I would really like to talk to you and Bill about us, inside."

Thankfully, my father walks out at that exact moment. I don't miss the way his eyes gravitate to our stance, but he recovers quickly enough to know it was just shock, and he's not completely repulsed like my mother is.

"How about you boys come inside?" My mother glares at him, but she doesn't argue with him when he backs her out of the entryway, allowing us to walk on through. "Head on into the living room and your mother can bring us a few beers."

Since my father has never been one to give such blatant orders I'm surprised when my mother listens, giving us a moment of reprieve to walk through the house like family and not strangers.

When she enters the living room Julian and I are sitting on the two-seater and my father is hunched forward on the recliner.

Mom returns with beers on a tray sliding it onto the coffee table in front of us. I don't reach for one, neither does Julian, but if my father could drink two at time, that would've definitely been his preference.

"I'm guessing you and Julian have something to tell us," my father states.

Begrudgingly I break our connection, my fingers feeling like stone, unable to bend or move from the stiff tension.

I rub my clammy hands up and down my thighs and keep my eyes to the floor. I will them to rise and use all my mental strength to look my mother in the eye and tell her exactly what we came for.

"Julian and I are together," I say calmly. "He's moving to Seattle, to live with me."

My father's face is expressionless, and my mother's is bloody murder.

She shoots up off her chair. "What do you mean 'you're together'?" she hisses. "You can't be. It's impossible."

Fully expecting her next words to be about my sexuality and how it doesn't make sense to have always been with women only to switch now, I'm completely floored when she storms up to me and slaps me across the face.

The collective gasp from Julian and my dad ensures I

didn't just conjure that up as fragmented pieces of my nightmares.

My hands immediately react, cupping my cheek. "What was that for?" I ask her calmly.

With not an ounce of remorse or shame for the slap, her shoulders are squared, her head held high as she looks at Julian and back at me. "He's Rhett's," she deadpans.

My head drops in disbelief, hanging between my shoulders. I feel myself wanting to shrink inside myself at her words.

I can feel things move around me. I can hear my father shouting, but all I can focus on are her words. *He's Rhett's.*

"You can't have him," she continues, her voice getting colder. "He's not yours to have, he's Rhett's."

Before I can process anything more Julian moves at record speed. He stands between my mom and me and raises a hand to stop her. "You're not doing this to him." He whips his head around to my father. "Are you listening to me? I will not stand by her ruining him."

Feeling numb, feeling everything, I manage to push myself up off the seat.

Before I even manage to take my first step Julian is on me, using all his strength to keep me in a tight hold, whispering into my ear repeatedly. "Please don't listen to her. Please don't listen to her. Please don't listen to her."

If this were a movie, and I was a superhero, my mother and her ruthless tongue would be my kryptonite.

"I love you," Julian chants. "I love you. I love you. I love you. I love you."

My shoulders begin to involuntarily shake, and I can feel myself unraveling. My knees buckle, and I force myself to let Julian carry my weight.

If I fall to the floor, I won't be able to get back up. The

hurt will seep out of me with an audience, and regardless of the fog I'm in right now, I know I will not let my heart bleed in front of her.

"Please, get me out of here," I cry into his neck. "Please."

It all happens in a blur, my head swimming, my throat coated in bile. Every part of me feels broken. Her words were like a sledgehammer cutting me off at the knees, giving me no reason to stand tall.

The scenery around me keeps changing in a blur, and before I know it, we're in the hotel room, and Julian is tipping the porter who has just brought up our bags.

I'm sitting on the edge of the bed, staring into nothing, when I feel Julian climb on top of me. He sits on my lap, his long, lean legs wrapped around my waist, and his arms around my neck.

He rests his head on my shoulder, still chanting the same three words. "I love you. I love you. I love you."

Eventually, I wrap my arms around him and let myself bleed.

"Am I enough for you?" I shamefully ask Julian. Refusing to meet his eyes, I continue, "I know I said I was fine with everything you shared with him, but I need to know the truth, because I'm so sick of being the fucking consolation prize."

Julian untangles himself from me, and I turn my head to avoid his gaze. Tears run down my face, and I don't have any more vulnerability to give.

"Deacon," he calls out.

I don't look at him.

"Deacon, please." He's now a little closer, grabbing my hand. "Deacon, if you're going to ask me a question, then you have to look at me when I'm answering it."

Reluctantly, I oblige, and I see Julian looking as heartbroken as I feel. When he's right next to me he reaches for the zipper on my jacket and I move. "What are you doing?"

"You want to know if you're enough, right?" he says angrily. "If what your mom said was right?"

Swallowing hard, I meet his gaze. "You have two options. Take off your clothes or I will."

"Julian, I don—"

He doesn't let me finish, his hands now roughly pulling at my clothes. I don't help him. Instead I rebel, being as petulant as possible, giving him a defense mechanism dressed up as attitude.

When it's only my pants left, and I don't help him get them off, he glares at me. "Now."

I raise a challenging eyebrow, and he completely ignores me and begins taking his own clothes off.

"What are you doing?" I ask.

"Take. Your. Pants. Off."

Standing up I shuck them off, and then feel a hand slip in mine. It's a lot softer and gentler than his mood, so I take it.

He leads us to the right side of the bed, pulls back the blankets, and throws off all the pillows.

"Sit on the bed."

Out of curiosity, I do what I'm told, waiting for some kind of fucking explanation.

When Julian climbs on top of me, naked, and wraps himself around me like a vine, I'm genuinely surprised.

"What are you doing?" I press.

He twists half his body and extends his arm so he can reach the blanket in the middle of the bed. Once he's got it, he lifts it over his back, and then over us completely, so we're doing nothing but holding on to one another in the dark.

Like our own little bubble, I return the sentiment and squeeze him to me. He sighs at my touch, and I know neither one of us is here unscathed.

"A few weeks ago, it was your time to talk," he tells, me referring to our conversation about moving forward. "Now, with no interruptions, and absolutely nothing between us, it's mine. To say I didn't love your brother with everything I had would be the biggest lie I've ever told." Uncontrollable tears begin to fall down my face. *Do I even want to hear this?*

"I was so lost, and so alone. I felt that loneliness in my bones, and one day he just shined his light on me, and I couldn't stay away even if I'd tried. He was my best friend. He taught me how to laugh, and he gave me the confidence to be myself. And there were times when I really needed that. We started as boys in love, trying to build a life out of naivety and hope. When he got sick plans and dreams for the future gave him hope." Julian's breath hitches, and I feel wet tears land on my shoulder. "It was young love, first love, puppy love. It was forged out of friendship, and it lasted as long as it did out of necessity.

"But this, with you..." He pauses catching his breath. "My heart didn't beat for him the way it does for you. The rush, the ferocity, the desperation to be with *you*—I have never felt anything with such strength and conviction, about anybody or anything."

He flips back the covers, and our eyes adjust to the light. He wraps his arms back around my neck, and lines up his face perfectly with mine. "So, you want to know if you're enough for me?"

He grips my chin in a tight and commanding hold. "You're the beat of my heart, the blood in my veins, the strength in my bones. None of me works without you. And if you need me to tell you every fucking day for the rest of our lives, then I will, because you are more than enough. You're *everything*."

My hold on him tightens, because words don't work and the only answer he's going to get is the frantic beat of my heart, responding to the matching rhythm of his.

"He might've had a piece of my heart, Deacon, but you own it. It's yours till the day you say you don't want it."

"Never," I breathe into his neck. "I will never not want you."

"I'm so, so fucking sorry she said that to you," he cries. "You are not less than or undeserving of anything, Deacon Sutton. You deserve to be happy, and you deserve to feel whole, and I won't let anyone, not even your mom take this away from us."

26

DEACON

I'm holding on to Julian for dear life, my body still sporadically hiccupping from the crying. I've been stripped down to nothing but bone, and being wrapped in his arms feels like the only way I may be able to beat this emotional fog.

Long, smooth fingers trail up and down my spine, as if he needs to feel me, soothe me, calm me down. I'm so incredibly grateful for his attentiveness, every touch a reminder that I'm still here with him, and we're still together.

My body shifts imperceptibly closer to him as the brush of his naked skin against mine lights a small fire within us both.

I bury my head in the crook of his neck, allowing my lips to skim across his collarbone and dance the length of his nape. His skin is like silk underneath my lips, and I can't stop myself from leaving a trail of soft, slow kisses as I make my way up to his mouth.

Julian lays a firm hand on my chest, halting my movements. "There's nothing I want more than you, but we can just lie here," he suggests. "I can just hold you."

For the sake of honesty, I shake my head, lower my hands to his ass, and pull him into me. Holding me just isn't enough right now. I need to feel centered and grounded, and Julian and his body are the only way I can find it.

In tune with my turmoil, he rears his head back to get a better look at me. The move forces me to raise my head and meet his eyes.

He's heartbreakingly beautiful in our role reversal, taking care of me, protecting me, fighting for me. I've never had a single person love me enough to do that. And now, tangled up with Julian, I wanted to say thank you. I wanted to thank him with my words, with my body, and then repeat the process till I couldn't anymore.

Julian was it for me, and after the way he made me feel today, even forever wouldn't be enough.

Squeezing his ass cheeks and holding his stare, I grind his naked pelvis into mine. "I want you," I tell him. "I want nothing but you."

"I'm here," he reassures me breathlessly, our cocks stirring to life. "I'll always be here."

Sliding a hand between us, I grab our solid dicks together in my fist and begin to stroke. I capture Julian's moan with my mouth, kissing and jerking him senseless.

"Deacon, baby, stop," Julian pleads. "You can do whatever you want to me, but please tell me you're okay."

Putting a hand on his mouth, I lock eyes with him, so there's no mistaking my honesty.

"I feel so raw right now," I confess. "Every part of me feels battered and bruised, and the only thing I want to do is get lost in the man I love." I drop my hand from his mouth, replacing it with a firm kiss on his lips. "I can't form the

words now. The ones you deserve to hear, the declarations
that'll last longer than my dying breath," I continue. "I want
all that for you and then some, but all I have right now to
offer is me."

"Make love to me, Julian." I beg longingly. "I need you
inside me. I need you to love me back to life."

He melds his mouth to mine, pushing against me, letting
us both fall into the mattress. "Let me take care of you," he
murmurs into my mouth. "Let me take care of what's mine."

Our legs straighten out underneath us, his body settles
between my legs, heavy and greedy on top of mine. The
tension in my muscles begins to uncoil, and I feel myself
slowly giving up my control to him.

I don't need it with him. Every touch of his lips and taste
of his tongue, he owns more of me. He owns more of my
body, more of my heart, and I have never wanted someone
to have every part of me until Julian.

Our kisses deepen, and our already hard cocks, rubbing
up on one another, feel like thick rods of steel. Julian navi-
gates my body with his mouth, moving down my torso, his
tongue loving on each of my nipples. Alternating between
flicking and twisting my piercings, his teasing is like a direct
connection to my cock, and now it's throbbing.

Grabbing the back of his head, I unabashedly push him
down the length of my body. "I need your mouth on me," I
pant.

"I've got a better idea," Julian says as he slides off me. He
stalks over to our duffel bags, and comes back with a
condom and a square packet of lube. He shakes them in the
air. "And for my next trick, I'm about to blow your fucking
mind."

Grabbing my cock and stroking it, I smirk. "How about
you just blow *me*?"

"Turn around," he demands. "Get on all fours."

I do as I'm told, but this position is new for me, and I'm feeling all kinds of exposed and naked—both on the inside and out. I can feel Julian behind me, the sound of foil tearing as he gets himself ready.

When large hands are splayed out on my ass cheeks, a small, scared part of me stiffens.

Julian takes his hands off me, worry and sincerity in his voice. "You want me to stop?"

I whip my head around to face him. "No."

"Watch me," he demands.

He lowers himself to his knees, and his hands now pull my cheeks apart instead of just resting against them. When my mind finally catches on to what he's about to do, my breath hitches in anticipation.

It's a simple swipe of his tongue, but my whole body trembles; my head falls forward, my breaths come quick and shaky.

When the next lick doesn't come, I turn to look at him.

"I was wondering how long it was going to take for you to catch on," he taunts. "If you look somewhere else, I'll stop."

I swallow hard and give him a small confirming nod. It's all he needs to get back up close and personal, his tongue licking my hole with much less tentative swipes than before.

"Fuck," I groan loudly. "Nobody ever tells you how good this feels."

When a hand circles my cock, stroking me up and down, while his tongue darts in and out of me, my body jolts off the bed. "Too much," I cry out. "Too much."

"Okay. Okay," Julian soothes. "How about we try this?"

His face is all smug and sexy, and I know whatever he

does next is going to drive me just as insane. "Grab your cock and start stroking yourself."

It's momentary relief, to be in control and set the pace, but when I watch him lube up his digits, my balls tighten and my cock shamelessly leaks all over my hands.

Cold, wet fingers begin to circle my hole. Julian's thumb repeatedly ghosts the rim, until all I can think about is him sticking it inside me.

"Please," I beg. "Please. Please."

Julian wastes no time slowly sliding a long finger inside me. It feels foreign, but it feels fucking good. His thrusts become a little faster, his finger probing a little deeper, and when he grazes my prostate, a litany of unintelligible sounds roar from my mouth and bounce all over the room.

With his voice dripping with lust, Julian asks, "Can you take two fingers?"

"Yeah," I pant.

When the second one slides in, I begin to imagine how Julian's cock will feel, how it'll fit. And how when he touches me, he takes away all the pain, and I can do nothing else but bask in all the pleasure.

"You want one more or you want my dick?" He stands to his full height when he says this, his thick cock and heavy balls desperate for attention.

I anticipate it being somewhat uncomfortable, and even hurting, but having us connected in that way, especially after today? I need it.

I need to feel his love. The insecure guy I've always been, *needs* to feel his love.

"I want you inside me," I answer.

Julian gives my ass a little slap. "Come and ride me."

He climbs onto the bed, sitting with his back against the headboard, his legs splayed out, open wide, and his sheathed dick hard and ready. I crawl up to meet him, maneuvering myself so I'm kneeling above him.

"Now, just lower yourself onto me. Slow and steady." As I get into position, he says, "If you want to stop at any time, just say the word."

When I feel his crown probe my entrance, I bite on my bottom lip to stifle any sounds that leave my mouth. Julian keeps his gaze on me, and I hold his stare, using him as my anchor. I repeatedly breathe in through my nose and out of my mouth as inch by inch I push through the new and different, and momentarily uncomfortable, sensations and finally take all of Julian inside of me.

He lets me set the pace, and I slide up a little bit more each time, the sting turning into a dull, addictive ache.

"You feel so good around me," Julian groans. "You want to quit your job and spend all day on my dick?"

Chuckling, I lean forward and kiss him, not caring where his mouth has been, my body rising and falling in a new rhythm. "I won't quit my job, but I promise to come home to you every night and you can have me anyway you want."

"I fucking love you," he growls, slamming his lips to mine.

Julian's well-mastered control falls to the wayside with every plunge into his mouth my tongue takes. His hips begin to piston into me, and the angle, hitting my prostate, is a delicious interlude to my imminent orgasm. I fist my cock and begin to unleash, desperate to chase my release.

"Fuck, Deacon, baby, come with me." His movements become frantic, and with one last thrust into my prostate, I'm doing exactly what he demands.

Just as I feel Julian quake beneath me, my come squirts

and spits on to his chest, my release looking like dessert after I just had my main fucking meal.

I watch as he closes his eyes, tips his head back, his chest rising and falling in exhaustion. I lift myself up off his dick and wince, feeling the sting.

"Hurt?" Julian asks, obviously noticing my discomfort.

Lifting my leg over him, I let myself fall in a heap of spent limbs beside him. "Best pain I've ever felt," I answer.

"I'm going to get rid of this," he says, motioning to the condom. "I'll bring back a wet cloth."

"No," I shout from the bed. "I want to sleep in our mess."

"Fine," he calls back. "But don't get used to it, because at home I'm not fucking washing bed sheets every day."

My face splits in two. Nothing else matters right now as I feel myself drifting off into sleep with a ridiculous smile.

Home. My home. Your home. His home. Our home.

The room is pitch black when I wake up, except for a small bright light coming from Julian's phone.

"You're awake," I say groggily.

He's sitting up against the headboard, dressed and presumably all showered. "Hey, sleepyhead."

"How long have you been up for?"

His eyes dart from me to the cell. "Maybe a little over an hour."

"Why didn't you wake me?

He runs a hand through my hair. "You had a big day yesterday, I figured you'd earned the hours."

My stomach revolts at the reminder, just as Julian's rumbles. "When was the last time you ate?" I ask, worried.

"I couldn't tell you, but now that you're awake we'll get room service."

"I hope you didn't wait for me," I scold while pulling the blankets off so I can head to the bathroom.

"Oh," Julian mock gasps. "The horror of waiting for your boyfriend to eat with you."

I spin on my heels, smiling. "What did you say?"

"Get out of here with that damn look on your face and your semi hard cock," Julian warns, even though his smile is now even bigger than mine. "We've got to eat and talk before your mind is allowed to revisit the gutter."

Sauntering off into the bathroom, I quickly piss and have a nice relaxing shower. I'm dressed and on the phone to room service ordering two turkey subs and two Cokes when his phone rings.

He doesn't hesitate to answer it and it's easy conversation with the person on the other line. When he catches me staring, he holds my gaze while still talking on the phone. "Yeah, I'll let him know. Thank you. Bye."

I raise an eyebrow at him. "Why do I get the feeling you're about to tell me something I don't want to hear?"

"Nothing like that," he says. "It was just Victoria."

"So, I take it she knows then?" He doesn't answer my question, so I narrow it down a bit further. "About you and me?"

"Yeah," he nods. "Your dad called her and told her. He figured Christmas was canceled."

"Fuck. I forgot it was Christmas," I say. "How the fuck did I just forget it was Christmas?"

A muffled voice along with a quick knock alerts us it's room service. "Let me get that," Julian offers.

He walks back in with a huge silver tray holding all our

food. He puts it down on the edge of the bed, and then walks to me.

He rests his hands on my waist. "What's the sudden freak out about Christmas?"

"It would've been our first Christmas together," I acknowledge. "I didn't want it to be like this."

"We're still together, though, aren't we?"

"I know." I mirror his stance and drag him to me. "What did she say about us?"

"There was a lot of that fake swearing she does when Lia is awake."

I smile, but it doesn't reach my eyes when I ask, "Was she okay about us?"

"Hey," Julian coos. "She isn't your mom, and she was very okay about us. More than okay even."

I release the breath I was holding, relieved that's one less thing we have to think about.

"She did want to know if you were going to try and stay and maybe work on—"

"I can't," I cut him off. "I know this makes me seem like a horrible son, but she already thinks I am one, so what does it matter at this point?"

"Listen," Julian says firmly, his annoyance escalating. "Your one job is to not worry about your mom. Quite frankly, she doesn't deserve it."

I don't know why, but a stab of guilt pricks at my conscience. She was always nice to Julian; I can't expect him to hate her because of me.

"You don't have to defend me," I tell him. "I know she's been good to you over the years. It can't be easy just dismissing her like that."

"No." He shakes his head vehemently. "No, don't do that."

"I wouldn't be mad," I try to explain.

"It's not about that. I can't look at her," he admits. "The only time the image of her slapping you wasn't playing on a loop in my head was when I was inside you."

His face is nothing but anguish and distress, and I don't want to see that, not because of me.

"I know you're not familiar with how this piece of the puzzle works, but you're mine. You are *always* going to be mine." My lips turn upward at his hint of possessiveness. "So, if you think I'm going to let anyone treat the man I love with anything less than the respect he deserves, and then think I'm still keeping them around?" He clicks his tongue. "Then maybe you're underestimating how much I love you."

"Come here." I pull him close to my chest and hug him. "If I'm underestimating, then you should give me a quick little refresher course on how much you love me."

"I love you more than my past," he says. "I love you more than the obstacles the present has thrown in our way. Because you're my future. And I'm going to love you forever because you're my always."

27

JULIAN
NEW YEARS' EVE

"Can you please put a shirt on?" I begrudgingly reprimand.

"Why? I polished my nipple rings just for you."

I side eye Deacon. On a normal day, I would be all over those rods of metal, using both my tongue and my fingers, but today is a different story; we're expecting company.

"Nobody polishes their nipple rings," I deadpan.

He waggles his eyebrows. "I'll let you polish mine."

Deacon laughs at his own joke when the doorbell rings. His eyes widen. "Who's that? Is this why you've been busting my balls to put a shirt on?"

"Ding. Ding. Ding," I joke.

"Okay, fine," he starts, as he walks backward to our room, "But that still doesn't explain why I don't know who's at the door."

"It's called a surprise," I answer back.

When Deacon is out of sight, I quickly pull my phone out and send a quick text.

Me: Opening up soon, just waiting for Deacon.

When Deacon returns, his eyes dart between me and the entryway. "Why didn't you open it?"

"Since when do you ask so many questions?" I tilt my head to the door. "Go on, open it."

If I didn't know surprises weren't his thing, I do now. The glare he aims my way, paired with his heavy and unhurried gait, is a clear indication he's not impressed.

As a result of not warming up to surprises, he opens the door slowly, as if on the other side Pennywise the clown is ready to pounce on him.

When the door widens, I hear a collective "Surprise," and watch Deacon take a step back in complete shock.

I make my way to him and the small group of people on the other side of our door. Excited that they're all here, because I asked them to be, gives me hope that not all is lost for Deacon and me on the family front.

Smiling, I step out in front of a still very shocked Deacon and greet Victoria, Hayden, Christy, and Wade, with quick one-armed hugs. Lia is too busy trying to get her Uncle Deacon's attention, so I take her out of Victoria's arms and see if I can give her a little help.

I call out his name, and it takes him a few minutes to process I'm actually talking at all. When he looks at me, I hand him Lia.

He wordlessly places her on his hip, giving her a kiss on the cheek, and then turns to me. "Did you know about this?"

"I might've had a hand or two in it," I say, feeling a little under the microscope. "I thought we could end the year on a good note."

Unshed tears shine in pools of happiness in Deacon's eyes, and my heart expands exponentially. My love for him is unable to be contained; it grows daily. Endlessly. Always.

Without a care in the world, he cups the back of my neck and unapologetically fuses our mouths together. "I love you so fudging much," he murmurs against my mouth.

The chorus of laughter surrounding us pulls us apart. Hesitantly, I let my gaze wander across the four sets of eyes, knowing that if they didn't want to see us together or support us—I was mostly concerned with Victoria's reaction —they wouldn't be here.

I'm more than surprised when I see the happy tears fall down Deacon's sister's face, but it's the proof I need, to know with certainty, that with her, we don't have anything to worry about.

Deacon, Wade, and Christy say a casual hello, since we've already seen them and spent time with them as a couple, and their excuse to come over was to show off Christy's new engagement ring.

Hayden takes Lia from Deacon when Victoria throws herself at him, crying a never-ending well of tears. I give the beautiful little girl a kiss on the head, and then can hear Deacon calling me over.

They're both red-eyed and smiling, and it's a bittersweet moment for me. Seeing how happy he is, and knowing how much he's lost just to get here makes me see red.

But I do my best not to think about it, because from here on out we have each other, and that will make us unstoppable.

When I reach their two-person circle, they both throw their arms around me. The moment isn't just about Deacon and me getting together. With the addition of Victoria, it's three people who share a special, life-changing bond. And even though Rhett is no longer with us, it's the first time in a long time I've felt him and felt peace instead of guilt.

When we separate, Victoria looks between us, her arms

on either one of our biceps.

"Fudging pregnancy hormones," she supplies while wiping her nose with a tissue. "I'm so happy you two are together," she says. "Never in a million years did I ever imagine you two together," she says. "But the way he kissed you in the doorway? The way you are so in sync together? It's like..."

"It's like they're made for one another," Wade pipes in, finishing her sentence. "I told Deacon the same thing a few weeks back."

"I've never seen my brother kiss anyone in public," she gushes. "And he's happy. Just look at how different he looks."

She's right, he does look different. Content. Lighter. Centered.

The way he should always have been. Burden free and undeniably happy.

Amidst all the excited tones and conversations between us, I hear a low but consistent knock at the front door. Deacon raises an eyebrow. "Everyone we know is here," he muses.

I don't bother to get technical, but seeing as I didn't invite anyone else, I'm just as confused as he is.

"Give me a second," I say to the group.

I swing the door open, completely unprepared for the person who's on the other side. I'm rendered speechless, and it takes me a good thirty seconds to manage a 'hello.'

"Bill," I sputter. "Hey. What are you doing here?"

"JULIAN." He nods at me in greeting before looking into the apartment at the group of people, and no doubt at the man who's now pressing his hand into the small of my back.

"Dad? What are you doing here?"

He pulls a set of keys out of his pocket and dangles them in the air. They're my car keys. That only Victoria had. I spin around and give her a knowing look, and she just shrugs.

Plucking the keys out of Bill's hands I put them in my pocket, and then stand there awkwardly.

"Do you want to come in?" Deacon asks.

Mr. Sutton scrubs his hand over his chin. "Only if I apologize first."

"I'm going to..." I jerk my thumb back inside. "So you guys can have some privacy."

"No." Deacon straightens his back and holds my hand, daring Bill to say anything about us being together, to be on his mother's side.

But those horrible words never come.

Instead, he clears his throat. "I need to apologize to both of you about what happened the other day." His posture shifts toward Deacon. "And I need to apologize to you for so much more."

Feeling uncomfortable, Deacon shakes his head. "Don't worry about it, Dad. It isn't necessary."

"Bullshit," he says angrily, and it silences the audience behind us. "I did you wrong, son. Time and time again, I kept my mouth shut, and I need to earn my forgiveness."

Deacon's fingers interlace with mine while his father unloads years and years of guilt. It's moments like these I feel our strong connection, where words aren't needed and that our hearts are synchronized in every way that matters.

I squeeze his hand, telling him the only thing he needs to know. The one thing that will never change.

I'm here. I love you.

"I should've said more," Bill confesses. "I should've stuck up for you more when she was being impossible. And the other day." He shakes his head. "She hit you. Her son, a grown fucking man, and she hit you." Bill's voice cracks, along with his heart, and the thick emotion in his voice makes it hard for all of us not to feel it.

I glance over at Deacon and the tears falling down his cheeks are an absolute knife to my heart. I lean closer to him, wrapping my arm around his torso, holding my man up.

"I know it's late and the damage is already done, but she's going to get help, son," Bill explains. "I told her it was non-negotiable. My family and my marriage are not going to survive if she keeps doing this, and it was time she needed to know. I know she's the reason our family is falling apart." He apologetically shakes his head. "Not because of Rhett." He taps at his chest. "I let her use that excuse for far too long. I didn't pull her up on so many things, swept so many things under the carpet, but I'm not going to do that anymore at the expense of losing my son."

He turns his face toward me. "Both my sons." Now it's Deacon's turn to squeeze my hand.

"I'm happy for you both," he tells us. "And if you need anything at all, you need to let me know." Mr. Sutton steps closer and places a hand on my shoulder, squeezing it. "I know it's a lot to ask of you, but even after all is said and done, she's my wife—in sickness and in health, so if there's any way you can find it in your heart to forgive her, then I'm grateful."

"And if I can't?" Deacon asks.

Bill shrugs. "Then you can't."

"I'm sorry to have interrupted your night together. I didn't know you were busy." He lifts his chin up at the people inside. "But I wanted to bring Julian's car back, and apologize."

"You can stay for dinner," Deacon offers.

"I'm not much company at the moment," he confesses. "But, please, please stay in touch."

The man walks away without a second glance, or another word. Almost like the whole conversation never happened.

I look back at everyone behind us, all staring at Deacon, their eyes as sympathetic as they can be.

"Are you okay?" I ask him.

He takes a deep breath and releases the energy. "I think so."

"We can go home," Wade offers, breaking the ice.

"No way. We're going to order dinner, that was the deal," Deacon insists. "I promise I'm fine."

"Ok," Wade puts his hand up in surrender. "If you say so."

"Do you guys want to hear how Wade proposed?" Christy interjects, her voice cheerful.

"No," Wade groans. "Please don't."

His plea only forces us all to look at Christy expectantly.

"So, Wade didn't even end up proposing," she announces. "I found the ring and decided to wear it until he noticed it."

"Oh my God," Victoria exclaims. "I can't believe it went down like that."

"Thankfully, it wasn't that long till he noticed," Christy confirmed.

"Please don't tell this story," Wade begs.

"Why? It's my absolute favorite," she says, her eyes giddy with mischief.

"I noticed it when she was giving me a hand job," he blurts out really quickly. The bark of laughter that sounds from multiple people around the room is deafening, but the revelation is hysterical and none of us can stop laughing.

"Holy shit," I gasp. "Then what happened?"

"He was speechless, I was almost sure he was about to pass out," she laughs. "He was stuttering, and his eyes were bugging out of his head. 'Uh. Uh. Uh. Where'd you find that ring?'" she mocks.

"I just asked him if he wanted to finish." Christy gives Wade a knowing smile, and then looks back at her interested crowd. "Or if he wanted to know my answer."

"Why do I feel like that was a test?" Deacon says.

"Because it was," she agrees. "Thankfully, he asked for my answer. I told him it was too pretty for me to take it off, so he was just going to have to deal with the fact that the wrong girlfriend found it."

The room breaks out in laughter as Deacon sidles up next to me, throwing his arm around my shoulders and kissing my temple. It's an 'I'm glad you're here' move. He does it often, and I always plan on being here.

"Now I know why you were skimpy with the details," Deacon accuses Wade. "Christy always tells a killer story."

"I still can't get over it," I say, still laughing with Christy.

"Just wait until it's your turn," Wade says nonchalantly, pointing between Deacon and me.

Looking up, I expect to see a freaked out Deacon, or even feel a little taken aback by the assumption, myself, but it neither happens.

He's got his blue eyes and bright smile aimed at me like he just realized that was an option for us. He lowers his mouth to my ear. "Are you going to marry me one day?"

"Are you going to ask?"

"Forever is a long time," he points out. "I guess we're going to have to see which one of us caves in first."

28

RHETT

D ear Deacon,
  Your letter was the hardest one to write, because I
  always wanted to kick cancer's ass so I could say it to
your face.

You were my dying wish. A brother who could be my best
friend, a best friend who could be my brother. I'm sorry we never
got that, I'm even more sorry that Mom was the reason why.

I want you to know, you grew up to be an amazing human
being, one you should be proud of, because that's all on you. You
suffered in silence, with your heart of gold, so everyone else didn't
have to.

I hoped one day I'd be able to stand my ground with Mom
and make her stop hassling you, and we'd be able to make up for
the missing years. But cancer's got a hard-on for me and she plans
to take me sooner rather than later.

So instead of moping and talking about the afterlife I don't
think even exists, I have some big brother tasks you need to fulfill
for me when I'm gone, so you can keep your best big brother
status (don't even think about responding and saying you're my
only brother. It's totally irrelevant).

They're not much, but they're important to me, because when I die, I need to make sure everybody I love is content and happy and loved.

Task One: Please bury me with candy corn.

Task Two: Tell Lia I love her every day.

Task Three: If Vic has another baby and it's a boy, make sure they name him Rhett. What's the point of dying young if you don't get a legacy out of it?

Task Four: Stand up to Mom.

Task Five: Be nice to Julian.

I know the last one is a weird thing to ask, but he doesn't have anyone else. You have Seattle, Vic has Hayden and Lia, and Mom and Dad have each other.

He's been my best friend for so long, and he's given up his whole life to take care of me. He deserves happiness.

Please, for me, help him find it. Maybe, he can help you too.

Love you, Big Brother.

Forever and Always.

Rhett.

∾

For more Deacon and Julian, visit my website for their bonus epilogue.

http://www.marleyvbooks.com/bonus-epilogues/

∾

Want to read more MM Romance from Marley Valentine?
Check out Devilry , her student/teacher romance.

Available on AMAZON in both e-book and paperback

MARLEY VALENTINE

Attending King University was at the top of my bucket list. Falling in love with my professor wasn't.

Earning a full scholarship to King University was my hard earned ticket out of hell. I'm happy to be away from the small town I grew up in and all the equally small minded people who live there.

King was going to be my safe haven. A place where I could leave the old me behind and finally grow into the young man my family had desperately tried to hide away.

Diving head first into new experiences, new friends, and parties, I didn't expect to run straight into the one thing I wasn't ready for.

His arms are welcoming, his body is addictive and his lips are heaven. Cole Huxley is everything I could fall in love with, except for one problem... I never wanted to fall for my professor.

Devilry is part of the King University Series, but can be read as a complete standalone.

AVAILABLE NOW ON AMAZON: PAPERBACK + KINDLE

ACKNOWLEDGMENTS

Andrew, thank you for all your support with this book, especially towards the end. You are the best husband and father to Jax, a girl could ever ask for.

Jaxon, I love you. Always.

Mum, Steph, and Chris, I love you. Rita, and Harry, thank you for being the best in-laws and always helping me when I need it.

Sybil, I think we for real broke the internet with this cover, what do you think? I'll love it til the day I die, just like I love you. Wander thank you for a beautiful photo, and Jacob and Luke, expect a copy in the mail real soon.

Jodi. There aren't enough words to explain how much easier you make my life. You are as neurotic as me, and I love that it's between us is a judgement free zone, always. Thank you for everything you've done with and for this book. And everything you do every day.

Kacey, thank you for talking me off the ledge a million times, thank you for supporting me in the eleventh hour, when I thought it had all turned to shit. You are an amazing listener, and an amazing friend and I cant wait for us to do this crazy thing all over again.

Laura, thank you for always being there to talk through a story line, to read a scene, or to calm me down when I'm being stupid. Your excitement about my books, always helps me push past the finish line, and this one was no different.

Jacob, thank you for the motivational memes. Now that I'm done, I'll be sure to return the favour #BelfastIsComing

My beta team: Jodi, Michelle, Monica and Shauna. Thank you for loving Deacon and Julian as much as I do, and sharing that love with the rest of the world every chance you get. This book got to the end and published because of each of you. Your roles, suggestions and support is everything and I couldn't write books without you.

Michelle and Annette from Book Nerd Services. Your work with my ARC team is always phenomenal. The organisation, the support, the general boost you have given my books and my brand will never be forgotten.

ellie and Shauna, thank you so much for taking the time to read and edit Without You. Your work is invaluable, and I look forward to more books together.

Donna, my music guru. You nail the song suggestions every time, and my books thank you.

My street team. You ladies kick ass, each and every day. Thank you for your faith and support, always.

The ladies at Enticing Journey, thank you for your work. Always above and beyond professional.

To all the people who listen to me bitch and moan on the regular. Sybil, Laura, Jodi, Monica, Celia, Bianca, Haley and Jenner, you all get me through life. Thank you.

If I forgot someone, I'm sorry. I still love you, and you guys know the drill by now. Eat McDonalds on the regular and stalk Charlie Hunnam.

Much Peace and Love.

ABOUT THE AUTHOR

Marley Valentine

Living in Sydney, Australia with her family, Marley Valentine is a USA Today bestselling author and a former social worker who uses her past experiences to write real life, emotional and heartfelt contemporary romance.

She enjoys mixing it up with all types of romance pairings, incorporating all forms of life, lust and love as her characters embark on their journey to their happily ever after.

When she's not busy writing her own stories, she spends most of her time immersed in the words of her favourite authors.

Marley enjoys interacting with her readers so please feel free to reach out to her via Facebook, Instagram, email and/or subscribe to her newsletter.

For more information please visit www.marleyvbooks.com

Other Books by Marley Valentine

Light My Way | Find My Way | Reclaim | Revive | Rectify

MM Romance Books

Devilry | Without You | Ache | Unforgettable (Vino & Veritas)

The Unlucky Ones
Unwanted

Find Marley

Facebook | Facebook Reader Group | Amazon Author Page | Goodreads Author Page | Twitter | Instagram | Website | BookBub | Newsletter